The Dragon's Familiar

The Dragon's Familiar

A Novel

Lawrence J. Cohen

iUniverse, Inc.
New York Bloomington Shanghai

The DRAGON'S FAMILIAR

Copyright © 2008 by Lawrence J. Cohen

All rights reserved. No part of this book may be used or reproduced by any means, graphic, electronic, or mechanical, including photocopying, recording, taping or by any information storage retrieval system without the written permission of the publisher except in the case of brief quotations embodied in critical articles and reviews.

iUniverse books may be ordered through booksellers or by contacting:

iUniverse
1663 Liberty Drive
Bloomington, IN 47403
www.iuniverse.com
1-800-Authors (1-800-288-4677)

Because of the dynamic nature of the Internet, any Web addresses or links contained in this book may have changed since publication and may no longer be valid.

This is a work of fiction. All of the characters, names, incidents, organizations, and dialogue in this novel are either the products of the author's imagination or are used fictitiously.

ISBN: 978-0-595-51413-7 (pbk)
ISBN: 978-0-595-61889-7 (ebk)

Printed in the United States of America

Chapter 1
▼

TWISTED MIRROR

THUNDER RUMBLED IN THE DISTANCE, HERALDING THE APPROACHING STORM. Large, gunmetal-gray clouds dominated the northwest, blown into an otherwise clear blue sky. The air carried the scent of moisture and ozone. Skinny, twelve-year-old Cory peered at the old Victorian mansion. It was a completely burned-out hulk, sandwiched between two well-kept houses on a side street near Brooklyn College. The burnt, blackened walls, once coated in sparkling white paint, gave the house a sinister look. Leaves and dead plants covered the front porch, and all the windows were boarded up, except for one window with broken glass in the turret. A chill went through the boy, and he shuddered.

"We're not supposed to go in there," Cory said, watching his friend climb the rusted chain-link fence that surrounded the weed-enshrouded property.

"What's-a-matter Avalon? Chicken?"

"No, John," Cory said as the older boy jumped the remaining few feet to the ground. "But that sign says the building's abandoned."

"I knew you were a wimp."

Cory's voice wavered. "I am not! It's just that," the younger boy hesitated, checking the darkening sky. "It's almost dinner time. I gotta get back soon—"

"Oh! So your Mommy won't let you, huh?" John said with a disgusted sneer.

The boy shot his new friend a nasty look. "You know my Mom's in the hospital!"

John held his temper. "Sorry. Look Cory, there's nothing dangerous in there! I've been in there several times. It's great!"

Cory hesitated. Something about this place chilled him. Still, he didn't want to lose John's friendship. *Well, I did always want to explore a haunted house!*

"Alright," Cory gave in, gripping the rusting chain links with his fingers. "But one more crack about my Mom and I'm gonna knock you through a wall!"

Cory carefully grasped the links, putting his sneakers into the holes for support. When he reached the top of the six-foot high fence, he slung one leg over, careful not to tear his Lee jeans on the sharp spikes at the top. Cory glanced sideways at John, who looked to be getting impatient.

"Just jump down!"

"Wait-a-minute," Cory replied, and slung the other leg over. He was never very athletic, and John knew that. After carefully climbing a few feet down, Cory did jump, the force of landing causing his knees to bend.

The younger boy turned around to see John already heading towards the house, wading through the broken beer bottles and blown pieces of newspaper. Cory looked nervously around to make sure nobody had seen them. If he got arrested now—

Who would care? His mother was still in a coma from the plane crash at JFK last year ago which had killed his father. Cory had been passed from one foster home to another, from Greenwich Village to

Forest Hills to Co-op City, further and further from his real home in Brighton Beach. This was the closest he'd been to home in months.

What was the point in making friends, when he knew he'd only be shuffled off to another home in a few months? He finally ended up sitting alone in his room, or on the front stoop, his sapphire blue eyes glazed over, staring off into space, the breeze gently blowing the bangs of his black hair. Sitting daydreaming his life away was worse than the temper tantrums he'd frequently had since the jet crash. While Danvers didn't tolerate the boy's outbursts, he'd insisted that Cory do something constructive with his time, like going to the Boy's Club after school. Danvers didn't understand. Cory felt alone. He missed his room and toys and friends. It was safer to sit and daydream than risk getting hurt again. Besides, all these grown-ups didn't matter beans to him.

Cory sat on the stoop, watching the street, waiting for his mother to come and take him home. Danvers knew this, and had to threaten to hit him with the belt to get him to go to the community center.

John was different from the other kids Cory had met in the Boy's Club. For one thing, John was already in high school, and the youngest star on the track team. That meant he'd be a junior, a big man on campus, by the time Cory started. To have John for a friend was an 'in' to the 'cool group.' Now if Cory just didn't screw it up, or have to move away again, everything would be fine!

The two boys dashed up the rotting wooden steps, and Cory started to stare at the boarded-up windows, wondering how they were going to get in. John simply reached for the brass doorknob and opened the front door, to the complete amazement of the younger boy.

"It's always been unlocked," John explained, and went on in.

Cory followed, careful to shut the door behind him, so nobody would come to investigate. Inside, it was very musty; it smelled of the fire, which had gutted the entire building. A carpet of dirt covered the floor and rotting rug. Dust danced in the light shining through cracks in the windows, looking much like the little toys filled with water and plastic snow. Ancient cobwebs hung everywhere, and had the boys examined them closely, they would've seen that it wasn't just insects trapped by the spiders; small mice were also cocooned in the silken threads. The place felt very large, empty, and scary. Any sound they made echoed in the vast space.

Something about the place wasn't quite right. The chill that gripped Cory when he saw the place from the outside intensified in here. His insides quivered, his breath came in short gasps. He was afraid, and not sure why. Somehow, the boy had the feeling that someone ... or some*thing* was here, hiding in the dark.

Ghosts? the boy thought nervously. Something squeaked off to his left, and Cory's head spun. He saw a small, brown mouse skitter across the dusty floor, and breathed a sigh of relief.

Immediately in front of the two boys was an enormous staircase, the same kind found in hotels or mansions. The rotting old rug covered the steps, which led up to a landing. On both sides of the stairway were finely carved wood railings, very dark from age, neglect and the fire.

Cory stared at it, wide-eyed. "Wow. Rich people must've lived here once."

John shrugged. "Dunno. Come on, there's something I wanna show you."

John bounded up the steps, Cory following eagerly. The stairs creaked under their weight.

"What's upstairs?" Cory asked.

"You'll see."

They stopped at the first landing. The stairway split off and continued up behind them. The boys paused before an enormous mirror, which dominated the entire wall. Its massive, ebony frame was carved into demons' heads, and there were some strange letters inlaid on the top, which Cory didn't recognize, but which looked oddly familiar. One thing the boy did notice: an inverted pentagram, carved into the very top of the wood frame. The stylized star looked as if it had once been highlighted with some kind of blood-red paint.

Cory realized something else. There was no dust on the mirror at all. Not a speck! And it didn't show any signs of smoke damage, unlike the remains of the furniture in the living room downstairs.

"You been cleaning this thing?" Cory asked, turning to his friend, and gasped. John was taking a red crayon and writing on the smooth glass. A pentagram. Cory grabbed the older boy's wrist.

"Don't! You'll ruin it!"

Suddenly the mirror's surface fogged up, and rolling mist showed through it as if on a giant television screen. While Cory stared, a pair of arms reached out for him from the surface—right through the glass—arms with dark blue skin and long, tapered fingers ending in razor-sharp nails. They grabbed Cory's outstretched right arm, taking a firm hold.

Cory screamed, pulling back, but the demon hands had too tight a grip on him.

"Ohmigod! John, help me!"

John just stood there, watching his young friend being pulled towards the mirror. The terrified boy flailed out with his free hand, instinctively trying to loosen the demon's hold on him. One of the demon hands grabbed Cory's other arm, and his limbs disappeared into the glass, meeting less resistance than entering water.

"HELP ME!"

"Sorry, sucker. But I gotta."

Cory was dragged further and further into the solid looking glass, his feet planted firmly on the wooden floor, the rubber from his sneakers screeching.

"HELP MEEEEEE!" the younger boy cried, and was drawn completely into the glass.

Inside the mirror, it was bitterly cold. Cory dimly sensed being drawn through thick mist, which chilled his lungs on the first breath. He still struggled to go back, but there was nothing beneath his feet any more. Before he had taken his second breath, the boy was back in the warm air again, and the mist was gone.

Held helplessly aloft by powerful arms, Cory looked straight into a hideous mockery of a face, with pointed ears and long, sharp teeth. The creature was seven feet tall, had glowing yellow eyes with no pupils, and dark-blue scales covering its massive muscular body. The creature wore an ebony toga of jet-black silk with gold trim, and folded bat-like wings protruded from its back. Cory suddenly realized what it was, and *where* he was.

The boy screamed and was immediately handed to a second demon, as easily as one would pass butter at the dinner table. The second demon stripped Cory's clothes off with his razor-sharp talons, and threw them into a burning pyre, where they smoldered in the golden urn. Before the terrified boy realized what was happening, he was wearing nothing but a slave's loincloth, like in the Tarzan movies. Then the demon quickly snapped manacles onto his thin wrists. The monster now held Cory by the chains, his skinny arms stretched above him, his bare feet not even touching the floor.

"BUT YOU PROMISED!" Cory heard John's voice cry. The twelve-year-old looked up and saw his 'friend' clearly through the hideous mirror, which Cory now knew to be some kind of a doorway. There were obviously two mirrors, one here, and the other back on Earth. The first demon angrily pointed his finger at John, more of a talon, really.

"And you promised me six hundred and sixty-six human children! This one is only the ninth! You will get your brother back when I see results!"

The demon waved his hand and the portal disappeared completely. Cory's heart went to his throat as he realized he was trapped here. Quivering while held in the second demon's iron grip, Cory watched helplessly as the first creature walked up to him. Asmodeus held the boy by his chin and inspected him as if he were a prize thoroughbred horse at a show.

"Hmmmm. The youngster shows improvement. This one has hair like untainted night, and eyes of clear sapphire. Obviously, he's the get of a magus. Even from here, I can sense his power! Take him to a cell, Cambian, and see that he is not damaged … yet."

"Yes, Asmodeus," the servant replied, and dragged Cory away. The boy struggled uselessly, being pulled by the chains on his wrists. The stone floor was cold and wet under his bare feet, and offered little friction with which to fight back. Looking over his shoulder, Cory saw a third demon throwing his clothes onto a smoldering pyre. The boy saw his dungaree jacket slowly burning as he was pulled out of the chamber, and he knew he'd never see Earth again.

* * * *

The underground caverns were dark, gloomy, and endless. Periodically, torches burned from iron sconces bolted into the rough stone walls, providing dim illumination. The boy absently noticed that the torches didn't produce any smoke, and the flames were orange, yellow, red, and even blue. The stone floor was smooth, but surprisingly warm, this far underground. Cory had a sudden, horrifying image of the flames of hell on the level just below this one, heating the floor.

"Stop fighting, boy. It will go easier for you."

Cory had always regretted being small for his age, but never so much as now. He had long since lost the strength to yank back on the chains forcefully, but still resisted now and then, in spite of the manacles biting into his wrists.

"W—where ar-are you taking m—me?"

The demon laughed. "To your new home, boy."

"M—my new home?" Cory's face screwed up, and he was about ready to start crying. "Why am I in Hell? I was good!"

The demon stopped walking along the torch lit hall, and laughed long and hard. Cory didn't know what he said that was so funny.

"If you were so good, what were you doing standing in front of the mirror?"

The boy swallowed, his mouth dry. "I didn't mean to—"

"Silence!" The demon pointed a razor-sharp fingernail at Cory's bare chest. "You are a human, the lowest of all creatures in Abydonne, good for nothing more than slavery. You have the night-hair, which gives you a certain amount of status among your fellow slaves—but don't expect it to save your miserable life if you break our laws. Now, on with you!"

The demon yanked on his chains, and Cory went flying forward, falling to his knees. His right knee received a cut on the stone floor, and it began to bleed. Now Cory did begin to cry, the tears running from his cheeks to the floor. He couldn't understand why he was brought here and enslaved.

The boy was pulled up again, and the demon gasped when he saw the blood. The blue finger was pointed at Cory again. "You tell Asmodeus I damaged you and I'll whip all the flesh from your back! Do you understand me?"

Sobbing, Cory nodded. He suddenly realized why slaves wore loincloths; it made it easier for their masters to whip them. The demon dragged the limping young boy through the dark hall. They eventually came to a large, torch lit chamber, filled with wooden cages, their bars as thick as tree trunks.

The demon produced a key, unlatched the padlock holding the cell door's chain together, and pushed Cory inside before snapping the chains into place on the door again.

Cory sat down on the cold, straw-covered stone floor, hugging his bleeding knee and crying. He wanted to cry out for his mother, but he knew she was back in the hospital, unable to even wake up.

"Are you all right?" a young voice asked, and Cory looked up to see another boy, about thirteen, kneeling next to him. The boy's skin was all grimy with soil and his shoulder-length blond hair had taken on a darker tinge from the dirt.

Sobbing, Cory shook his head. "I—I'm s—scared!"

The older boy sighed, shaking his head. "Is that all? I thought the Kelloids tortured you!"

Cory's sobs grew even more hysterical, in spite of his attempts to control them. If he had listened to his mother's warning not to go into abandoned buildings, this never would have happened!

"Will you please stop wailing!" the boy said in a commanding voice.

"I—I'll Tr-try," Cory sobbed, and wiped his wet eyes. "Wh—where are we?"

"The slavepits of Abollydd. When did the Kelloids capture you?"

"J—just now. I got pulled through the mirror."

The older boy frowned. "Mirror? You mean they brought you here magically?"

"I guess so. Who are you?"

For the first time, the other boy smiled, revealing perfect white teeth to contrast with his dirty face. "You really must be from far off, not to know me! I am His Royal Highness, Prince Taliesin of Caer Dathyl."

Hearing this, Cory forgot his throbbing knee and a slight grin came to his lips. "You're a real prince?"

"Yes, although the youngest son. I can't inherit anything save a minor piece of land on the other side of the hills ... if I ever get out of here to rule *anything*, that is. Where did you come from?"

"New York. But I get the feeling I'm no longer even on Earth." Cory ran his tongue across his dry lips and swallowed.

The prince's frown deepened. "Indeed you're not. I've studied many of Abydonne's cities, and New York is not one of them."

"Hey, Kid!" A boy called from a neighboring cell. Cory looked through the thick wooden bars and saw that a tall, fourteen-year-old youth with brown hair had addressed him.

"Yeah?"

"You're from Earth too?"

Cory nodded, and started to get up, but his knee was already getting stiff. Wincing against the pain, Cory limped over to the bars. "Yeah. Brooklyn."

The other boy smiled. "Me too. John Coonan tricked you into that building?"

"Uh huh."

The older boy's features changed, and he clenched his fists. "When I get my hands on that punk, I'm gonna break his nose!"

"Heh. I'll help you do it! What's your name?"

"Nat Sommers. What's yours?"

"Cory Avalon. I live a few blocks from the school."

Nat smiled. "Me too. I don' remember seein' you around. You just move to the neighborhood?"

Cory nodded, and thought he had seen Nat somewhere before—

Yes ... on that carton of milk in the 'fridge! So this is where he got kidnapped to! Cory had a sudden image of his own thin face gracing a milk carton, too. "*Cory Harlen Avalon, Age 12. Height 4'9", Weight 76 lbs. Runaway.*"

If Danvers even bothers to report me missing, that is, Cory thought bitterly.

"Hey, Cory! I asked you a question."

"Huh? Oh, yeah. I was in a foster home."

"Oh, sorry. Bad break."

The Prince put his hand on Cory's shoulder. "I thought you said you hailed from New York. What's this about Brooklyn?"

The boy turned. "I am. New York is a big city. Brooklyn is one of the five boroughs that make it up."

"Ah, I see. Brooklyn is a village within the city's walls."

Cory frowned. "Something like that. You'd have to see it to understand."

Taliesin grinned faintly. "Not much chance of that, my friend. Only a wizard can send you back, and I don't think the Kelloids are going to give you the chance to find one."

Cory suddenly looked to be on the verge of tears again. "You mean I'm stuck here for life?"

The prince saw his young friend was ready to go into hysterics again, and tactfully rested his hand on Cory's shoulder. "No. We're going to get out of here. That I promise you."

Cory smiled weakly. "Thanks, Tal. When can we leave?"

"You've got a plan?" Nat asked hopefully.

Taliesin put a finger to his lips. "Shush! Don't let the Kelloids hear! Yes, I have a plan. Kelloid demons can't stand bright light, especially the Sun. I think I remember where the passage leading to the surface is. All we have to do is make our way there during the daytime-"

"*All* we have to do? Excuse me, your Royal Highness, but have you seen the whips those monsters are packing?"

Taliesin scowled. "Perhaps you prefer to spend the rest of your life in the slavepits?"

Nat's face suddenly fell. "No, of course not."

"Then you'll risk it with me."

Nat swallowed. "Yeah, I guess so. But have you thought of what might happen to us if we get caught? They can do worse than just whip us!"

The Prince turned away. "Fine! Then stay here and rot!"

Cory caught Taliesin's arm. "Waitaminute! What does he mean by 'worse'?"

"Shut up and listen for a minute," Nat called to him. Cory did so.

"I don't hear—" Cory began, and then heard the sound of kids screaming and moaning. It was coming from down the other end of the long hall. "What in God's name is *that?*"

"Torture chamber," Taliesin said tonelessly.

Cory's eyes ballooned. "They *torture* us?"

Nat peered solemnly at the younger boy between the bars of their cells. He turned, and pointed to several long scars on his bare back. "This is what they did to *me*."

Taliesin swallowed, and then sneered. He reached out, touched Cory's shoulder, and turned him gently in his direction. "Don't worry. If we get caught, we'll probably just get the stocks. I hope your feet aren't ticklish."

"Yes, they are!" the boy protested, curling his toes protectively.

Taliesin sneered. "Don't be such a baby! It isn't *that* bad!"

"Yeah, it is," Nat injected, and Cory turned to him again. "It's humiliating! First they cover you with itching powder, and you can't even scratch! Then they make you drink a whole gallon of water, so you have to use the bathroom real bad!"

"Nat!" Taliesin said, trying to get him to shut up.

"Then they tickle you so badly you can't even breathe!"

"Nat!"

"Then, there's the ducking board. Hold you underwater till your lungs are bursting," Nat said, counting off the tortures on his fingers. "Strapedo, hang you by your wrists with weights on your ankles. The rack, where they stretch you till your bones pop out of their sockets—"

"Nat, you're *not* helping!" Taliesin snapped.

"He's just trying to scare me, right?" Cory asked.

"Look, you wanna get out of here?"

Cory nodded slowly.

"Then trust me," the prince said, and saw the dubious look in Cory's eyes. "Look, I won't lie to you. For really serious offenses, like escape, the slaves don't survive the torture. Such offenders are run through the gauntlet, all the tortures, ending with a slow death by constant magic lightning at low power. Cook us slowly from the inside out. Feels like you're burned alive. But if we have one good shot at getting out of here, will you trust me?"

Cory saw Nat shaking his head, and swallowed. Then he thought of spending the rest of his life down here, as a slave to demons, and slowly nodded. "Alright, I'm with you."

A whip cracked on their cell bars, and Cory jumped from the sound. It almost sounded like a gunshot. A Kelloid was standing there, tall and imposing. He slid a wooden bowl of steaming food under the door and a waterskin between the bars. "Eat your meal, slaves. Then get to sleep. Tomorrow you go to work on the Wheel, and we want you rested."

The demon pushed a cart to the next cell, where he gave Nat his evening rations. Cory approached the bowl and tried the hot mush. It was strange, but bland and tasteless. He looked up to see Taliesin taking a swig from the waterskin, and then reached for a spoon.

"Enjoy this. They don't feed us very often, only twice a day."

Cory nodded and sipped two more spoonfuls of the meal. He didn't realize how hungry he was until now, and immediately wished he hadn't skipped breakfast this morning.

"Tal, what's the Wheel?"

The prince looked up, stirring his food. "You'll see. The Kelloid wasn't lying when he said we'll be working hard."

The boy swallowed audibly, his blue eyes wide with fear and glistening in the torchlight.

CHAPTER 2

THE WHEEL

Waves roared as the ocean waves pounded the golden surf at Brighton Beach. High above, sea gulls cried as they circled about in the clear, sapphire-blue sky, searching for food. The earth was warm and pleasant beneath Cory's knees as he dug into it, carefully building a sand castle. The sun was hot, and the salt water beaconed for Cory to run into it and go for a swim. First though, the boy was determined to finish this last turret. He put one of the thin sticks on top of a spire, and then added a clamshell for the main gate. A cool breeze fluttered his dark hair, and Cory looked up. His mother was about to insist he put on a T-shirt and straw hat to protect him from the intense sunshine—

"UP, SLAVES!"

Cory's eyelids bolted open and he lifted his head to see two bowls of gruel and a waterskin lying on the floor. "Eat quickly. I will be back for you in five minutes," a Kelloid ordered, and wheeled his cart to the next cell. The Earth boy had slept near the door, so he barely had to sit up in order to reach the morning rations. Cory was extremely thirsty, and took a few swallows from the waterskin while Taliesin ate.

Fearing the young prince would eat most of their breakfast, Cory put the skin down.

"It's cold," Cory complained after sampling the meal.

"Shut up and eat," The prince said. "We can't be choosy. The next time we get something to eat will be tonight."

Cory nodded and ate another mouthful. Within five minutes the two boys had consumed the contents of the wooden dishes and the demon had returned, as promised. The cell door was unlocked, and the Kelloid came walking in with a sneer on its reptilian face. A long whip was coiled in his scaled hand, and his voice rasped when he spoke.

"Finished your banquet, slaves? MOVE!"

The younger boy shuddered, not moving from fear.

"Come on," Taliesin sighed, and lifted his friend by the shoulders. Cory tested his weight on his right leg, and winced. During the night, his knee had grown very stiff, and a scab had formed.

"What's the matter?" The prince asked, helping Cory to stand up.

"My knee," the boy whispered back. "It hurts."

"Your knee hurts?" the Kelloid asked, a mocking grin on its face. "A few hours on the Wheel will cure that, boy! MOVE!"

As quickly as possible, Cory limped out, supported by Taliesin. Outside there were several more young slaves, mostly boys, and all wearing chains like the two of them.

"What's he mean, 'the Wheel will cure it?'"

The prince had a sour look on his face. "Soon, everything will ache. Your knee will be the least of your worries. I hope you're in shape."

"Well, I'm pretty good at softball during gym."

Taliesin looked at Cory quizzically. "Nothing you ever did will have prepared you for this."

Cory swallowed, trying to keep his mind from his fate. He again stared at the manacles on the slaves' wrists, and wondered how they were expected to get any work done.

"Don't they ever take the chains off?"

"No. They don't know which of us can perform magic and which of us can't, so they chain all of us. Your dark hair doesn't help."

"My hair?"

"The more powerful wizards always have black hair and blue eyes. Royal magi family from thousands of years ago."

Cory frowned, staring at the manacles. "And how do chains stop magic?"

Taliesin's eyebrows rose. "You really are from another world, aren't you? Even a six-year-old knows cold iron stops magic!"

Cory thought about that for a minute. "Wait. If iron is immune to magic, then how are magic swords made?"

"The enchantment is set soon after the weapon is forged, while it is still hot. Once the metal has cooled, nothing can enchant it again."

"Oh," Cory replied, and gasped when he saw the size of the room they were being led into. It was twice the size of Giants' Stadium, and torchlit. Dominating the center of the room was an enormous wooden wheel with long poles sticking out from it. The Wheel was attached to a thick axle, which disappeared into the floor and ceiling. Connected to that was a giant gear with paddles for walking on.

Manning the long poles were about sixty ragged-looking kids, making the Wheel turn at a constant rate. Several of the kids looked to be beyond exhaustion, and most were leaning on the poles, trying to rest while walking in an endless circle. Those who looked about ready to collapse were whipped by Kelloids, and told to get back to work. Some fainted dead away and were pulled out of the work team by frail slaves, mostly girls.

Cory and Taliesin were led to one of the poles, keeping pace with it while the tired kids were told to leave. Many looked at the boys with gratefulness in their eyes. They were finally being relieved.

Cory followed his friend into position, and grasping the pole, began to push. It wasn't hard, since there were many kids contributing to the job, but he could see the effects of constantly walking with no rest. To his right, five more boys and a sixteen-year-old girl came into position, completing the new team.

"What are we doing?" Cory asked.

"It's a magic engine," Nat answered, who stood to Cory's immediate right.

"It charges the crystals around the demons' necks," Taliesin explained. "Then they use the crystals to cast spells."

Cory nodded, then looked down at his right knee, which was beginning to throb again. "How long do we have to do this for?"

"Just keep pushing," the prince sighed.

* * * *

They were walking in the endless circle for so many hours Cory lost track of the time. His knee had grown worse, and he mainly limped throughout the whole thing. The scab had broken and pus leaked out, running down his leg. Taliesin and Nat saw this and tried to cover for him, hoping a Kelloid wouldn't see and whip them for it. Still, Cory thought, Taliesin was right. His legs, his back, and his arms ached for rest. He was also desperately hungry, and tried to ignore the rumbling in his stomach.

Two hours ago the team was allowed for a short break to rest and drink as much water as they wanted, but not given any lunch. A kind girl with disheveled red hair had brought them water, and poured some on Cory's bad knee. It helped somewhat, but now, after two more hours of walking and pushing the Wheel, it hurt so much Cory wished someone would come along and cut his leg off.

"YOU!" a demon shouted, and cracked his whip on Cory's naked back. It stung worse then anything the boy had ever felt, leaving a long red mark where it struck. Cory screamed, releasing his hold on the pole. He immediately tried to reach for his back, but the chain stopped his hands less than halfway there.

"WALK FASTER!" the Kelloid ordered, and flogged the boy again. This time Cory nearly collapsed, sobbing.

"He's injured!" Taliesin cried to the Kelloid. "His knee is hurt!"

From the look the demon gave the boys, it looked as if he wanted to lash Cory again, but wisdom got the better of him and he lowered the rawhide whip.

"Come here!" the Kelloid barked, pointing his razor-sharp fingernail at Cory, and the boy made his way past his fellow slaves, limping. It wasn't easy, trying to go out while the poles were coming at him, but it was moving slowly enough so that Cory managed.

The thin child stood quivering before the hulking demon, mindful of the fresh pain on his back and the whip still in the creature's hand. His heart beat so quickly he thought it would burst, and his breath came in short gasps.

The demon looked down at Cory's knee and frowned. "So, you told the truth. Come here."

Cory hesitated, quivering, and the Kelloid grabbed his chain with a scowl, lifting the boy off his feet with one arm. The monster put the whip on his belt and gripped the injured knee with one hand. Held aloft with his arms stretched high above him, his toes ten inches from the dirt, Cory could only watch in terror as the demon handled his bare, bleeding leg.

A orange stone hanging around the neck of the Kelloid began to glow. Taliesin had told him earlier that was a magegem, which the demons used to spellcast. Then the boy felt a tingling sensation on his knee where the demon's hand rested, which quickly spread all over his skin. Cory giggled, and the creature stared up at him with glowing yellow eyes.

"Ticklish, stripling? Good. Break the law and you'll end up in the stocks!" The demon put him down and Cory was forced to test his weight on the leg. It no longer hurt. In fact, no part of his body ached anymore!

"Now, back to work with you!" the Kelloid ordered with intent in his voice. Cory eyed the whip and quickly rejoined his friends after taking a moment to locate them on the large wheel.

"You okay?" Nat asked.

"Yeah," Cory replied. "The pain's all gone—all of it! How come they don't do that for everybody?"

"Magic drains them," Taliesin explained. "And for the hours we're expected to work on the Wheel, it wouldn't make sense for them to cure all sixty of us of fatigue. They only save the healing spells for the seriously injured, as you were. And even that's rare."

Cory frowned. "It hurt a lot, but it wasn't that bad."

The prince shook his head, amazed at the innocence of a boy only two years younger than he. "Yes, it was! Concentrated magic here speeds healing and disease up. I've seen the case before, and would have told you, but I didn't want you to start crying again. You came very close to losing your leg, and if they hadn't healed you, you would have."

Cory stared at his friend and swallowed, realizing he wasn't kidding. "Thanks."

Taliesin shrugged. "You are one of my subjects now. I'm responsible for your welfare, even at the cost of my own life."

"Thanks anyway," Cory repeated in a small voice, thinking of how close he had come to having his leg sawed off below the knee, and his own blood flowing all over the place. The boy shuddered at the image and looked straight ahead, pushing the great Wheel.

* * * *

By nightfall Cory was exhausted again, in spite of the two twenty minute breaks they were given. He couldn't even tell how long he had been walking, because they were inside a cavern with no sun. Cory was falling asleep on his feet, tired and hungry, but didn't say anything when he saw the condition of the other boys around him. Cory had been healed once during the day, and had in effect started fresh. The others had been working since dawn, and for all he knew, it was probably well past sunset now.

Some of the boys leaned against their poles from extreme exhaustion, only to be whipped awake again by the ever-vigilant Kelloids.

After a little while longer, a few of the boys collapsed. The others, tired as they were, tried not to step on their fallen comrades as the girls rushed forward to pull the unconscious slaves out of the work area.

Not long after that and the relief teams were herded into the immense chamber. Cory followed Nat and the others out of their position on the Wheel. The kids were put into groups and led off, back to their cells for the night.

Cory recognized the Kelloid who escorted his group as Cambian, now that he was noticing subtle differences in their features. Cambian was in charge of Cory's cellblock, according to Taliesin. He was responsible for their training, brought them their rations, and, when needed, brought them to the torture chamber for punishment.

Cambian shoved the two boys into their cell, locked the door behind them, and signaled a slave to dispense their evening rations: two bowls this time. Cory eyed the food, not sure whether to lie down and fall asleep immediately or eat. Smelling the aroma of cooked meat, the boy made his decision and wolfed down the warm food.

"I told you," Taliesin said between gulps, "we would work hard today."

The younger boy eyed his friend fearfully. "You mean we have to do that every day?"

The prince shook his head. "They don't want to wear out good slaves. They have enough to keep the Wheel going in shifts. We do it every third day, and handle other tasks in between. The only good thing about working on the Wheel is that we get extra rations."

Cory nodded and noticed with horror that his meal was already half gone. He tried to chew more slowly and asked Taliesin something else.

"I haven't seen any adults. What happens when we grow up? They don't kill us, do they?" Cory asked the last sentence in a very meek voice.

The prince swallowed before answering. "No. We're in training, and the hardest task we have is to work the Wheel, or breaking apart stones with pick-axes to free magegems from the rubble. When we've grown we're sent to the mines themselves, or so Cambian tells me. The Kelloids need precious gems and the magic to charge them, and this mountain range is filled with both."

Cory nodded. "Why do they need that stuff?"

"The gems they use to focus their magic powers."

"Oh. Wait!" Cory said, a big smile on his face. He crawled closer to his friend, whispering. "If we stop working, their power will be turned off, and we can escape!"

Taliesin started to laugh, dropping the food in his hand. "Oh, Maker! You *are* naive! They'll kill us if we refuse to work!"

"Oh," Cory said in a small voice, and went back to finish his dinner. He ate the last two pieces of meat and opened his waterskin, draining it almost completely; he wanted to save a little in case he got thirsty at night. For the first time since he got here, Cory felt content, his belly full. The young boy lay down in the straw, curling up to keep warm. He was asleep the moment he shut his eyes.

Chapter 3

ESCAPE FROM ABOLLYDD

Weeks passed before the boys saw their chance. In that time, Cory saw that the "lighter tasks" Taliesin had mentioned included unloading carts from the mines, and breaking apart the chunks of rock with hand-picks, looking for the precious gems so prized by the demons.

Cory, like most kids here, was a thin child to begin with; the lack of nourishing food didn't help matters. He was expected to carry chunks of broken rubble from a metal cart fresh from the mines, swing a long, sharp pick-axe, and chip away the rock particles until he had freed a beautiful, faceted crystal. This gem was then brought to a special chamber beneath the Wheel, where it would be charged with magical energy, then set in a piece of jewelry. The demons could then tap into the awesome magic power contained within to cast spells.

Taliesin had accidentally shattered one of the gems while breaking apart a rock, and was sent off to the torture chamber for punishment. Cory watched helplessly as his friend was taken away. The boy swallowed, fighting back tears, until a demon ordered him to get back to work. He hefted the pickaxe once more, and chipped away at his piece of rubble even more carefully, his mind filled with the hideous tortures these creatures could inflict upon their helpless captives at will. In particular, the boy feared being tied to a wooden plank, held underwater until his lungs were bursting, and he drowned, staring in vain at the shining surface of the water, high above him, precious air just out of reach.

The next day, Cory was put to work in the kitchens. It was a huge chamber filled with long tables and enormous cauldrons on heaps of burning wood. The boys beat the meal into powder, adding it to a lot of boiling water, to make a thin gruel. On other tables, several slaves cut apart small pieces of meat into even smaller pieces of meat, before putting them into pots of boiling water. This was the reward for those who worked the Wheel.

There was only one demon in the room, supervising. Most of the slaves working here had been punished at least once, and didn't dare sneak some food for themselves, no matter how hungry they were, but some did. Cory saw a boy named Jonathan pop some meat in his mouth when the demon's back was turned; he didn't even take the time to chew it. The boy just swallowed it whole.

Cory was just thinking of doing that same thing when a yell startled him out of his daydreaming.

"Young fool!" the demon bellowed, squeezing Cory's skinny arm, and twisting it painfully. Cory dropped the knife.

"Cut the pieces smaller! We can't afford to feed you miserable humans a banquet!"

Cory's eyes ballooned. The demon was practically lifting him off his feet. "S—sorry. I'll try to do better."

"Better? I'll bet. I saw you looking at that food, human. Hungry?"

Cory's face went two shades paler. "N ... no."

The demon smiled. He was so close; Cory could smell his foul breath. "No? Then perhaps you can skip supper tonight. I'll tell Cambian."

Cory didn't know what to say to that. He was starving as it was.

"Meantime, we can use some salt for the meat. Helps preserve it. Down the hall to your right. Stay to the right, and you'll reach the storerooms. Lots of crates and barrels. You want the small barrel with two white stars on it. Even a young idiot like you should be able to find it."

Cory was given a push toward the entrance, and he started walking. He paused at the door, his heat beating quickly. There was nobody in the tunnels. Could it be this easy?

The boy stopped, his hand resting on the stone wall. He had to find Taliesin. He couldn't just leave without him! Even if he could find the exit by himself, he was *not* about to abandon his friend!

But where, in this maze of tunnels, was Taliesin? Torture chamber. How was he supposed to find it?

Then, from down the hall, he heard the screams. Of course!

Cory silently made his way down the tunnel, following the screams. His mind filled with horrible images. There was a book in the school library on tortures of the Middle Ages. It usually involved red-hot pokers, knives, and wooden splinters under fingernails. He had a sudden, horrible image of his friend being lowered into a huge pot of boiling oil.

He finally reached an open doorway, which was obviously the entrance to the chamber. Steeling himself, the boy snuck a peek inside.

Cory was both revolted and relieved by what he saw. Most of the tortures were intended to punish, not to maim or kill. Why should they? The human boys were their slaves, after all. Maimed slaves could not work. Toward the back of the huge chamber, several boys were chained to the wall, their hands stretched above them. One boy was being whipped by a demon, leaving long, red marks; but the wounds healed completely a moment after they were made. A magic whip, intended to inflict pain, but leave no lasting injury. Cory rubbed his knee, remembering how quickly infection could set in here.

Near the whipping was a huge wooden tub, filled with water. A boy who was about fourteen was tied tight to a flat board, being held underwater for several long seconds. Cory saw bubbles float up to the surface of the water, and the boy was heaved into the air by a second demon, coughing and allowed to catch his breath before sinking beneath the surface again. Cory swallowed in sympathy.

The most common punishment by far, closest to the door, appeared to be the stocks. Two rows of wooden frames lined the walls, with young slaves sitting in most of them. The first frame had holes for immobilizing a boy's wrists just in front of him at chest height, while the other secured his ankles, legs stretched out, with the exposed bottoms of his bare feet presented for tickling. The victim could do nothing but watch, completely immobilized by the restraints.

Nat hadn't lied. Cory remembered from history that in the Middle Ages, the stocks were used to humiliate law-breakers in public, usually ill-behaved children. It was an insidious torture, almost as bad as being held underwater, for the victim could hardly breathe during the endless torment. First, each boy had been forced to swallow a gallon of water, and told to hold it, or *else*. Then his skin was coated with itching powder. The trapped boys couldn't even scratch themselves to relieve the awful itching. Finally, magical feathers floated in the air and relentlessly assaulted the exposed soles of their feet. Even if a kid's skin wasn't especially sensitive, those enchanted feathers were bewitched to be ticklish beyond belief. The young offenders all collapsed into hysterical laughter, unable to draw a full breath of air for hours. Faces beet-red, the boys squirmed, with no hope of escaping the endless torment.

The twelve-year-old remembered a few summers back, when four of his camp counselors tickled-tortured him and another kid for playing with illegal fireworks. They were each tied spread-eagle to their beds and attacked all over, on their feet, underarms, neck, and ribs. Cory had laughed so hard he couldn't breathe and his chest ached. The torture didn't stop until both Cory and Ben had wet the front of their shorts, and then their counselors marched them across the open field like that, in full view of all the other kids. The diaper jokes went on for days. It was not a pleasant experience, and Cory had no wish to repeat it.

Cory finally spotted Taliesin, sitting right next to two ten-year-old boys who were caught stealing food: blond-haired Aren from Kaleva, and Thomas, a skinny little kid from Earth. A demon was using two feathers at the same time to tickle torture a kid. When the demon let go of the feathers, they floated in the air and continued to automatically torment the youngster, from heels to wriggling toes.

"HAHAHAHAHAHAHA! PLEEEZ! CAN'T STAND IT!" Thomas begged. His black hair was matted with sweat, his face was red, and tears streamed from his glistening brown eyes. The boy's thin arms and legs strained with the effort of trying to squirm free, but the solid wood prison held him fast. The poor boy couldn't even kick, could only rock back and forth, hysterical with helpless laughter. Cory thought the kid was about ready to pass out from lack of air.

"*AWW!* Is ickle Thomas *icklish?* Too bad, you little thief! You only have another six hours to go!" The demon mocked, leering down at the young slave.

Taliesin also squirmed in agony, next to Thomas. He laughed so hard he thought his sides would split. The young prince's face was beat-red as the feathers relentlessly stroked his ribs and the tender bottoms of his wriggling feet, toes curled in a vain effort to protect himself. Cory was amazed his friend could draw the breath to beg. "HAHAHAHAHA! PLEEEZ! I HAFTA GO! HAHAHAHAHAHA!"

For stealing a whole pound of beef, Aren had it worst of all. Feathers assaulted his feet and probed his exposed ribs and underarms, all at the same time. Aren squealed like a girl, his long blond hair flying as he struggled in vain to free himself. "PLEEEZ! MAKE IT STOP! HAHAHAHAHAHA! CAN'T … BREATHE! HAHAHAHAHA!"

The demon leered down at them, a sinister gleam in his eye. "Did I give you *permission* to *breathe*, human stripling? Look at you all *squirm!* Your bladders must be *BURSTING!* How *HUMILIATING!*"

"PLEEEZ! HAHAHAHAHA MAKE IT STOP! HAHAHAHA! I'LL BE GOOD!"

The demon snarled down at them. "You slaves have to learn *DISCIPLINE!* I'll be back in thirty minutes. If any of you boys *dare* to wet my floor, first you'll get the *belt*, then I'll tie you to the *ducking board!*"

The demon stormed off to the opposite side of the vast torture chamber, his hooves clacking on the stone floor as he walked, leaving the young boys to suffer. Cory snuck across the floor, constantly glancing at the demons. If caught, Cory knew he'd get far worse than this inane tickle torture. He hadn't mentioned it to Taliesin, but he was terrified of drowning, and he was certain the demons would tie *him* to the ducking board.

"Tal, it's me," Cory whispered.

The young prince blinked tears from his eyes and tried to focus. His long blond hair fell into his flushed face, and his lungs burned for lack of air. "Coreeeheehee! PLEEEZ! LET ME ... OUT OF THIS THING! HAHAHAHA! CAN'T ... BREATHE! HAHAHAHAHA! CAN'T STAND IT!"

Cory's face fell when he saw the stocks were secured with padlocks. The boys were trapped, but good! "It's locked!"

"KEY! BE ... HIND YOU! HAHAHAHA! HURRY!"

Cory stole another glance in the direction of the two demons. Their backs were to him. The boy grabbed a key ring from a hook on the wall. Then Cory approached his friend with a mischievous gleam in his eye. He couldn't resist the urge to tease him a little. "I dunno. You kept telling me how tough you were, and here you can't even take a little tickle torture. Tsk, tsk...."

"HAHAHAHA! CORY, PLEEEZ! I HAFTA PEE! HAHAHAHA! I'LL ... DO ... ANYTHING!"

With an impish grin, Cory unlatched the padlocks with the key, and lifted the wooden frames open. Tal immediately yanked his feet back, his hysterics dying down to giggles.

"Just remember you owe me one."

"ME, TOO! PLEEEEEZ! HAHAHAHAHA!" Thomas squealed, tears running down his face. He gasped for breath, then hoarsely yelled. "MAKE IT STOP! HAHAHAHAHA!"

"HAHAHAHAHA! CAN'T BREATHE! HAHAHAHA!" Aren begged. The kid's face was beat red, and he obviously couldn't last much longer. Then Cory heard the distinctive sound of urine tinkling to the stone floor.

"One at a time!" Cory whispered, unlocking the stocks and freeing as many kids as he could. All of them drew air in huge, grateful gulps, wiping tears from their eyes. Cory didn't know how long they had been trapped like that, relentlessly tickled into submission, but he knew he didn't want it to happen to him.

"WHAT ARE YOU DOING?"

The boys all turned as one. Cory was so startled he dropped the keys. The demon with the rawhide whip was striding toward them. Cory recognized the demon as Cambian, and knew he was doomed.

"Time to go, Cory!" Taliesin cried, and grabbed his friend's arm while running for the door. Cory felt his bare feet slap the stone floor as he ran, and wished he still had his sneakers for better traction. Dashing into a side-tunnel, Cory rolled the chain links into a ball to prevent it from making noise. He looked around frantically around, searching for someplace to hide.

"You sure you know where you're going?" Cory asked, beginning to panic. The stocks didn't seem so inane anymore, and he was scared. He also couldn't get the image of that poor, half-drowned kid out of his mind. He didn't even notice they were in the storeroom he had originally been sent to.

"Yes," Taliesin answered, ducking behind a huge crate. "They brought me through here from the surface the day they captured me, and I have a perfect memory. Besides, it's daytime now, and the

Kelloids can't stand the sun, so there should be very few guards near the entrance. The Sun'll finish them."

"I hope you're right," Cory said, and got a scowl as a reply. Taliesin grasped Cory's arm and squeezed, a warning to keep quiet. Cory cocked an ear, trying hard not to breathe. He heard a demon walking around in the room and feared it might be Cambian.

Cory heard his heart beating rapidly in his ears, was afraid that would give them away. The Kelloid moved crates and barrels around on the floor, obviously looking for something. The demon's breath exploded from his nostrils like a steam press.

"Lousy human striplings!" a voice said, and Cory felt relieved, if slightly. It was not Cambian. "First I'll drown them, then I'll flay them alive!"

The boys stared at each other, their eyes wide with terror.

"Cambian!" a deep, rasping voice called from another tunnel. "Down here! I found three of 'em!"

The stone floor vibrated beneath the boys' feet as Cambian stormed off, his hooves clomping loudly. The boys stared at each other, hardly daring to breathe, sweat pouring down their faces. In the distance, they heard the distinct sound of kids screaming and begging for mercy, and the deep baritone of the demons threatening everything from whips to magic lightning. It was several long moments before the cries for help faded, and the pair dared peek over the top of the crate they'd been hiding behind.

Cory swallowed audibly. The room looked like a tornado had hit it. One wooden crate was smashed open, flour spilled all over the floor. Another crate that must have weighed two hundred pounds had been casually tossed against the far wall.

"Eeep, was all Cory managed to say, his throat tight and dry.

"They catch us, and we're done for. We've gotta escape, right now!"

"M ... ma ... magic lightning?" Cory asked.

Taliesin nodded grimly. "At low power, slowly cooking our insides alive. I've heard it's a very painful death."

"Ma ... maybe they'll just—" Cory started to say.

"Maybe nothing! You freed a bunch of slaves from the mildest torture they have! They're gonna kill us, Cory! We've got nothing to lose anymore! Come on," the prince said with determination, and Cory followed, walking as quietly as possible. After ten minutes of wandering through the slowly inclining cave tunnels, Cory saw daylight beginning to illuminate the cavern walls. His heart flew. They were really going to make it out of here!"

Taliesin grabbed his friend's arm and forcefully pushed the two of them against the wall. The prince put a finger to his lips and signed that a demon was right around the corner, guarding the last tunnel to freedom.

What are we going to do? Cory mouthed silently.

Taliesin shrugged. Then his face lit, and he held up a finger.

You be the decoy, Taliesin signed. *And I'll jump him from behind.*

Cory's eyes grew wide. Was his friend planning suicide? The Kelloid could rip chains in two with his bare hands! Cory wondered how bad it really would be to go back and face the music. As if hearing the thought, Taliesin squeezed his friend's arm and gave him a sour look.

If we go back now we'll both be killed, the prince mouthed.

Cory swallowed and knew his friend was right. Cambian was sadistic. He preferred punishments which prolonged the agony as long as possible. Their deaths could take days.

Taliesin continued to put pressure on Cory's arm, and the younger boy nodded. Better the quick, painless death. Better to have his head ripped off by the demon—

I must be out of my mind, Cory thought as he stepped out of the shadows and saw the hulking demon. It had its back to him, watching the cavern, which narrowed as it climbed towards the surface. Maybe the Kelloids were expecting an attack from outside, Cory thought. It was inconceivable for any of their slaves to attempt an escape. Death by slow torture, or a quick and gruesome end by those razor-sharp claws. Cory had seem them eat, tearing raw meat apart, using those claws as a knife.

So what in the name of God was he doing? Cory drew a deep breath, steadying himself, and walked right in front of the demon.

"Hi, I'm lost," Cory said, trying to sound calm, but his voice still quivered.

The Kelloid frowned at him. "What are you doing here?"

Cory looked the Kelloid directly in the eye, seeing Taliesin approach with his peripheral vision. If the demon didn't turn around—

"I—" the boy began, trying to sound realistic. "I was sent from the kitchen for some seasoning, and got lost. Can you help me?"

The demon scowled and pointed a razor-sharp fingernail at him. "You're a little liar! The storerooms are a long way from here! Who's your master, boy?"

Taliesin jumped up, slinging his chain around the demon's neck. The thirteen-year-old pulled back with all his strength, only to be yanked off his feet when the guard resisted.

Cory saw his friend in dire need of help and kicked the demon in the groin. Mom said to do that only if his life was in danger, and now it surely was! If the demon dragged the two boys back to the torture chamber they would both die with agonizing slowness.

The Kelloid bent forward in pain, trying to scream, but the chain was crushing his windpipe with cold iron. Taliesin wrapped his legs around the demon's waist to get a better hold and pulled even harder. The manacles were digging into the boy's wrists and they began to bleed, but Taliesin ignored it. The pain would be a lot worse if he failed.

The Kelloid dropped to his knees, groping for the human boy on his back. Cory gasped when he thought of what those long fingernails could do to his friend if they ever reached him. The boy rushed forward and poked the demon in the eyes, jumping back when scaled hands moved forward to cover the Kelloid's face.

The demon gasped for breath and the prince saw his chance. Putting all of his strength into a final, bone-breaking pull, Taliesin crushed the demon's throat with the chain. The guard flopped forward, dead.

Both boys breathed hard, realizing how close they had just come to being torn to pieces by the monster. Then Cory saw the black blood running on the stone floor and his face turned sour.

"You killed him!"

Taliesin looked up, startled. "No kidding! Do you realize what he would have done to us?"

"Yeah, but you didn't have to kill him!"

The prince sighed, shaking his head. "You're too innocent to realize, I suppose. I'll bet this is the first dead body you've ever seen."

Cory's jaw shifted. "Well, now that you mention it—"

"Never mind. Just keep watch," Taliesin ordered, and began to examine the body.

Cory tiptoed back the way they had come, listening carefully for anybody coming. A slight metallic sound made the boy jump, but he realized it had come from behind him, where Taliesin was. He went back to see what the problem was.

"Coast is clear," Cory reported.

"Darnit!"

"What's the matter?"

"He doesn't have the keys on him. Some guard!"

"Keys for what?" Cory asked, walking up to his friend.

"The manacles, you dope! Oh, well. At least we have his knife and whip."

Cory didn't see the connection, but followed the older boy silently, not wanting to raise any alarms. There also might be a second guard up ahead, near the cave entrance.

The cave floor changed from stone to sand and narrowed as they neared the surface. Fortunately, Taliesin was right, for the room where the monster's body lay was as close as the Kelloids dared come to sunlight. The boys saw the entrance ahead of them and ran for it, eyes wide with joy.

Emerging, Cory squinted against the bright light, smiling. The boy had spent the last three days in darkness, but it seemed more like three weeks. The sky was clear blue with few clouds, and a moist wind blew against his face, whipping his dark hair. Cory took a deep lungful of the sea air, enjoying his freedom, now fully appreciating what the word meant—

Sea air?

Cory opened his eyes as best he could against the glare and saw the water, the waves lapping softly against the beach. But they weren't as large as sea waves, and he could clearly see the opposite shore, the mountains outlining the horizon. Cory turned to his friend with a quizzical look on his face.

"Since when are there salt lakes in the mountains?"

"The Kelloids did that magically. It's now called the Dead Lake because they cursed the water and killed all of the fish."

"Lovely," Cory murmured, and looked around. They had emerged from a cave entrance in the face of a large cliff which went straight up for seventy feet before leveling off. The beach stretched for as far as Cory could see.

"Now what'll we do?"

"This way," Taliesin said, pointing. "The cliff is too steep to climb, but the land becomes level with the beach further on."

Cory slowly nodded and followed his friend. The sand was hot and stung their bare feet as they went, until Cory suggested they walk in the water. The sensation of cool wetness around his ankles was pleasing, and Cory gave in to an impulse, running and splashing in the lake, drenching himself.

"What are you doing?" Taliesin asked.

"Come on, you lug! The water's great!"

The prince's jaw fell. "Have you lost all your senses? The Kelloids will look for us the minute the sun is down!"

That remark sobered Cory, his smile fading. Water dripped from his wet, black hair and down his chin as he checked the position of the sun. It was nearly noontime, which gave them roughly five or six hours to get wherever they were going.

Cory sighed, swimming to shore as best he could with the manacles on his wrists, dog paddling. He emerged from the water with the look of a small child told to leave the bathtub.

"I don't believe you did that!"

"Gimme a break, Tal! I haven't had a bath in six weeks!"

Taliesin fairly exploded. "You stupid little kid! You want water, fine! So do I! *Fresh* water! We don't even have anything to drink, and you go playing around as if nothing were wrong!"

"I'm sorry," Cory said softly, and then noticed the drying blood on Taliesin's wrists, under the metal bands.

"Oh, my God! Are you all right?"

"No, you knave! I have to wash this before it becomes infected!"

Cory stared at him. "So? We've got a whole lake to wash it in!"

The prince hesitated, then dipped his wrists in the water, wincing as he did so. "We can't stay here too long. Certainly not swim and play! Maker, how can you be so naïve and survive in this world?"

"I didn't come from this world," Cory reminded him.

"Then how did you ever survive in your own?"

The water lapped Cory's ankles and he stared out at the water. It was Summertime here, where it was Fall back home. The soft breeze blew against his cheek, and he inhaled it, trying to calm himself.

"My parents protected me," the boy said softly.

"Well, they're not here for you now. All you have are yourself ... and me."

Cory turned to the older boy and Taliesin saw the tears welling in his friend's eyes. "I'm sorry, but it's the truth."

"I know," Cory said, his voice breaking up. "My mom ... she's been in the hospital for four years. Nobody will even tell me how she is—"

Rising, the young prince nodded slowly, not completely sure what a hospital was. He reached out and put his hand on Cory's shoulder. "Don't cry."

"I'll cry if I want to," the boy breathed, and turned away again, staring at the water.

"No you won't. That's a royal command."

"Go and order somebody else. I'm in no mood—"

Taliesin grabbed Cory's arm and spun him around. "Now you listen to me. I don't know what kind of world you come from, but here I am the law. You live or die at my word, and until you manage to get back to your home, that's the way it will be. Do you understand me?"

Cory shrugged Taliesin's hand off and back away, further into the water. "No, I don't! How can you tell me—order me not to cry?"

The Prince stared at his friend uncertainly. Never before had someone—*anyone*—talked back to him, a prince. Still, something in Cory struck a chord in him, and Taliesin explained.

"We don't have any drinking water. Until we do, don't cry, or you'll dehydrate yourself. Understand?"

Cory looked at him for a minute, then nodded. "All right."

"Good," Taliesin said, and gestured at the beach. "We have a long way to go before nightfall. I just hope we make it in time."

Chapter 4

FOREST

The two boys made their way along the beach for four miles before the slope of land was low enough to climb up onto the rocks. After traveling inland for some time, the occasional brush gave way to a dense forest, with maples, elms, and oaks. Thorns cut their unprotected legs, and Cory almost stepped into a patch of poison ivy. The city boy was saved by the intervention of Taliesin, who pulled Cory out of the way in time.

"Is this jungle your idea, or do we really have to go through here?"

The prince scowled. "Perhaps you'd rather stand around in the open? And this isn't a jungle."

"Seems like it," Cory complained, rubbing the scratches on his calves. Then he noticed the water and his eyes grew wide. "Tal!"

"Yeah, I know," the prince said, walking up to the brook. "Where there's trees, there's bound to be water."

The boys rushed forward and knelt at the shore, cupping their hands and drinking deeply. The water was warm, but fresh and good. After a few minutes they waded into the creek, dunking their heads and shaking the water out.

"Whoa! That's good!"

"Just wish we had some soap, Tal."

"I'll make some later."

Cory looked at the older boy quizzically. "How?"

"Plant fat," Taliesin explained, and examined his wrists. Dried blood caked the metal bands, gluing them to his wrists. The Kelloids had made the manacles so they were loose-fitting and allowed room for growth, but they were still small enough to cause problems if there was an injury.

"How're your hands?"

"Not good," the prince answered, pulling at his chain. "These are going to have to come off."

Cory's face fell. He hadn't thought of that until now. "Where are we going to get the keys?"

"We don't need them. A smith back in Caer Dathyl could take them off, but I don't think I can wait that long."

The young prince left the water and knelt beside two Kelloid weapons in the grass where he had left them. Taliesin picked up the knife and began to insert the point into the keyhole.

Cory dunked his head one last time, then followed Taliesin out. Dripping wet, the boy sat down next to his friend.

"You're trying to pick the lock?"

Taliesin nodded. "Wish I had the chance to take these off earlier. Not many people can pick locks—"

Cory frowned, watching intently. In a moment there was a satisfying click, and the shackle snapped open. "Ah," Taliesin said, and pulled it off. The skin was broken, as expected, and a thick scab lined Taliesin's wrist. Cory winced.

"It isn't that bad," Tal said, and began on the other shackle.

Cory watched his friend trying to maneuver the knife with his left hand, and realized how hard it must be. Then it dawned on him. "Since when does a prince know how to pick locks?"

Taliesin grinned. "Learned it from Badger, our keep's blacksmith. I have to learn a bit of everything, as a prince."

"Prince of Thieves," Cory accused, and Taliesin glared at him.

Cory's smile faded. "It's a joke!"

"I don't find it very amusing—" the prince said, and the second lock popped open. "Ah! Now let's see—OUCH!"

"What's the matter?"

Taliesin squeezed his right wrist. "Metal was stuck to the skin, and I pulled some of the scab off. I have to clean it before infection sets in."

Taliesin crawled back over to the water and soaked his wrists. Cory watched, swallowing. "Is it bad?"

The older boy sighed. "No. I think I'll live."

"Good. I'd hate to get caught in this jungle all alone."

Taliesin knew *that* was a joke, and laughed.

After a moment, Cory lifted his hands, holding the chain taut. "Ummm ... Tal ... when you get a chance?"

The prince of Caer Dathyl nodded, glancing back at the grass. "Hand me the knife."

Cory did so, and the older boy got to work. Once the knife almost slipped, and Cory winced. "This isn't going to hurt, is it?"

Taliesin smiled. "Coward."

"Am not a coward. I just don't want my hand cut off."

"Have a little faith in your liege," Taliesin said, and the shackle popped open. Cory smiled as the prince got to work on the second one.

"What's a liege?"

Taliesin looked up at the younger boy in shock. "Don't they have kings where you come from?"

Cory shook his head. "No ... wait. Yes, they do, but not in my country."

"Who rules you?"

"The people rule," Cory explained. "It's called a democracy."

"Strange," Taliesin murmured, and the lock clicked with a final, gentle twist. "There!"

Cory nodded, letting his chains drop into the water with a plunk. The boy smiled at his free wrists. "Thank you. For everything."

"Forget it. I was only doing my duty to protect you," Taliesin said, and threw the knife into the grass before wading into the water again.

Cory stared after him. "You mean you only helped me because you had to?"

"Of course not! I helped you because I wanted to."

Cory accepted this, and went into the water again himself. Finally free of the chains, Cory could swim for real now, and went deep into the creek, diving under several times. He found the sandy bottom, covered with water plants, and saw a school of fish.

The boy surfaced, blinking water from his eyes, and threw a dripping lock of his black hair away. "Tal?"

"Yes?" the prince answered. Cory noticed most of the grime was gone from his friend's body, and his blond hair was plastered to his head.

"What are we going to do about dinner?"

The prince looked around and pointed with a dripping finger to the trees. "We can eat berries tonight—"

Cory frowned. *Berries?*

"And by tomorrow, we'll be back in a town, hopefully."

"Oh."

Cory swam for shore and lay down in the soft grass, letting the warm breeze blow against his skin. Resting his head in his arms, the boy pulled the grass with his toes and closed his eyes. "This reminds me of the time we went up to the Adirondacks, when I was little."

"Where are the Adirondacks?"

"Earth, in Upstate New York."

"Earth is what you call your world? What's it like?"

"A lot like this one, except we have buildings and cars and stuff. We don't have anything like demons, that's for sure!"

"Sounds like a nice place."

Cory sighed, taking a deep lungful of the mountain air. "It is, Tal. But it can be rotten, too. Some of the people watching me weren't very nice."

"They beat you?"

Cory winced at the memory, and nodded. Suddenly, something plopped onto his chest. Cory opened his eyes, sitting up. "What the?"

Taliesin giggled, standing over the younger boy. "Your dinner."

Cory gathered the berries from his chest and tasted one. It was sweet, and the boy quickly ate another. "Thank you."

"You're welcome," Taliesin said, sitting down next to him. "When you want more, that bush over there is full of them."

Cory nodded and quickly consumed the few berries he had, before walking over for more. He glanced back at his friend. "You want some more?"

Taliesin nodded, gazing out at the creek, letting the Sun and breeze dry his hair. The prince's blond locks began to shine, finally free of dirt. The boy combed them roughly with his fingers, licking his lips as he stared at the water hungrily. "If only we had a fishing rod...."

"I was thinking the same thing. There's a whole bunch of fish down there."

"Yes, I know. I saw them too. Math would be able to catch them without a rod!"

Cory sat down next to his friend, his hands full of berries. The boy set them down between them, and the boys ate.

"Who's Math?"

"A great wizard who lives at Penllyn. In a mountain cave on Penllyn, actually. I was on my way to see him when I was kidnapped by the demons."

Cory swallowed a berry and reached for another. "You never told me much about that."

"That's right, I didn't. I was riding with my personal guards. We were resting for the night, out in the open, like fools. The demons made a raid that night, and saw us as they flew overhead. I was sleeping at the time. My two guards were also, apparently."

Taliesin scowled, and Cory grabbed another berry. "How long ago?"

"Three months."

Cory's jaw fell open. "You spent three months in that hole?"

The older boy nodded. "I tried escape before, and got sent to the torture chamber for it. This time I managed to escape, with your help."

Cory gaped. "My help? Tal, you're the one who saved me!"

Taliesin eyed his friend. "Do you really think I could have done it on my own? If you hadn't distracted the demon when you did, I would have been captured easily."

"Oh," Cory said, and leaned back. "Cambian told me that they weren't really demons."

Taliesin laughed. "Well, yes and no. I heard tales that say they were once humans who were turned into demons. But I doubt it. No human could possibly be that evil!"

Cory nodded, rubbing his cheek against the soft grass, watching the lake lap the sand.

The prince crawled the few feet to the water, and, cupping his hands, drank some more. Cory realized the fruit had made him thirsty too, and joined him.

"Water's too warm," Cory complained.

"Here, hold it up."

"Huh?"

Taliesin lifted his friend's hands gently. "Hold the water out in front of you, like this."

As Cory watched, Taliesin closed his eyes and waved his hands over Cory's. The younger boy felt the water change temperature even as he held it.

"Now taste it."

Cory did so, and looked up with a smile on his face. It was cool now, as if it were tapwater.

"How did you do that?"

"Magic! I know a few cantrips, or minor spells. My brothers taught me, after being tutored by Math."

Cory stared at the prince, wide-eyed. "Can you teach me?"

Taliesin shrugged and drew some water, holding it out in front of him. "Sure! Hold your hands over the water like I did, and close your eyes."

Cory did so. "Now what?"

"The water is made up of a lot of little parts, so small we can't see them—"

Cory nodded. "Molecules."

Taliesin frowned. "Whatever! You have to picture these small parts in your mind, and will them to slow down, and then come together."

The younger boy wriggled his fingers and opened his eyes. "Anything happening?"

Taliesin shook his head. "Try again."

Cory sighed, waved his hands over the water, and tried to force the molecules to slow down with his mind. This time the boy felt a tingling charge on his fingertips which grew stronger as he built concentration. The water hardened with a loud pop, turning white.

"OW!" Taliesin cried, and dropped it to the grass.

"I'm sorry! Are you alright?"

The prince rubbed his palms together, trying to get warmth to return. "Ice! You made *ICE!*"

"I'm sorry!"

Taliesin shook his head, awe on his young face. "You don't understand! I can only cool it down a little! You turned it to ice! Are you apprenticed to a wizard in your world?"

Cory shook his head, staring at the frozen water lying in the grass. "No, there aren't any. This is the first time I've ever tried anything like this!"

Taliesin gasped. "The first time? Are you sure?"

Cory nodded, a smile forming. "I did good, huh?"

The older boy picked up the ice chunk, turning it over. "Uh ... yeah."

Cory looked at his friend with a gleam in his eye. "What's next? Fire?"

"Waitaminute! I can't do that—"

"You can't make ice, either," Cory pointed out.

Taliesin scowled jealously. "Showoff!"

Cory giggled. "Sorry. You want me to make some more ice? It's the next best thing to ice cream, on hot days."

"You're taunting me," Taliesin accused.

"No, I mean it! Here," Cory said, taking the frozen chunk from him. The boy put the ice in his mouth and began to suck on it. "You never had a popsicle before?"

The prince frowned. "No, but I think I see what you mean. I do the same thing with icicles that hang from my window in the winter."

"It's even better in the summer," Cory said, and broke off a piece before handing it to Taliesin.

The blond boy hesitated a moment before putting the piece into his mouth, then decided he liked it. "They eat this in your world?"

"All the time," Cory said, enjoying his homemade treat. Then he glanced up at the sky. The sun had sunk below the black mountains in the distance, and the whole world seemed to grow big and terrible. An owl hooted in a nearby tree, and little creatures rustled through the grass. Every sound seemed to rattle him, and the boy shuddered. "It's getting darker, Tal."

"Yeah, I know. Fortunately, we can sleep under a tree tonight. I doubt they'd find us, hidden like that, even this close to Abollydd."

"Good. I never want to see them again."

Taliesin shot his friend a look. "Oh, you will! Until you find a way home, you'll see them all the time, flying over the towns and cities, looking for humans to kidnap into slavery."

Cory shuddered again. "They'll kill us, won't they?"

"If they catch us," Taliesin answered, got up, and sat under a wide oak, stretching. Cory followed, watching the sunset nervously.

"You sure we're safe here?"

"Sure," Taliesin replied, but there was fear in his eyes.

The boys sat there, watching the wind make small waves on the surface of the water, trying not to notice the darkness gathering around them. When it grew very dark they spoke in whispers, then not at all, afraid the demons might somehow hear. Before long the boys were sleeping, glad to be finally free of their captors.

Chapter 5

▼

MATH

Feldspark cursed softly as he found the long, coiled whip lying in the grass. The two runaway slaves had actually killed one of them, taken his weapons. While armed knights and powerful wizards had slain Kelloid demons before, that was in combat. None of their young slaves had yet had the courage or the will to challenge them within their own stronghold. Until now. The two little brats would pay dearly for this. Feldspark silently coiled the leather whip, and circled around the thick trees, peering at the two boys. His left hoof accidentally snapped a fallen twig, and he cursed his own carelessness. The sound of wood snapping was like a thunderclap in the silence of the woods.

"Cory," Taliesin whispered, gently shaking his friend.
The boy's eyes fluttered, and he moaned. "Wha?"
"Shush!" the prince said, putting a finger to his lips.
Cory remained silent, listening to the sounds of night. The creek gently lapped the shore, crickets sung in the brush, and owls hooted in the trees. But in a moment Cory heard it: the sound of giant, leath-

ery wings beating the air, high above them. The boy looked up and gasped.

Outlined against the crescent moon were Kelloids, dozens of them. Cory shuddered when he realized the demons were looking for the two of them, searching in droves. He looked at Taliesin, hoping the older boy, raised on this world, knew what to do.

But the prince's blue eyes were just as wide, showing just as much fear. Cory swallowed, then held his breath as the demons flew off into the distance.

For a long moment, there was no sound besides the crickets and water. "I think they're gone," Cory whispered.

Taliesin nodded, and slowly rose, crawling away.

"Where're you going?"

"I left the weapons over by the shore," Tal whispered back.

Cory nodded, staying right where he was. The boy hugged his legs with his chin resting on his knees, hoping they wouldn't need to use the weapons.

"Where is it?" Taliesin murmured.

"What?"

"The whip. I found the knife, but I can't find the whip!"

Taliesin rubbed his hands along the grass, searching. In a moment his groping fingers felt hard leather, but it wasn't in the shape of a whip. It was a boot. Tal slowly looked up.

"Looking for *this*, slave?" a Kelloid hissed, baring large teeth. Its amber eyes glowed brightly in the blackness, but the dark body was almost totally invisible at night.

The boy screamed, jumping back. The whip cracked, catching Tal on the left shoulder.

"You'll both die painfully! Perhaps I'll dunk you repeatedly in this creek, and let you drown slowly!"

Taliesin, frightened as he was, was still trained to fight. He rolled in the grass, avoiding the whip, and came up on his feet, throwing the dagger. The blade embedded itself in the demon's chest. The creature screamed, dropping the whip.

Rushing forward, Taliesin quickly snatched up the weapon, but the demon was too quick, in spite of being injured. In a moment the demon had the boy in a viselike grip. The young prince struggled, screaming.

Cory gasped, and knew he had to do something or his friend would be dead. The demon's razor-sharp fingernails were beginning to cut into Tal's flesh, which is why he cried out.

Cory picked up a rock, ran as close to the Kelloid as he dared, and threw it. It hit the demon squarely in the head. Taliesin was released, and immediately rolled away.

"Lousy human brats! I'll roast you over a firepit!"

Cory swallowed, his knees trembling, threatening to give way under him. The young boy's vision fell on his friend, who lay in the grass, squeezing his bleeding arm. The demon had obviously cut Taliesin with his claws, and now was getting up to finish the job.

No! I've gotta save him!

"HEY, YOU BIG JERK!" Cory shouted, waving his hands above his head. The demon turned in his direction.

I must be out of my mind! He thought, and ran down the shore, away from Taliesin. The demon followed as Cory had expected, and the boy immediately regretted it.

"Run, boy! Run as far as you wish! Soon you'll tire and I'll have you!"

Looking over his shoulder, Cory could see that the Kelloid wasn't lying. Even now his pursuer was gaining, and the slight boy was running as fast as he could. Cory wondered why the demon wasn't flying after him with those enormous, leathery wings. *He's toying with us. He could've easily killed both of us by* now. He ran into the creek, hoping the water would slow the demon down a bit. Unfortunately, it also slowed down Cory, but he was soon deep enough to swim.

"Over here!" Taliesin cried from the shore. "Swim back here!"

Cory didn't know why, but saw his friend was back on his feet, and decided to do it. He pumped his arms and legs furiously, in spite of the fact that he was getting tired. The boy ignored it and continued forcing his arms over his head and into the water, pulling himself in the prince's direction.

"Enough of this!" The demon growled behind him, and Cory heard the whooshing sound of great leathery wings beating air. In a moment a pair of strong adult fingers gripped the boy's shoulders and lifted him from the water.

Cory felt the claws begin to puncture his skin, sending fire up his nerves, and he screamed. The boy kicked frantically, hitting something, but it didn't seem to make any difference. The winged creature just laughed at him. Then the demon screamed as a rock hit him, and he let the boy go. Cory fell to the water five feet below.

Cory opened his eyes, wincing as the pain from slapping the surface stung his flesh. He was underwater and tried to swim upward, but sharp pain shot through his bleeding shoulders. He let out a little air from his lungs and realized he couldn't stay down there forever, injury or no injury. He began to pump the water with his legs, swimming upward.

Cory's lungs began to burn for air, and he paddled by moving his arms below the elbows, moving a bit faster. This brought him to the surface just barely in time. The boy coughed, filling his lungs, and looked around to see the demon hovering over Taliesin. The young prince had managed to recover the whip, and was holding off the Kelloid with it.

Cory felt the cuts on his shoulders and knew he was bleeding heavily, but couldn't just sit there while his friend fought the monster alone. He steadied himself in the water and shouted,

"Hey, you big dope! You forgot about me!"

This distracted the demon, and he was nicked by the lash as he turned to face Cory in midair. The demon gained a little altitude, putting himself out of Taliesin's range, and flew swiftly in Cory's direction.

The boy took a deep breath and dove under again, swimming for shore. If he and Tal could get something of a strategy going, maybe by fighting the Kelloid together, they might stand a chance of surviving this.

Moving his arms were agony, but Cory ignored the pain by keeping his mind on the demon above who wanted his life. The boy broke the surface when he reached shallow water, looked back to where he'd just been, and saw the demon still searching for him out near the center of the creek.

Standing up, Cory ran for shore, aware that the Kelloid had noticed him. Then he had an idea. When the water he stood in was just a few inches deep, the boy turned to face his attacker, hands held out in front of him.

Please, God. Let this work!

Cory shut his eyes and concentrated, trying to block the pain and everything else out of his mind. He envisioned the water and willed the molecules to slow down their motion. In a moment he felt tingling at his fingertips, even stronger than before, and heard the sound of water cracking as it hardened instantly.

The boy opened his eyes and saw the demon, half in and half out of the water, trapped in solid ice. Wisps of cold air floated above the suddenly frozen water, into the summer night sky. The massive demon struggled to free himself, screaming and cursing in a language so ancient, nobody even spoke it anymore.

Taliesin's jaw fell open. "I don't believe it! You've frozen the creek! *The entire creek!*"

"Thank you, Lord," Cory said hoarsely, and turned to his friend. "Come on, we've gotta get outta here before he manages to escape!"

Taliesin nodded, pausing to roll the whip so it would be more convenient to carry. "I know of a shortcut. Come."

Amid the demon's curses, the two boys ran quickly away, along the shore of the creek, then further into the forest.

* * * *

Twigs broke under Cory's bare feet and they hurt, but not as badly as his shoulders. The blood had become sticky and hard, covering his wounds, and the muscles seemed to get stiffer as time went on. Finally Cory stopped walking, bending over and taking deep breaths.

"Come on!" Taliesin shouted at him.

"I can't ... too tired."

The prince of Caer Dathyl went back, a sneer on his face, checking the trail behind them carefully. "What's the matter with you? He could be right behind us!"

"Doubt it. That ice was pretty hard, Tal."

"You don't know anything, do you?" the older boy shouted. "The Kelloids are impossibly strong! He must be free by now!"

Cory looked up at his friend, and straightened. "Look, your Highness, I can't walk any further without resting, okay?"

"Fine!" Taliesin said. "Stay here and get captured! See if I care!"

The boy turned to go, and Cory stared after his friend, unbelieving. "Wait-a-minute!"

Taliesin kept on walking in silence.

"You stuck up, half witted—"

"Who's half-witted?" Taliesin cried back, turning around.

"You are," Cory said, hardly able to suppress a grin. This prince was obviously not used to being insulted. "How long do you think you'd last against him, all by yourself?"

"Longer than you could!"

"Ha! You can't even make ice!"

Taliesin's face twisted into a good imitation of stormclouds. "You take that back, common dog!"

"I will not! This is a free country—"

Cory stopped short. He wasn't home anymore, and as much as he hated to admit it, Taliesin *was* the law, like he said.

"Only if I say so! I could make you bondservant to a goatherd if I want to!"

Cory giggled. "A what?"

"Don't tell me they don't have goats on your world!"

"Oh, they do! But what's a goatherd?" The younger boy giggled again at the mere sound of it.

Taliesin saw Cory laughing and began to snicker himself, their plight forgotten for the moment. "Someone who tends goats," he said, then sobered slightly. "You really don't know, do you?"

The Earth boy shook his head, his hysterics growing more intense. "Little Boy Blue, come blow your horn, the sheep's in the meadow, the cow's in the corn! Hehheheheheh!"

Taliesin frowned. "What?"

Cory rolled in the soil, holding his sides and laughing at the prince's ignorance. How could Tal come from such a backward world and not know simple nursery rhymes?

"You're making sport of me," Taliesin accused, but Cory didn't answer. The boy simply wiped tears from his eyes.

"Stop that right now!" Taliesin barked, arms akimbo. "I order you to stop laughing!"

That only made Cory laugh harder, and after a moment, the prince began to snicker too.

The two boys sat down in the grass, and eventually the hysterics died down. The wind blew their hair gently, and a bird flew from one tree to another.

"How much further to your castle?"

Tal shook his head. "We should be back in Caer Dathyl by nightfall, I think. Or we'll at least find a small village near it. There isn't a man in Father's realm who wouldn't shelter me for the night."

Cory looked awed. "It must be great to be a prince."

"Yeah, but it's worse too, sometimes. I have ten different tutors teaching me everything from history to swordcraft. I very rarely get holidays, except for when my brothers and I sneak off to the lake."

"In other words, you play hooky," Cory accused.

Taliesin looked at the younger boy quizzically. "I guess so. What do you do where you come from?"

"Pretty much the same thing. I hafta go to school, except in the summer ... and when I play hooky."

Taliesin frowned. "Hooky?"

"Skipping school!" Cory explained with a grin. He'd love to bring this kid back to New York, see his reaction to all the skyscrapers, the subway trains, even television sets and computers. He'd freak out!

"Your father must be wealthy," Taliesin observed. Not many medieval children were educated.

Cory's face fell at the comment. "My dad died in a plane crash four years ago."

The prince didn't know what a 'plane crash' was, but it didn't sound too good. Sympathy filled him. He'd known many children from their kingdom who'd been orphaned by the demons over the years. "Sorry. Then you're an orphan?"

"No," the boy said in a soft voice, feeling his stomach tie itself into knots. "My mom just won't wake up, that's all. When she comes out of the coma, everything will be just the way it used to."

Taliesin wore a deep frown and had sadness filled his brown eyes. He put his hand on Cory's shoulder. "Until then, you can live in our castle. We have plenty of room, and Father will reward you for saving my life."

Cory frowned. "Aw, come on. I didn't—"

"Yes, you did. Twice."

He remained silent, not wanting to argue. "If you say so, Tal. Come on, I wanna sleep in a bed tonight."

"It's almost morning," Taliesin observed, giggling.

"I'm a late sleeper," Cory replied, and rose. "Which direction again?"

* * * *

It was mid-morning by the time the boys reached the outskirts of a small village. The fields were filled with corn and wheat, twice as tall as them and golden. The crops scraped against their bare legs and arms as they passed through and brushed against the plants. Except for the sound of a lonely crow or the wind which caused the plants to sway like a golden sea, it was quiet and calm. The boys walked endlessly through fields, and finally stopped at a farmhouse. It was a ramshackle cottage with a patchwork roof and loose boards in the porch. Thick smoke poured from the chimney, and the aroma of cooking stew greeted their nostrils.

They climbed onto the dusty porch and Taliesin knocked at the locked door. There was no answer, and Tal knocked again. Silence. The boys exchanged glances.

"Maybe nobody's home," Cory offered.

The prince shot his friend a dirty look. "You have a talent for stating the obvious. I wonder why the farmer left meat cooking on the fire. Come on, there must be somebody on the next farm."

Cory nodded, turned, and nearly tripped over something soft which had tangled itself between his bare ankles. The boy fell to his knees, hearing something gently cry out.

"Cory! Are you all right?" Taliesin asked, helping his friend up.

"Yeah, I guess so," his friend said, looking down at his feet. A small black cat was there, hissing at him.

"Stupid cat! It tripped me!"

"A black cat," Taliesin said softly, then whispered, "Oh, no! Come on, let's get out of here!"

"Why? What's wrong? It's only—"

"Don't you know anything? Black cats are the familiars of witches! One might live here!"

Cory scowled. "Gimme a break! I'm too old to believe in that kinda stuff!"

"How can you believe in magic and not in witches? You froze a creek, didn't you?"

The boy stared at him in shocked silence. "Maybe you're right," he whispered, licking his dry lips nervously.

Taliesin led Cory off through the high, unharvested wheat again, roughly in the direction of Caer Dathyl, but in truth, the prince wasn't sure which of the mountains in the distance was home. He kept looking back nervously.

"It's following us!"

Cory turned. "Oh, no! It's probably hungry, and hooked onto us, hoping we'll feed it. That happened to me a few summers ago. My foster family wouldn't let me keep it, though."

The cat meowed as the boys started to walk again, the sound very much like human laughter. For some reason, it filled the children with dread, and they shuddered. It suddenly occurred to them, too late, that this cat might be more than it seemed.

"Tal, you don't think the demons are onto us again, do you?"

"You should be so lucky, mortal!" a deep, thunderous voice echoed from behind them. The boys whirled and gasped at what they saw. The cat wasn't a cat at all!

It stood fifty feet tall on its hind legs, the tail as thick as a telephone cable and twenty feet long, the neck long and sinuous. Its head resembled a crocodile's, and huge, basketball-size eyes were staring at them.

"A black dragon," Taliesin whispered hoarsely.

Cory shuddered again. He had seen pictures of dragons in books, in the movies, and on *Wizards and Knights* posters ... but to see one of the things in real life, this close up, was enough to make him wet himself.

"I haven't had much for breakfast this morning, boy ... how very perceptive of you. And I find human children so very delicious."

Cory's eyes were wide as saucers, staring at the dragon, which loomed over his small, skinny body. Cory couldn't move a muscle out of sheer terror, but somehow Taliesin found his voice.

"Wait! You don't want to eat us! We ... we're escaped slaves from Abollydd! We're all full of grime ... and we're much too small to satisfy *your* great appetite!"

"I like tasty snacks, child," the dragon quipped, steam billowing from its nostrils. "But you *are* wearing loincloths. Tell me, boy. If you are escaped slaves, where are your chains?"

"I—I took them off. I'm a thief."

The dragon chuckled and the vibrations from his voice pounded into the boys' chests like an explosion of thunder when a storm passed directly overhead. "How very interesting. I ate a group of thieves last month. They were delicious!"

"Nice going, Tal," Cory whispered. The boy tried closing his eyes to spellcast, but found he was too nervous to concentrate.

"You ate the farmer of this land," Taliesin suddenly accused, and the dragon smiled as best as his features would allow. "Then you must not be very hungry."

"Indeed. Perhaps I'll bring you back to my cave and save you for later. You seem to have more meat on your bones than your friend here," the dragon tapped its long digit on the ground near Cory.

"Oh, no!" Taliesin cried. "We're really quite bony—"

"Enough of this!" the dragon roared, smoke flowing thickly from its mouth. "I hunger sorely, and you have ceased to amuse me. Prepare to be eaten, Breakfast."

Taliesin gulped audibly and Cory squeezed his eyes tighter. He could feel the barest hint of magic on his fingertips, but couldn't calm himself enough to freeze the dragon!

Suddenly the beast let out an awful sound the likes of which Cory had never heard before, and the boy opened his eyes in spite of himself to see what was happening. Bright flashes of blue lightning struck the great beast, jolting it and obviously causing extreme pain.

The boys' eyes followed the line of flashing energy to a tall, stout man with a white beard, dressed in robes of noble finery. The mystic energy was coming from the man's fingertips, and his lips were forming strange words.

"MATH!" Taliesin cried, shaking with relief. Cory stared at the wizard, having much the same reaction. He was too scared to do magic, but a real wizard would have no problem at all with a dragon!

At the old mage's bidding, the gentle breeze increased in force to a strong wind, so that the wheat was bent over in waves like the sea, and the moss-covered rotting shingles on the farmhouse roof were lifted and blown away. After a few moments, the air seemed to enclose the dragon, and its movements grew slower and slower until it stood as a statue, unmoving. Finished, the tall wizard walked up to the children.

"The king had almost given up hope for you! 'Tis a good thing I was tracking this particular dragon. His Majesty would be quite upset with me if I had let his son perish due to neglect of duty."

Taliesin collapsed into a nervous smile, and Cory closed his eyes again, breathing heavily and praying softly. That was about as close as he ever wanted to come to dying.

"Well met, good magician! I do believe that dragon was interested in consuming us. Ah, where are my manners? This is my friend, Cory. I never would've escaped the slavepits if not for him!"

"Truly?" Math remarked, raising an eyebrow. "Your father will reward him handsomely! Come, my demesne is not far from here, and I'm not sure how long the Winds of Time will hold this creature."

The wizard pointed a finger at the motionless dragon. That was all the urging the two boys needed, tired as they were from the night's marching, to leave the farm swiftly.

Chapter 6

PRINCE OF CAER DATHYL

"Come here, boy," Math commanded, and Cory rose from the table where he and Taliesin had consumed four full bowls of stew.

The firelight flickered off the wizard's elegant white beard, casting long shadows in the darkened room. Math's velvet deep-purple cloak had been hung on a peg in a corner of the room, and the boy could see that the wizard was wearing an ebony robe, trimmed with magic runes. He seemed kind, but there was a hint of darkness in his deep-set grey eyes. Math held out a gnarled, trembling hand.

"Let me see your palm," the old man's voice rasped, and Cory put his soft young hand in Math's leathery wrinkled one. The old wizard traced the lines in the child's palm with a thin finger, and his eyes grew wide. Where the lines in most people's palms form the letter "M", Cory's formed a perfect triangle, called a Triangle of Power, which covered the boy's entire hand. After a moment, the beginnings of a smile formed at the edge of Math's lips.

"What?" Cory asked.

"Nothing, lad. I was just curious about you, after His Highness told me what you did." The old man patted the boy's hand lightly, then let it go.

"Oh. What did you find out?"

"Nothing you would understand," Math replied, and even Cory could see he was evading the question. "You boys must be tired. There are a pair of cots down the hall in one of the apprentice's rooms. You can rest there until tonight, when we will travel to Caer Dathyl."

Cory was about to ask why, when Math clapped his hands loudly and a nine-year-old boy came into the room. He was bony; with dirty-blond hair cut in a Dutch boy haircut, and wore a simple tunic not unlike the one Math had.

"You summoned me, Master?"

"Yes. Show the prince and his friend to a room down the hall, and prepare a couple of beds for them."

"Yes, Master," the boy replied, and waited patiently for Cory and Taliesin to follow him. As they left, Cory cast a final glance at Math. He was everything Cory thought a wizard should be, yet there was something hidden beneath the surface—something which glinted in the eyes. The boy looked at his hand, flexing his fingers, and wondered what Math had seen in him.

"What is your name?" Tal asked of the small boy.

"Gwion, my lord."

Gwion led them into another chamber, much smaller than the sitting room. The wizard's entire home was a maze-like cave dug into the mountain. It was safe from attack, but there were no windows to let light and air in. A single candle held by the boy was placed on a rickety table, and that provided the room's dim illumination. The 'guestroom' was sparse, containing only a moth-eaten rug, a small table with scratches in its surface, a three-legged stool, and a pair of cots against a wall. Still, this was a palace compared to the cell Cory and Taliesin had shared in Abollydd.

"Are you a slave?" Cory suddenly asked of the boy.

Gwion turned to Cory and gave him a queer look. "Of course not! Why do you ask such a question?"

"Because you called Math your 'Master,'" Cory replied.

Taliesin sighed and explained to Gwion, "He's from another world."

The boy's face lit up. "Truly?"

Cory nodded, and Gwion began to put fresh bedding down on the cots. "I'm from Earth."

"I see."

Cory frowned. "If you're not a slave, why do you call Math—"

"He's apprenticed to him, you dope!" Taliesin snapped. "Math is a master of the mystic arts, and Gwion is his student!"

Cory's mouth formed a big 'O.' He tossed the cloak and sat on the soft bedding as the child began to work on the prince's cot. It wasn't much of a mattress, but it was soft compared to what he had been forced to sleep on the last four nights, and it felt good. Cory lay down, resting his head in his folded hands, staring up at the ceiling. It wasn't a freshly painted one like the one at home. This one had cobwebs on it, with spiders spinning them ever-larger. Fascinated, Cory watched the little creatures working, gradually making the web more and more intricate.

"I could get to like it here, Tal. Is your castle like this?"

The prince laughed. "Are you joking? My father is a king! I have a suite all to myself, with a bed half as large as this room!"

Cory's blurring vision locked on his friend, and he yawned. "If you say so, Tal. Think I'll go to sleep."

Gwion's blue eyes grew wide. "You let him sit, lie down and sleep in your presence, Highness?"

"He's been through a lot, and I owe him my life twice over. The boy can do whatever he wishes in my presence."

So saying, Taliesin lay down himself and closed his eyes, feeling just as tired as Cory. For the first time in as long as he could remember, his belly was full and he could feel a soft bed underneath him. The boys were asleep before the candle wax had run, and never noticed a dark-cloaked figure checking on them an hour later, smiling.

* * * *

A hand shook Cory gently, and his eyes fluttered. "Wha?"

"Wake up. Master Math wishes you to get ready to leave."

Cory's sleepy eyes fixed on the little boy fearfully. "Leave?" he asked in a groggy voice. "Did I do something wrong?"

"No," Taliesin said from the other side of the room, moaning and stretching. "We have to get ready to go to Caer Dathyl ... my home."

Cory eyed the lone candle on the table, which had burned down to a stub, and the new, fresh one next to it, which Gwion had apparently brought. "What time is it?"

"Five of the clock, just before dawn," Gwion answered, and began pouring the contents of a pitcher into a washing basin, and set a pair of towels next to that.

"Does Math think it wise to travel at night?" the young prince asked.

Cory sat bolt upright. "Hey, that's right! The demons will be out looking for us again!"

The nine-year-old giggled. "You forget who protects you, Highness. The Kelloids are no match for my master."

Tal smiled. "Heh! I'll bet."

Cory looked at his friend, still worried, thinking of the Kelloids' whips. "Just how powerful is he, Tal?"

"Very. Math is one of the wisest men alive!"

"Wisdom is the loom of power, little prince, but it is not the thread," an adult voice said from the doorway. The three boys looked up and saw the old wizard standing there in a different robe, this one purple. "I thought I taught you that."

Taliesin cast his eyes down. "You did. I'm sorry."

"It is not good for a prince to forget. You would do well to improve your memory. Now Gwion will help you two get ready, while I prepare something to eat before we leave. It will be a long trip."

Math turned and left, and Cory shuddered—why, he was not quite sure. There was something definitely frightening about that old man.

"I know," Gwion said to Cory, and the Earth boy turned. "You'll get used to it. I am told all wizards are frightening ... but that doesn't mean they're evil. They're just ... spooky."

Cory nodded. "How did you get to be his student?"

"I'll tell you some other time. I've got to help you get ready to travel, and Master hears almost everything."

Tal giggled. "Then it's true that he hears every word uttered?"

Gwion grinned. "Almost."

The prince got up from the cot, walked over to the small table, and splashed his face with the cool water. "That's good! Tonight I'll bathe in my own bathtub!" He grabbed a towel and dried his face with it, then turned to Cory. "You can use it too, of course! The hot water will make your muscles feel better. How is your leg, by the way?"

Cory got up and walked over to him. "Much better! That demon healed me pretty well."

"Appropriate, seeing as how they caused the wound in the first place," Taliesin muttered, and Cory grinned.

"At least we're out of there, Tal. I've never been so happy to leave a place in my life!" Cory splashed some cool water on his face from the basin, which woke him. He groped for a towel and dried his face so he could see.

The young prince clapped Cory on the back. "And we won't be going back there, Maker willing."

Gwion laid out clothing for the boys on their cots. Cory dried his hands and walked over to it, feeling the fine silk between his fingers. "My mom has a blouse like this ... but I never thought I'd get a shirt made from it!"

Tal's eyebrow raised at his friend's remark. "You must be of at least noble blood, then."

Cory shook his head, "I don't think—"

But the prince was busy getting dressed already, not paying attention. Cory shrugged and slipped into real cotton clothes for the first time in four days. These people had never heard of underwear. They just slipped into a long tunic and maybe pants, called breeches. Still, sensation of clean cloth against his skin felt good after wearing that filthy loincloth for six weeks. He sat down, and slipped into a pair of tights. He had to straighten his legs to pull them on, much like long underwear. Cory frowned, a slight grin on his face.

"What is this, ballet?"

"Huh?" the prince asked, turning around while fastening the buttons on his tunic.

"The pants. Didn't you people ever invent jeans?"

Taliesin frowned. "What are jeans?"

Cory gave him a look which said now-who's-ignorant. "Pants made of cotton, which take a lot of wear and tear and are a lot more comfortable than these things!"

"Perhaps you can have a word with the tailor at Caer Dathyl."

"Definitely."

"Your Highness, the master requests your presence in the kitchen ... NOW."

Taliesin nodded, and Cory tried to hurry into a pair of soft shoes. "Gimme a minute. I'm not used to these things."

"Then you prefer the loincloth?" Taliesin asked sarcastically.

"Very funny! I'd love to see you put on a pair of roller blades."

The young prince frowned, then decided to ask about that later. If there was one thing he learned, nobody keeps Math waiting ... especially not children! The prince sat down next to his friend and helped him slip the shoes on, as if Cory were a small child.

"Thanks," the Earth boy said, looking up at his friend.

"Save the gratitude for later. Math wants us."

Taliesin and Cory followed the young apprentice through the winding, torchlit corridors, until they had come to the sitting room again. On the table were four loaves of fresh-baked bread and two bowls of steaming soup. The aroma of the hot bread and soup suddenly made Cory realize how hungry he was, and he and Taliesin sat down to eat.

"You may join them, Gwion. I shall not be home again this evening to cook you supper. There is some cold oatmeal for the others in the kitchen. Have them reheat it when they finally return."

The boy smiled at the old wizard and obeyed. He went to the cauldron over the fireplace, poured himself a bowl of soup, and joined Tal and Cory at the table. While sitting down, he noticed the fourth loaf of bread lying on the platter, and looked up at his master, who had his back to them.

"Aren't you going to join us, Master?"

At the question, Cory also looked at Math. The wizard was staring into the fire, rubbing his long beard with a gnarled hand. Cory had a weird feeling that although Math was facing in the opposite direction, he was looking right at him.

The corners of the magician's lips curved into a slight smile, and he turned to face the boy. Their eyes locked, venerable old man and twelve-year-old child. For a moment, Cory thought something passed between them; what, he wasn't quite sure, but he knew that Math did. Cory thought Math knew things about him that he didn't know himself yet.

"You show promise," Math muttered. "You are worthy indeed."

"Excuse me, Master?" Gwion asked meekly, thinking he had done something to displease the wizard.

Math shook his head. "No, lad. Eat." And with that, the old man joined the boys at the table and began to tear apart the last loaf.

*   *   *   *

The King of Gwynedd hugged his youngest son so tightly that Taliesin complained he couldn't breathe. Then the king laughed mightily, holding the prince at arm's length.

"You have grown, Taliesin," King Llewelyn said, then frowned. "And so has your hair." Before the young prince could reply, Llewelyn muttered, "Maker, I had almost given up hope of seeing you alive again. Where is the one who has wrought this miracle?"

The boy turned to face Cory and Math, who stood nearby. "That boy, Father! He saved me from the slavepits and my life twice."

The King smiled warmly at the young Earth boy, whose face flushed a bright red. Cory had saved the kid's life and this was the thanks he got: embarrassing the heck out of him.

"Come here lad, and tell us your name."

Cory took a cautious step forward, and the man reached out and held his shoulder firmly. His throat was tight, but he still managed a meek reply. "Cory Avalon, Sir."

"I see. And where are your parents?"

Cory looked down, and felt the emptiness in his chest. He wanted so badly to see his mother! She must have woken up by now, and begun asking for him!

"He's an orphan, Father. Kidnapped from his world by Asmodeus."

The King's eyebrow raised, and he gripped Cory's shoulder tighter. "Indeed! Then we must correct that."

Cory looked up at the man, his bright blue eyes growing wet. He could not even bring himself to correct Taliesin's remark that he was an orphan.

"Here now, no more tears, lad! You have saved the life of my son, and shall be aptly rewarded."

The King stared at the boy, thinking. Then he said aloud, "Indeed, there can be only one reward for such an act of uncommon bravery! Henceforth, you are my adopted child, a prince of the Royal House. You shall have our love and protection for as long as we shall live."

Cory's lower lip trembled. "Prince?"

The king's expression grew dark. "Aye, lad. And a prince does not weep openly."

Cory nodded, trying to gather what little pride was left to him. "Thank you—"

"Be silent," Taliesin whispered firmly, and Cory's mouth closed, his eyes staring at his friend, now his foster brother.

"Now boys, go play. The wizard and I have much to discuss."

"Of course, Father," the young prince said. Gripping Cory's arm tightly, he led the dark-haired boy from the room.

"What did you think you were doing?" Taliesin asked harshly, once they were in the hallway, beyond the closed doors.

"Couldn't help it," Cory sobbed, wiping his tears away with his right sleeve. "I thought of my Mom. She's still alive, *darnit!*"

Taliesin's face softened and he put a comforting hand on Cory's shoulder. "Sorry. I forgot."

"She must be awake by now, calling for me ... and I can't ... even—"

"It's all right," Taliesin said, and glanced around at the guards. "Come. It is not proper to cry here, out in the open."

"Right," Cory said, raising his chin. "Where's ... my room?"

Taliesin smiled. "This way."

* * * *

Cory looked around his new bedchamber, struck dumb. Light poured from the windows, shining on the enormous canopy bed and fine oak furniture. Tapestries covered the stone walls, showing great battles between mythical beasts and men armed with magic swords. And that was not all, for they had passed through two more rooms just as luxurious as this one, and all three were Cory's. He stared at his foster brother, eyes wide.

"This can't be real, Tal!"

"It is," the older boy said softly. "I really expected you to be made into an earl or a Ward of the King, but adoption...." Taliesin shook his head. "Father must have taken a quick liking to you."

The younger boy nodded, smiling. "I guess. I've had a room to myself before, but never three, and not like this!"

Taliesin gave Cory a knowing smile. "You haven't seen my suite yet! Come."

Cory followed the prince through stately rooms and long, richly decorated corridors. There were rooms enough for each member of the royal family to have their own apartment, and many did. The prince led Cory through four rooms and a bath before lounging on a sofa in one of the sitting rooms.

"You like?"

The boy slowly walked to the terrace, where the air slowly swayed the sheer drapes. He moved the veil aside and gazed out at the rolling meadows, full and green in the summer Sun. "I don't believe this! And you've lived like this all your life?"

"Uh huh," Taliesin sighed, at once taking in the softness of the entire room. "I missed this."

"I can see why."

There was a knock at the main door down the hall, and Taliesin answered it, not getting up. The two boys watched as footsteps were heard walking towards them on the cold stone floor. In came a young man of perhaps nineteen years, smiling widely, wearing silk clothing of princely design.

"Taliesin! You little pirate!"

"Joukahainen," Taliesin said, grinning. He started to get up but never made it. The older prince was upon him, hugging him almost to death.

Joukahainen laughed, tousling the boy's hair. "You look well. A little skinnier perhaps—"

"Yeah, and you've gotten fatter."

"What, this?" the young man asked, patting his tummy. "Baby fat!"

"Baby fat my eye," Taliesin muttered, and frowned at him. "Where are the others?"

"On their lands. Manannan is hunting in Morfran, and is returning in the autumn. He'll be sorry he missed this! He and I were going in to rescue you, but Father stopped us."

Taliesin nodded. "I got myself out ... with a little help."

The boy regarded Cory, who was standing by the terrace, smiling sheepishly. "We helped each other, Tal."

Joukahainen looked kindly upon the boy, who stood there, looking as out of place in the palace as a fisherman in the desert. "So you're the one who saved our youngest brother. Father couldn't have done enough for you!"

"Oh, come on," Cory said hesitantly, taking a step forward. "Anybody would've done what I did!"

"Spoken like a true nobleman."

"He's a wizard-born," Taliesin explained. "I've seen him spellcast!"

Cory shook his head. "One little spell!"

"One little spell?" Taliesin repeated, in a mocking voice. "You froze an entire creek in the heat of high summer!"

Cory vividly remembered the Kelloid chasing him through the water, claws thrusting for his thin flesh. "I wish you'd just drop it."

"Drop it nothing," Joukahainen said to him. "Math is in the Great Hall with Father now, telling him of your power."

Cory frowned, staring at him. For some reason that frightened him more than the demons returning. The old wizard had seen something in him, and Cory knew he wasn't about to let it go now.

CHAPTER 7

▼

APPRENTICE

When Cory was called into the throneroom a few days later, he felt dread in his heart. He feared that the King had changed his mind and was going to send him away, all alone into this strange, alien world. The feeling grew worse when he saw Math standing there next to the King, and no one else in the large room. Llewelyn bade the boy come close to him, and Cory could do nothing but silently obey.

"Are you angry with me?" Cory managed to ask in a small voice, and both men smiled at him.

"No, boy," the king said kindly. "How could I be angry with you?"

Cory stammered, not knowing how to tell Llewelyn he feared being cast out. The king put a calming hand on top of Cory's small trembling one, and leaned toward him. "I have made you my son, and wish the world for you." His eyes passed to Math for a moment, and Cory could not help but look at the mage as well.

"A prince must learn many things, Cory. Not the least of which is magic."

The boy swallowed, suspecting where this conversation was leading. Llewelyn went on. "Math tells me you show great promise in the

Arts. More than a great promise, perhaps. He wants me to bind you to him as an apprentice."

Very softly, fearfully, Cory asked, "You're sending me away, then."

"Not permanently, lad."

Cory envisioned young Gwion, whom Taliesin said would be the wizard's student for many years yet. "Long enough," he lisped.

Llewelyn's face turned serious, and his grip on Cory's hand grew tighter. "Listen to me, lad. To be a magician is to be very powerful indeed, and the gift is rare. Math tells me you have that gift. To be a prince is also to have power, though of a different kind. Now a magician from a royal house is almost unheard of, since there are few of noble blood who truly have the power in them. I am now giving you that chance."

The boy tried to avert his eyes from the King, to look at Math and search for some reason for all this, but he could not. His voice breaking, Cory pleaded with him. "But I don't want power! I just want to go home!"

"That is not possible," Math intoned, and this time Cory's head did turn in his direction, as if pulled. "There are worlds beyond number. Only Asmodeus knows where you came from and can send you back there." The edges of the wizard's mouth upturned slightly, the beginnings of a smile. "But he will not, eh? So your fate, young one, remains in our hands, on this world."

Cory's uneasiness with Math grew to utter fear now, and he definitely didn't like that half-smile which was almost a leer. He turned back to Llewelyn, screaming, "No!"

The King pulled Cory closer, holding him in a half-embrace, his voice calming. "Easy, lad. The spellweaver is right. Your destiny lies on our world, and it is mine to decide, as your father and King."

"I've been in a lot of foster homes. They send you away when they get tired of you!"

"Nay, I will never abandon you, child. But you are twelve. It is the custom here to send a boy your age away to learn a craft. You can still come home for holidays."

Cory watched him, speechless, his blue eyes silently pleading.

The King studied him, exhaled noisily through his nose, and nodded. "I think it would do you good to be with him. You are from a mundane world, devoid of magic. Your fear is the fear of the unknown, and to be rid of a fear you must face it.

"Math, take the boy and go. Return him to me a wizard or not at all."

With those words, Cory was led out of the throneroom of Caer Dathyl, away from the only friend he had come to know in this strange place, taken by a tall, strange man to a gloomy and uncertain future.

He did not go quietly.

* * * *

"You will sleep here," Math told him with a note of finality in the tone of his voice. Cory sat on the wood frame straw mattress bed and looked around, almost in fear. The room was nothing like the suite he was given at Caer Dathyl. It was plain, with walls and floor of grey stone. A chest and a small table with a stool were the only other furniture besides the bed. Two long wooden shelves were on the opposite wall, the first filled with scrolled parchment, the second empty.

"Dinner will be ready in an hour. I shall send Kellyn to show you around and speak with you, but I advise you to get much rest tonight. Tomorrow begins your schooling."

With that, Math left the boy alone. Cory stared at the walls for awhile, then grew tired of that and went to the shelf. He took some parchment down and unrolled it. He frowned, for it was blank.

"It will be written on soon enough," a young voice said to him from the door, and Cory spun. A barefooted boy about his own age stood there, bearing a small bottle of black ink and a quill. The boy looked Nordic, like most people from Gwynedd, and his skin was sheet-white from long hours indoors, constantly studying. He went over to the shelf and put it beside the blank scrolls.

"They will be filled with incantations. The second shelf is for the tomes Math will give you to study, and there will be many of those."

Cory stared at the boy for a moment, then nodded and sat down on the bed again. "I'm here by mistake."

The other boy smiled at him. "Math never makes a mistake. You are here because you either have power, aptitude, or both. I am Kellyn."

"I'm Cory."

The boy went to the stool by the small table and sat down. "Your coloring is dark. Are you from Kaleva, in the North?"

Cory shook his head. "No. I'm from New York."

"I've never heard of it. Is it a city?"

For the first time Cory cracked a smile. "Yes."

"What part of Kaleva is New York in?"

Cory laughed a little, shaking his head. "It's not on this world. It's on Earth."

Kellyn's eyes grew wide. Neither Math nor Gwion mentioned this! "You're from another world? At night Math sometimes tells us tales of such places, of other worlds through space and time and something he calls the Veil. What's it like?"

Cory's smile faded as he was asked that, and he glanced at the tall candle dripping wax onto the table. "Different."

Kellyn smiled wide. "The others will want to meet you. We've never met someone from another world before!"

Cory looked at him strangely, suddenly recalling that night he and Taliesin slept here. He had seen no other boys besides Gwion. "What others?"

Kellyn smiled. "There are ten of us—eleven now—and Math also sometimes tutors the sons of powerful lords in minor magic."

"Where were the rest of you before?"

"Before?"

"A week ago, when Taliesin and I were rescued by Math, and brought here."

Kellyn frowned, then his face lit up. "Ah! That must've been while we were down at the lake. Twice a week Math gives us the day off to play and learn of nature. Gwion was being punished, and had to stay behind to do our chores."

Cory nodded and was about to ask something else when a bell echoed throughout the halls, and the sound of many boys could be heard running and talking.

"That's dinner. Come."

* * * *

The first weeks at Penllyn went quickly. Cory found that as apprentice to a great wizard he had to do some work, usually shared by Kellyn, Gwion and the others. It also consisted of learning a whole new alphabet, made up of strange letters called runes. It was slow going at first, but Cory was a quick learner. He had mastered spell-reading in three weeks, and was chanting simple incantations in four.

At the same time, Math taught him the beginnings of spellweaving, the art of nameless enchantment. "There are threads of power running through the world: through the earth, the sea, the trees, the rocks, the animals, everything. These can be tapped, nudged, twisted, and woven into different patterns. And with that, reality is changed, warped about the new weft."

Cory learned to see these threads, call them to him, tap into them and bind them. Their energy could be used to boost psychokineses or telepathy. That was called tapping, a minor magic. Spellweaving was something else altogether, for there were hundreds of patterns which could be woven with the threads, all with different effects, and they all had to be learned.

Yet all of this came easily to Cory, as if he were born to it. All the while, his master stood in the doorway, watching his newest pupil's skill growing daily, and he knew Cory's power was great. As the weeks stretched on, Math's smile of pride eventually faded in the face of reality, for the boy was learning his lessons *too* quickly. Math's suspicions about the boy had been correct, but he had no knowledge on how to teach such a pupil. One such as Cory came along only once in a great many years. Still, the danger was clear: if the boy's power grew faster than his ability to control it, he might be turned to evil, and become the realm's ruin instead of its salvation.

One day in the second month of Cory's apprenticeship, Math called the boy to him. Cory stood by his master, expectant and respectful. All initial fear was gone, for Cory saw the wizard now for what he really was: a kind and wise, but lonely man, driven by reasons known only to himself. Math never beat any of his charges, nor spoke harshly with them, but there was sometimes an edge to his voice which made the boys in his care obey him unquestioningly.

So Cory stood silently at Math's side, waiting for him look up from his tome and speak. When he did, it was to frown at the boy, and Cory felt the beginnings of fear for the first time in a long while.

"Cory, you have gone into my library, have you not?"

The boy swallowed and nervously rubbed one bare foot on top of the other. Math heard everything that was said, and he seemed to see almost everything as well. Lying was unthinkable, so the boy simply nodded, throat tight.

"I must ask you not to do so again. There are spells in that room which you are not ready for yet."

Cory stared at the old man, wondering what to say. He decided truth would be best. That was the way with wizards. They might remain silent about the truth, but they always spoke it.

"Master. I—"

Math looked upon the boy, eyes widening. If it were any other child he would have dismissed him without another thought. This one was not only his prize pupil, but possessed of a greater power than he, and whose destiny shone in all scrying glasses.

"Which spell were you looking for?"

"The binding of ... familiars," Cory lisped, his mouth as dry as on that first night when he had been dragged back here as Math's student.

"I see," Math said, studying Cory as if he were a young child asking for a new pet. But this was different. *Very* different. "A familiar is a great responsibility, Cory, and the dangers are great. A wizard's powers are both augmented and weakened by one, as is his life. For that reason, few magicians take one—"

"I am aware of the dangers, Master. I'll take the risk!"

"Aware of the dangers, are you?" Math began, his voice dark and terrible. "I've seen what happens to students of mine who took a familiar, and it was killed by accident. A bitter, long, and very painful death. The boy would lie helplessly in bed, unconscious, and waste away for weeks, until death came to claim him. Even colleagues of mine, puissant wizards, grown men learned in ancient and secret craft, lost much of their power and nearly their lives—"

Math stopped, stared into young eyes, so full of life, so full of bright promise, and knew Cory had his heart set on the idea of a familiar, no matter what was said. The ancient mage sighed heavily. The boy would cast the spell with or without his permission in due time.

Slowly, Math nodded, thinking that it might as well be now, while he could still help him.

Cory beamed, rushing forward to hug him. His stomach loosened, relieved that he had actually gotten permission! "Thank you, Master!"

Math felt the thin young arms slip from his neck and watched his pupil run out the door, wondering if he had done the right thing.

* * * *

Cory prepared the potion as prescribed in the spellbook. Earlier he had both memorized the enchantment and copied it to a bit of parchment, since he was explicitly forbidden to go to the library again, and had expected it.

The boy walked out the cave entrance and went down the mountain to an open cliff. There Cory chalked the appropriate runes in a circle, around the stone's inner heart, then wove enchanted threads of force tight around them. The runes glowed brightly. In the center of this circle of power he placed a small brass dish filled with a green fluid, and mixed a vial of blue into that.

Then Cory stared at the gleaming dish, taking a long breath. There was one last ingredient to be added, one which hinted of dark magic. The boy pulled out the dagger he had taken from the kitchen and quickly pricked his finger, letting his own blood drip into the dish. The fluid bubbled and hissed, almost as if set on fire; in a way it was. Cory watched as the bubbling fluid slowly turned clear. It finally looked exactly like water, which was the trap.

Cory backed off and hid behind a boulder. Resting on his stomach, chin cupped in his hands, bare feet swinging above him, the boy watched the bowl from there, wondering which animal would answer his call. The circle would draw the first creature nearest to it, but there was no way of knowing which kind of animal it would be.

He lay still until his elbows hurt, then slowly reclined against the wall of rock, rubbing the circulation back. He listened for anything to finally come, but only heard the whistling of the wind across the mountain's face. Cory looked up at the blue sky, watching the clouds twist themselves into different shapes. Once, on Earth, that was all he could do with clouds. Now he knew how to mold them into any shape he wished.

Pointing his finger at a cloud, he whispered a single word, and the gaseous watery mass became an eagle, with wings spread against the wind. Would he have an eagle for his familiar? That would give him sharp eyesight and the power of flight. Of course, it would also shorten his life, for the spell would take years from his own natural lifespan and give them to the bird.

Cory did the same with another cloud, whispering the word for panther in the ancient tongue. It reshaped into a likeness of the creature, a great cat ready to leap at its prey. A panther would give him strength, nightsight and incredible agility.

The boy changed several more clouds as they passed by, finally becoming bored with the game and closing his eyes. The tome hadn't said how long it would take to lure an animal, it only said that it would. Cory sighed, wondering if he had possibly cast the spell wrong, or made a mistake in copying it down. He carefully unrolled the parchment, rereading the incantation.

Then, from the other side of the boulder, Cory heard the metal bowl clattering against the stone, and jumped. Carefully he poked his head around the rock and frowned at what he saw. It was a small shiny creature, no larger than a half-grown dog. Its golden scales gleamed in the noon sunlight as it played with the now-empty bowl.

"Oh no," Cory whispered, and slowly rose, horrified. Math had warned him of this! The animal that had answered his call was one of the strange creatures that wandered the hills and mountains of Gwynedd, and didn't even exist on his native Earth. The runes had ceased glowing, meaning the spell was finished. Cory had his familiar and was stuck with it—an ugly little animal he couldn't even name!

The boy stepped forward, frowning, trying to get a closer look at the thing. Hearing the noise, the creature turned, and Cory found himself staring into a pair of soft violet eyes. It stared back, knowing him but not knowing him, and unafraid. Cory fearlessly approached it, for the creature would not harm him after drinking his blood. That was the heart of the spell. The two were bonded together until one of them died.

The boy knelt and the creature came to him, lapping at his outstretched fingers. It was then Cory saw the small, leathery wings attached to its back, and his eyes ballooned, suddenly realizing what it was.

"A *dragon!* A baby dragon!" Cory laughed, not believing his luck. Of all the animals he dreamed of answering his call, this one hadn't even entered his mind! He remembered the time Math had rescued him from the monster in the field, but that had been a black dragon. This one was golden—benign toward humans, but the mortal enemy of virtually everything else.

Cory stroked the dragon's head, feeling the soft golden scales that would soon grow hard and impervious to injury. It couldn't fly yet, for the wings were still too weak, but soon it would be soaring faster than a hawk and more gracefully than a swan!

The boy stared into the deep violet eyes, feeling the mindlink beginning to take hold. He suddenly knew a few words in Dragon-Language, and the animal's name: **Benythonne**, "Son of Thunder." He also saw a cold, sunless cave, a clutch of unhatched eggs, and an enormous body, which provided fresh meat when it cried of hunger.

Cory shook his head, breaking the trance. This animal was the first to hatch, and had left the safety of the nest while his mother was out hunting. Had he stayed instead of answering the call of the spell, he would've had to compete with his newly-hatched siblings for food, and eventually one would kill another. With a trembling hand, Cory petted the dragon's head, thinking of how he had saved it from that fate.

The boy sighed and slowly rose, the animal staying close to him. He would have to feed it some of the meat in Math's cave, raw. But how would he meet the needs of a growing dragon in the years to come? The boy blew between his teeth, hoping Math would know some of the answers.

"Come on, Benythonne."

※   ※   ※   ※

The boys crowded around Cory and the little dragon, asking many questions, but kept their distance when they saw how the razor-sharp teeth tore apart the meat on the stone floor.

"Where'd you get it?" Gwion asked.

"The West face of Penllyn," Cory answered nonchalantly.

"And it just followed you here? A dragon?"

Cory nodded. In truth, he was just as hypnotized as the rest of them by the unusual creature's grace and horrible beauty.

"Math'll never let you keep it," Hanephour warned.

Cory looked up at him, mild anger on his face. "Shows what you know! He's not a pet. He's my familiar!"

"And a very good one," Math said from the door, and all heads turned. "A golden dragon is extremely rare. As it grows it will boost your power *tenfold*."

The boy beamed at him. "Really?"

Grimly, Math nodded. Cory had never seen the master's face so grim. "Tell me, do you know where the birth-cave is?"

"Uh huh."

"Show me. Now."

The boy immediately went to his master and formed an image in the air between them, showing the entire mountain and where the nest was.

The old wizard nodded. "Good. You boys stay here. I have a duty to perform."

With that, Math left the kitchen. The boys whispered between themselves, listening to their master's footsteps disappear down the hall.

"That doesn't sound too good."

"It isn't," Hanephour told them, poking his head out the doorway. "He's taking his staff with him."

The boys all blew between their teeth except Gwion and Cory. "I've never seen him use a staff," little Gwion said.

"Pray you never do," Hanephour told him. "It's only used for invoking dangerous magicks. He keeps it locked up in his room. I've only seen him take it out once before, to calm an earthquake five years ago."

"Uh oh," Gwion muttered.

Cory stood stock still. Hanephour was the eldest among them, seventeen. He had already earned his sorcerer's cloak and was almost finished with his training. Soon he would leave to find his fortune in the world, but for now the younger apprentices all looked up to him as their leader.

"You don't think ... he's going to kill...."

Hanephour looked at Cory and shook his head. "You mean the dragon? I don't know."

Math returned later that evening when the boys were sitting down to dinner. Silently he walked to the fireplace, placed his cloak on a peg, and sat down, staring into the flames. Silently the boys watched him, gradually resuming with their meal. Finally, when he could no longer bear it, Cory got up from the bench and approached the wizard.

"Master?"

"Yes, Cory?"

"Did you ... kill Benythonne's mother?"

Math looked up at the boy, staring him straight in the eyes. The boy's jaw began to tremble, his eyes growing wet. Math had warned him of the dangers of taking a familiar, and now he had to pay the price of his folly. Finally, Math spoke.

"The dragon did not take the loss of her child lightly."

Tears flowed down the boy's cheeks unashamedly. Cory tried to say something, but his voice was breaking, so he silently shook his head in disbelief.

"No, I did not kill her."

"W—what?"

"Dry your tears. The dragon yet lives. If she were any other clan but golden I would have done otherwise."

Hanephour came up from behind Cory and held the younger boy's shoulders, calming him. "Master, if this is so, why did you take your staff?"

Math did not move. He just watched the two boys as a statue might. Hanephour and Cory hardly dared to breathe, waiting for the dread answer, for a wizard's staff is not used lightly. Finally, he gave them one.

"I owed Gwendorianoah a boon. I have paid it."

Math said no more than that, and neither boy pressed him further. It would be months before Cory would finally learn what that payment was.

CHAPTER 8

GATHERS THE DARKNESS

Spring came, the dragon grew healthy and strong, and with it so did Cory's power. The boy's physical strength became monstrous, and he could soar through the sky in true flight while the other apprentices his age were still learning simple levitation. Contrary to Math's warning, the boy's lifespan was extended, not shortened, for years were taken from the long-lived dragon and added to his own.

One warm spring morning Cory's thirteenth birthday came, and Math gave the boy his true name. The rites of manhood were performed at this age even though the boy wouldn't reach full growth for many years. Cory bathed in clear lake water while Math wove powerful charms about him. He was named out of earshot of the other boys, for a person's true name was kept a close secret, especially among wizards; he who knew someone's soulname held that life in his hands. As he left the water, Math whispered the boy's true name to him: *Draigswynwr*, or "Dragon-Wizard" in the Old Tongue.

Neither of them noticed a peculiar raven in the trees, watching them with baleful, red-glowing eyes. After the wizard and his apprentice left, the bird took wing and flew south.

Later that same month, another powerful wizard came to visit Math, and the apprentices were all sent to the lake to play in the warm weather. Cory gathered a few things he'd need, a towel, lunch sack, and a small crystal ball he'd been learning to scry with. The boy held the marble-sized crystal sphere in the palm of his hand, and remembered that Math had a slightly larger one, more powerful than this little trinket, and that he'd had better luck viewing through that one. Cory slipped his small marble into one of the leather pouches that hung from his belt, and rushed to ask permission to borrow the larger crystal, when he heard voices from Math's study. This room was the Master's private sanctum, which the boys didn't dare intrude upon, unless summoned, or to ask permission to perform some magic spell which was beyond them at the moment. The thin child paused outside the chamber, the door slightly ajar, with golden candlelight seeping through the crack.

"You know why I have come," the strange, red-robed wizard intoned in a low voice.

Cory's blue eyes widened, suspecting something important was about to be said. He knew he really shouldn't be snooping like this, but curiosity got the better of him, and the boy crept up, putting one eye to the narrow slit between the door and its frame.

Math nodded, gently stirring sugar into his tea. He looked across the table at his guest, who wore a long flame-red robe and a matching skullcap. Resting against his chair was a long staff, made of Rowan, and a yellow wool cloak dried by the fire. There had been a recent downpour, Cory recalled, a sudden storm that came and went in fifteen minutes. Steam rose in a great white cloud from the cloth as the orange and gold flames dried it.

"I have the answer, Ilmarinen."

The ancient wizard stopped stroking his long, white beard. "Oh, do you now? Do you have the Demon Lord's true name?"

Math shook his head. "No. But I believe I have a boy who is his equal. The lad is an archwizard."

Ilmarinen inhaled sharply. "Careful...."

"No, he is the one. His power is already great, and he has learned his lessons with lightning swiftness. A mage born. And something else: he has a golden dragon for a familiar."

Cory swallowed, his heart rising into his throat. He'd of course known before now that his natural gifts were beyond most of the students here, but to hear Master speak of him in such glowing terms ...! *Archwizard!*

Ilmarinen's eyebrows rose, and he weakly reached for his steaming tea. He softly asked the question which hung in the air between them. "When do you expect him to outstrip you?"

Math sighed. That was the heart of it. Few wizards alive knew how to teach a budding archwizard, and Math was *not* among them. Resting the cup in his lap, not looking at his friend, Math answered.

"Three months."

Ilmarinen sipped his tea. "You know to whom you must send him."

Slowly, Math nodded. "I do. But will he take the boy?"

"If this apprentice is all you say he is, yes. But again, I must ask. You've been premature before."

The spellweaver shook his head. "Not this time. The boy's already hurling mystic bolts. Less than a year with me, and he's hurling mystic bolts."

Cory had heard enough. He made a quick pass with his hand, to ensure his footsteps were silent, and quickly darted down the deserted stone corridor. Fear gripped his heart.

Master Math wants to send me away again! Because he thinks I can stand up against Asmodeus? That's crazy! I'm talented, yeah. Quick in learning my spells. But I'm just an apprentice! *Asmodeus is a demon— Lord of all the demons. He's been practicing magic since before my great-grandfather was born! How can these wizards possibly think I stand a chance against a monster like that?*

The boy shuddered, his whole thin body quaking. It had nothing to do with the pervasive chill that clung to the corridors of the mountain fortress. Cory told himself that they'd made a mistake. That's all. They're as scared of the Demon Lord as much as any of the kids, and they think that he could somehow stop him, just because he'd fulfilled some moldy old prophecy by coming here from Earth!

They'd made a mistake. Yup, that's all there is to it, Cory firmly told himself, and rushed off to join his companions for a day of fun. The others were all assembled in the audience chamber, near the entrance to the vast network of tunnels and chambers dug within the mountain. Jern, the eldest, passed his hand before the imposing stone door, whispered a few words of passage, and the portal slid aside. Golden streams of sunshine flowed into the Caer, and the boys skipped outside into the warm spring air.

It took the better part of an hour to reach the huge, clear blue lake at the foot of the mountain. The boys doffed their boots and sandals at the foot of a huge oak tree, hung their tunics on some low tree limbs, and dashed naked into the cool water. Cory swam with his friends for a bit, then lay in the soft, green grass, while the gentle breeze and golden sunshine dried his skin. The young teenager lay there, eyes closed, listening to the sounds of kids splashing in the lake, and birds singing in the thickly-laden boughs, high above him. Suddenly, one of the thinner branches fell, the leaves and twigs landing on his face and chest, which scratched his skin.

"Hey!" Cory cried in surprise.

"Hey, yourself, lazybones!" the voice of a young child answered him. It sounded like a six or seven-year-old human boy, except Cory knew it wasn't a human boy at all. It was his dragon.

"Benythonne! What's—" Cory began, and quickly cut himself off when he saw the flash of sunlight reflect off the dragon's golden scales, as the yearling wyrm soared quickly above the treetops.

"Betcha can't catch me, Cory!" the little wyrm cried, and the young magic apprentice smiled.

"So, that's the way you wanna play, huh?" The thin child rose, padded barefoot across the soft, new grass, grabbed his tunic from the low branch and slipped it on. During these few seconds, Benythonne flashed high above once more, taunting him. Cory jumped into the air, and flew, quickly rising above the treetops. Benythonne shot past him, the thin membranes of his amber, leathery wings brushing the boy's skin.

"Tag!"

Cory couldn't help but smile, and flew after him, making loops and barrel-rolls in the air, chasing the young dragon like two planes on Earth in an old dog-fight from the First World War. Cory caught glimpses of the huge lake, spread out before him. Below, the boys magically sent huge waves of water across the lake at each other, thoroughly drenching themselves against the heat. Cory flew high above them, he and Benythonne flying around each other in the clear blue sky. A few of the older boys tried get in on this game but couldn't keep up. Even a year-old dragon could out-maneuver them, and Cory had that same talent as his familiar. Hanephour had left the day of Cory's naming, and, being highly respected by the others, Cory became their new leader.

Thus playing, none of them noticed the tide of darkness gathering at the edge of the southern horizon, gradually creeping across the sky. It was ink-black, night with no stars, eating all the light like a plague. Eventually the darkness grew close to the sun, and the boys noticed the shadow deepening, bitter cold replacing the warmth of spring. Caught up in the fun and sheer joy of magical flight, Cory didn't notice, didn't pay attention to what was going on around him until it was too late. Of course, he heard the concern in his friends' voices, his hearing far sharper than any human's, now. He just didn't realize it until Kellyn cried out in warning.

"Jern, what's that?"

"Dunno. It looks like some kind of spell."

"Very good, halfwit! Who's casting it?"

Jern, now the eldest of them, frowned. "If I knew that—"

"Oh, Maker! Look!"

They followed Kellyn's outstretched arm to the south and saw something moving in the blackness. It took a few minutes for their eyes to adjust, then they clearly saw several hundred creatures with batlike wings coming toward them.

Gwion swallowed, eyes widening in fear. "Kellyn, what are they?"

"*Demons*," the boy breathed. "They're attacking! CORY! GET OUT OF THE SKY!"

Cory was arcing around his dragon, avoiding its playful bite when he noticed the shadow passing in front of the Sun. At first he thought it was just a cloud, but the darkness was so total, so cold. Then he looked south, saw the Kelloids coming for him, and swallowed.

He froze. All that training, for months, and the boy's first reaction was to freeze and hover in mid-air. His sapphire-blue eyes widened, and his all the blood drained from his face. His breath came in short gasps. Incredibly fast, the demons closed the gap between them in less than a minute. The boy's enhanced senses made out their yellowing fangs, glowing, baleful eyes, and powerful claws that ended in razor-sharp talons.

Impossibly, it was nighttime. The demons had somehow managed to summon the night, hours early. It made no sense. Nobody was this powerful …!

Then, Math's words echoed in Cory's head, rousing him from his shocked stupor. The boy's training took hold of him, and something more, something innate to dragons. Ferocity unlike anything the usually timid Earth-child had ever known before in his young life.

"*Not this time. The boy's already hurling mystic bolts. Less than a year with me, and he's hurling mystic bolts.*"

Eldritch energy lanced from Cory's fingertips, burning the heart of the Kelloid, and it fell to the earth below. But the boy had no time to rejoice in his victory, for there were *dozens* of the demons surrounding him in the sky. Two demons flew straight for him, rammed hard into the invisible wall he had just barely finished conjuring, and stunned, they both spun away into the pitch darkness.

Below, the other apprentices were screaming, fighting for their lives against the creatures, which grabbed at them and carried them off. Taliesin had told Cory of this, the Kelloid raids, so feared by the humans of Gwynedd. But Cory knew that this was different, this conjured darkness. The light of day was deadly to demons, but they had finally found a way around that!

Cory flew straight at the monsters, striking several of them with a volley of mystic energy, and they painfully released their living booty. Thus occupied, a demon was able to come up from behind and throw a thick, leathery arm around the boy's neck.

"A prize for sure, this one. He fights like a true wizard!"

Choking, Cory couldn't summon the breath to incant. His fingers groped for the demon's head, and wheeling in mid-air, threw the monster over his head with all of his dragon-like strength. The Kelloid yelped in surprise, helpless to stop his flight path into a mighty oak, which shattered on impact. A great crack resounded through the field as the solid wood splintered, sounding like the report of thunder.

"He's as strong as one of us!" another demon warned. Holding an orange-glowing jewel in one hand, he began to spellcast, but a pair of powerful jaws closed about the demon's torso, sinking razor-sharp teeth into thick blue flesh. The demon tried to fight the monster, which was now as large as a pony, but Benythonne twisted his sinuous neck and threw the demon into the lake.

Cory nodded. The dragon was yet too young to breathe fire, but it was already a match for one of the demons. Together, the two of them were able to hold the Kelloids off and help the other boys to some extent. Kellyn had created a wall of flame to hold the demons back, but they walked right through it as if it were nothing more than a hot shower. Kellyn screamed as he was picked up by the leg, and the ebony creature laughed at him. Another apprentice tried to blind the creature with bright light. But even as the demon shielded his delicate eyes, he still held firmly onto his young captive.

From the air, Cory fired two spheres of emerald energy which exploded on impact, forming a green slime which burned the demon's wings. Screaming, the Kelloid dropped Kellyn, then soaked his wings in the lake to extinguish them. Infuriated with humiliation and pain, the demon started to approach the young humans again. But Benythonne landed between them, protecting the boys.

"Come here, ugly," Cory said, grabbing the demon's batlike wings and pulling him into the sky. Cory was careful to avoid the razor-sharp claws as he carried the monster over the lake and dropped him into it. The Kelloid quickly recovered, beginning to flap his wings, but the young apprentice turned the water to rock-hard ice. Then Cory landed next to Benythonne, ready to strike at the demon should he manage to free himself.

"Thanks for saving me," Kellyn said to his friend, and frowned at his arm. "Cory, you're bleeding!"

"He nicked me."

"Some nick! It's a couple of inches deep!" Jern warned.

Cory held the wound, which now began to hurt. Blood flowed thickly, drenching the torn tunic. The boy clenched his teeth, trying to ignore pain until the charm he cast on the gash could work. "It'll close. Listen, somebody's gotta go back and get Math. We can't fight them all."

"Don't have to. He knows by now. He hears everything!"

Cory frowned, looking back at the shadow of the mountain. "I don't think so. Whoever cast this spell must've found a way to block Math's detection, or he'd be here by now."

Jern nodded. "Makes sense. I'll go. Cory, you stay here and protect the others as best you can."

Kellyn shook his head, horrified. "No! Jern, we should stay together! They'll capture you!"

"I've almost earned my sorcerer's cloak," the older boy said, and his eyes and Cory's met. Cory almost had his cloak as well.

Gwion pulled at his elbow. "Jern, take me with you. Please!" The teenager looked down at the little boy, seeing how terrified he was. Jern put a hand on the child's shoulder, hoping to calm him.

"No. You'd only slow me down. Stay here with the others. They'll protect you."

"They're coming back," Kellyn cried, pointing at the sky.

Cory swallowed. "Second wave. Jern, take Benythonne. He'll get you there faster."

"Thanks," the boy replied, and climbed up onto the dragon's back. The boys watched as Benythonne flapped his golden wings, hardly able to take off with the extra weight, but in a moment the little dragon got used to his burden and climbed into the blackened sky.

"They're almost here!" Gwion cried.

"Cory, what'll we do?" Kellyn asked nervously, turning to his friend.

The boy stared at the ebony wings flashing in the greater darkness, and spoke through a dry throat. "We'll ... we'll build a wall."

"I tried that," Kellyn told him.

"No, not of fire. A web of *light!* We'll weave it. Kellyn, Bron, get behind me. Seloy, Pellor, to my sides. Gwion and Markrael, in front. Form a hexagram, with me in the center."

The boys did so, each standing at one of the six points, joining themselves together with lines of pure force, which concentrated energy in the center. The air around them gave off its own light, a flickering candle in the all-consuming darkness.

"This is never gonna work," Pellor said, his voice quivering. "I say we just run for it!"

"No! They'd catch us!" Kellyn yelled at the boy with a scowl. "Listen to Cory!"

"He's right. Just follow my lead. We'll start in the center and work our way out. Hurry!"

They began to weave, out of desperation, out of terror. A single circle appeared in the center of the sky, surrounded by threads of eldritch force like the spokes of a wheel, and the web grew. By the time the Kelloids reached them, the web was almost complete, being several hundred feet in diameter.

The creatures struck the barrier and were repelled as energy sparked through their leather hides and night-dark wings. The Kelloids cursed, those few with mystic crystals sending bolts of blue-white energy at the web, snapping several strands, but still it held.

"I don't believe it," Pellor breathed. "We're actually beating them. Hundreds of them and—"

"Shut up!" Kellyn screamed. "You'll break everybody's concentration!"

Gwion, the youngest of them, cast his eyes on Cory. The little boy was feeding all his power into the spell, and beginning to tire. Yet Cory looked worse, bearing the brunt of all their combined energies. Sweat poured from Cory's face and his body trembled.

"Hold on, Cory!"

"You little jerk," Markrael snapped. "Don't talk to him while he's—"

"Look at him!" Gwion cried, and Markrael did, with a gasp. "He can't take much more!"

"He's right! We're killing him!" Markrael screamed, and the boys turned.

"We're not killing him, halfwits," Kellyn told them. "He can take it. Just don't let your guard down or we've had it!"

"They're breaking through the web!" Bron warned, and all heads turned. The Kelloids had torn open a hole and were now flying through it. The boys screamed as the demons descended upon them, claws extended. The hexagram fell apart as the youths diverted their efforts to defending themselves, but most of the web still held.

Cory fell to his knees, no longer able to stand. He held his hands up out of sheer force of will, maintaining their one true defense. The boy panted for air and the muscles in his neck tightened from the strain. The spell was already cast, but it had to be maintained against demons that constantly fought the individual threads, making the hole larger.

Four demons came down, grabbing the boys, who thrashed about, no longer fighting with magic. Gwion sent blinding light into their eyes, doing virtually no good. The demon Cambian came ever closer, cursing the boy, finally taking him in a viselike grip. The ten-year-old cried, his most potent spells having failed him, now pleading with his comrades for help, but none came.

"GWION!" Kellyn cried, sending a bolt of force at the demon that held the boy, but Cambian merely shook it off. Kellyn heard his friend's screaming, begging for help, but couldn't do anything. Kellyn had to hold his ground, keeping the other three demons off Cory. "Back, you animals! Somebody go after Gwion!"

"I can't!" Markrael yelled back. "Oh, Maker! Somebody help me! He's almost on top of me!"

"Nothing can save you, pathetic *human*," the demon rasped. Cory recognized the dark form, the voice of death. Ahriman, Grand Duke of Abollydd, was personally leading this attack! "You are ours. All of you are! You'll work the Wheel until your puny little bodies break!"

Cory moaned, helpless to do anything. He heard the spark of magical energy discharging, heard Ahriman scream in agony. Heard the demon curse.

"Strike me, will you?" Ahriman snarled, his voice full of menace and loathing. Cory swallowed, knowing what was going to happen, helpless to stop it. "Time to die, little boy!"

A Kelloid demon was one of the most powerful creatures in all Abydonne. Impossibly strong, armed with razor-sharp talons, armored with tough, dragon-like scales. Quick as lightning and just as unfeeling, the demon stepped forward, and casually struck the human boy with one hand. Cory heard a sharp, wet crack, and knew human bone had just shattered. He saw through the fog of pain, through his tears, his friend fall. The once living, vibrant young teenager lay still, spread-eagled on the ground nearby. Markrael's skull was cracked open like an eggshell, his brains spilled all over the grass. The boy's blue-gray eyes stared at Cory, but there was no intelligence behind them. Markrael's soul was gone.

"BACK, HELLSPAWN!"

Helplessly, through his tears, Cory watched as the demon now turned on Jern, yellow eyes gleaming. He saw this other boy, as sapling-thin as the other one. Yet, Cory knew Ahriman could feel his innate power. No, not power, Cory realized—skill. Jern was almost a full sorcerer.

Ahriman smiled grotesquely. "Come and get me, boy. Do your worst!"

With a single burst of anger, Jern weaved the largest, most powerful bolt he knew, striking the thing full force. Ahriman was thrown back, setting the grass on fire. "Human filth! I'll destroy you for th—"

Before Ahriman could even complete his sentence, Benythonne clamped a firm hold on the demon, tossing him into the web, which then caught and discharged into his body. The demon fell, unconscious.

Cory finally dropped his arms, letting his face rest in the grass, breathing hard. The boy swallowed, knowing what his failure has caused, seeing in his mind's eye the web dissolving, letting the swarm of demons through. He fully expected the demons to pick him up at any minute and carry him off like the other three children. There had been ten of them. The demons had carried off the two weakest before Cory managed to defend the rest. Exhausted, he waited to join them, to be taken once more to the slavepits.

"Cory," a voice said, a hand gently caressing his back. His body ached, exhausted, but still he raised his head a little, ready to strike with the last dregs of his strength.

"Easy, lad. Let the enchantment work. You must regain your strength."

"Who ... who are—"

"Shhh. Easy. You have more work yet. But for now let your body recover."

Cory nodded, lying in the soft grass, looking up at the shadowy figure. He dimly recognized the man's voice, and straining his memory, finally remembered the wizard who had come to visit Math earlier that day. Through the corner of his eye, Cory could see the web still in place, and realized either Ilmarinen or Math must be holding it.

"How is he?"

"He'll be fine in a moment, lad. You did well."

"I did nothing," Cory heard Jern's anguished voice reply. "Markrael's dead. I tried—I tried to save him, but I couldn't ... and they've captured three of us! Kellyn just told me they've taken Gwion!"

Cory's eyes grew wide. "Gwion?" The boy tried to turn his head, but a firm hand held him down.

"Rest!"

Cory pictured the little boy, his mass of blond hair disheveled, his almond-brown eyes tearing, wide with terror. Standing in the center of the spell, falling to his knees, Cory had heard the little boy's cries of panic, heard and recognized the voice of the demon that had kidnapped him: *Cambian*. Cory doubted a child as fragile as Gwion would survive the slavepits. He violently shook his head, shutting his eyes against the image. "No, please! Jern, go after him!"

"I SAID BE STILL!"

"No," Cory sobbed, burying his face in his arms. "Jern, go after him! Take Benythonne. Hurry before it's too late—"

"*Cwsg bach tywysog*," Ilmarinen incanted, and Cory fell silent, into a deep sleep. Voices drifted through to him, through the veil of slumber.

"What did you do to him?" Jern asked, nearly stumbling forward. He ignored the wailing of the younger apprentices around him, crying like sheep, who were relieved that their master was finally there to protect them.

"He'll sleep. Now the enchantment will work on him. We'll need his power soon."

"What? I'll help you! Cory's done enough."

Ilmarinen shook his head. "No. It's all we can do to hold the demons back. Only this one has the power needed to win the battle, and he must do it soon, or all of us are doomed."

Chapter 9

ORIGINS

"How do you feel?" came the question.

Cory's throat burned as he forced words out. "Like death warmed over."

Ilmarinen smiled beneath his hood. The wizard put a waterskin to the boy's lips and let him drink a bit, then poured the rest on his head to wake him.

"We need you, lad. You must dispel this darkness."

"Dispel the ... I can't do that!"

"Yes you can. You're the only one of us who can."

The boy was helped to his feet, which surprisingly held his weight. But to spellcast ... Cory shook his head, doubting he could even weave a small fire.

"We are fortunate for the dragon," Ilmarinen said to Math. "It helps him to recover."

Math nodded. "The boy has been extremely lucky."

'Lucky!' Cory almost laughed. He could be home right now, on Earth, eating his mother's stuffed turkey for dinner. Why, oh why did he have to go into that abandoned building with John? Was he that foolish? Did he have to stand so close to the mirror so Asmodeus could reach out and pull him into this world?

"Cory," Math said firmly, and the boy raised his eyes. "I know you're weak, but this must be done. You can rest later."

Cory nodded. "Alright, Master. Tell me what to do."

"Look to the east. Do you see the threads?"

The boy strained his vision, barely able to manage that. Yes, he could see the dim outline of a pattern—the pattern which held the natural daylight back. But the pattern was so confusing ... he could change it, but change it to what?

"Be calm," Math said gently, putting a hand on his shoulder. "Weave the pattern I put in your mind."

Cory raised his hands, calling up the power. His palms glowed, but dimly. "Master—"

"I know. Draw upon Benythonne for strength. Let him provide the crutch for you to spellcast."

The boy closed his eyes, intensifying the link between him and his familiar, which was already very strong. Without even trying, he normally had many of Benythonne's powers. When he concentrated, he could draw upon the dragon's innate magic directly, using it boost his own energies. The glow on his palms grew brighter.

Cory's brow furrowed in confusion. There were so many threads, and he barely knew some of the patterns they belonged in. Gradually, he remembered a pattern here, a pattern there. But they were wrong, all wrong! To even begin to reweave them all could take years!

Then he saw the image Math had placed in his mind, which now burned bright and clear. Cory heard the words of power echoing in his skull, in Math's voice, and repeated them. He knew most of the words, but some were alien to him. He repeated them heedlessly, commanding the sky to cast out the foreign ebony cloud while gently nudging some of the more prominent threads.

The sky began to heave. The eastern horizon gradually began to change color. As he worked, the boy felt the reserves of power deep within him—not through the link to Benythonne, but his naturally—and tapped into it. The spell's force grew rapidly now, and the tide of darkness retreated against the onslaught of blue.

In the distance, Cory heard the demons screaming. He paid them no heed, for he needed all of his concentration to fight against the blackness ... the unnatural dark which existed only to shield the Kelloids against the power of the sun. In his mind's eye, he saw them retreating, knowing what was to come. They felt its heat, its life-giving warmth even before the artificial night was driven back.

Finally the darkness retreated past the third quarter of the sky, sliding past the solar disk as at the end of an eclipse. The Kelloids flew on, howling in pain, retreating from light of day.

As the last bit of night disappeared, a more total blackness claimed the young apprentice and he collapsed, falling into his master's protective embrace.

* * * *

For three days Cory saw nothing, heard nothing, felt nothing but all consuming darkness and wisps of dreams.

He saw young Gwion lying in a cell, the little boy's wrists bound in the magic-stealing iron chains Cory had once worn. Gwion was crying, his eyes red, wailing for food and water beside an empty earthenware dish. Cambian stood outside the cell door, cursing the small boy, twirling a long rawhide whip while ordering Gwion to stop crying. Cory reached out to his friend, running his fingers gently against the new, long scars on Gwion's back.

"Help me," Gwion begged. "Please, Cory! Get me out of here!"

"I'll get you out," Cory promised, his throat tight. "I'll get you out somehow."

"But how?" Gwion asked, pointing at his friend. "When cold iron stops you too?"

Cory looked down at his wrists for the first time in his dream. They were manacled again, robbing him of strength and blocking his magic. Cambian lifted Cory by the neck, hefted him over a huge, muscular shoul-

der, and carried him off, screaming, to the torture chamber to be whipped to death.

"No! I'll get you for this, Cambian! I'll kill you, I swear it!"

"Who is Cambian?"

"Our jailer," Cory heard Taliesin's voice say. The prince sounded like he was choking back tears. "Will he live, Math?"

"Yes, lad."

"But his fever—"

"Will break. The boy has overtaxed his power. He needs time to recover."

"I thought you said he has power to spare, more than you!"

"He does. Ilmarinen or I would be dead now. This one is an archwizard. That kind of gift is the rarest of all."

More voices: King Llewellyn, Ilmarinen, Kellyn. Cory knew they were standing over his supine body, looking down at him. Cory tried to speak to them, but his mouth wouldn't cooperate. He could just barely whisper, and his throat burned from thirst.

Helplessly, Cory slipped back into the dream, back to the cell with Gwion, playing the nightmare scene over and over again. Sometimes it changed. The cell melted into the torture chamber, where the two boys were locked in the stocks, covered with itching powder, and mercilessly tickled on their bare feet until they passed out. The torture chamber melted into the kitchen, where he and Gwion cut meat into pieces just large enough to keep the other slaves alive. The kitchen melted into the Wheel, where they walked alongside each other, pushing the Wheel in an endless circle while their injured knees grew painful and bloody.

On the fourth day, Cory woke screaming, his bedding soaked. Dimly he sensed that the place wasn't his room at Penllyn, but his suite at Caer Dathyl. Someone put a waterskin to the boy's lips and he drank greedily. Coughing, Cory looked up at his friend and spoke, very weakly.

"Tal."

"Take it easy, Cory. You've been ill."

"I know," Cory rasped, hardly recognizing his own voice. "I turned back the darkness?"

Taliesin slowly nodded. "You saved us all. But the Sun eventually went down, as it must. The first night nothing happened—I guess they were all hurt by direct daylight—but the second night came, and the demons swarmed from their cave by the hundreds.

"We fought them of course, but they were too strong. Most of the demons had magegems and cast spells against our armies."

The prince heaved a heavy sob, fighting back tears. He stood very still, staring at a wavering candle flame. "They took Arianrod. They took my sister!"

Cory watched his friend through glassy eyes, almost seeing right through him. "Did they ... they took Gwion. Was that real?"

Taliesin's face burned red. He turned on the young apprentice, screaming. "How can you think of a goatherd at a time like this? They kidnapped our only sister!"

Taliesin cruelly snatched Cory's arm, looking into his hazy blue eyes. Abruptly the prince once more saw that terrified little boy who had been wrenched out of his own world, crying, staring dumbly at the chains binding his thin wrists, begging to know what had happened to him and why.

And Taliesin saw something else: deep within those eyes a man, a powerful wizard stared back, burning for vengeance. For the first time he was afraid of Cory, the same fear he felt around Math. That, more than anything else, forced the boy to gradually let go of him.

"Tal, they took Gwion as well. I know you don't understand, but he's been very close to me. Where I come from royal blood means nothing. Everybody counts—and so help me, I'll get Gwion back if I have to kill every Kelloid in that mountain!"

"He means it," Kellyn warned, and both boys turned. "We're gonna have to lock him in this room 'til he gets better."

"You'll do no such thing," Cory bit off, but he knew Kellyn was right. His body was unbelievably weak; even the link with Benythonne was strained. He didn't know it was possible to be so tired, but he feared going back to sleep. A shadow of the long nightmare passed before his eyes, and Cory submitted to Kellyn's advice.

"Cory, I know how you feel. Gwion was close to all of us. We'll get him back—we *will*—but you have to recover first."

The boy nodded meekly. "We'll have to do it soon. He won't survive down there for very long."

Kellyn frowned. "Is it really that bad?"

"Yes, it is," Cory and Taliesin said as one, and for the first time, the boys shared a smile. Taliesin grew angry with himself for screaming at this poor boy—a brother to him now—who lay ill, having risked his life to save them all from the Kelloid demons. Taliesin drew Cory close and hugged him. "It is good to see you again ... Brother."

"You too, Tal. It's been too long." Cory let go, sinking back into his pillow. "I was going to see you soon, when I earned my sorcerer's cloak."

The prince grinned. "I heard. I wanted to see you many times. I made up excuses to sneak off to Mount Penllyn ... but Father always found something else for me to do. He sent me out hunting with Joukahainen, studying the Ruined City in the far north with Manannan, anything and everything to keep me busy."

"Heh. Don't feel bad. He did the same thing to me, shipping me off to Penllyn to be Math's apprentice."

Taliesin's face turned dark. "No. You there was a reason for. You have a power in you I don't understand. I don't even think Math understands it."

"Don't be ridiculous. Math knows everything."

"No," Kellyn said, sitting down next to the pair. "His Highness is right, Cory. I heard Math and the King talking. The Master wants to send you west, to an even more powerful wizard—an enchanter."

Cory's jaw set and he violently shook his head. "Oh no, he's not!"

"Cory," Kellyn said, holding the boy back with his hand. "He's right. Powerful as you are, you lack skill. This other magician, this ... Vain ... Vainam—"

"Vainamoinen," Taliesin gasped. "It can't be! He's a legend! A nursery rhyme!"

Cory shook his head. "He's one of the Elders. I read about him in Math's library—"

"*Cory*," Kellyn interrupted with a smile, and the boy returned it. They both knew the library was off-limits without permission. Cory didn't say a word about eavesdropping in on Master Math and Ilmarinen's conversation.

Taliesin looked out the window in awe. "If Math's sending you to *him*...."

Cory nodded. "An Elder would know how to defeat Asmodeus, and be able to teach me."

"Wait. If it's that simple, why doesn't this Vainamoinen come down here and beat Asmodeus himself?"

At Kellyn's simple question, Cory stared off into space, wondering. "I don't know. Maybe because he's very, very old."

Taliesin laughed. "If he's still alive, he must be!"

Kellyn snickered too. "Yeah, he probably gets around on crutches!"

"No. A wheelchair," Cory said, imitating a decrepit old man. "'Nurse, nurse!'"

Kellyn giggled, then frowned quizzically. "What's a wheelchair?"

Cory looked at him sideways. "A chair with wheels. Old people use them to get around on my world."

The other two boys tried to envision it and laughed.

"I see you're better," a deep voice said from the door. "Good. Now I can begin feeding you the potions I had prepared to speed your recovery."

Cory looked up fearfully at his master. "Why does that sound bad?"

"Because it smells and tastes worse," Kellyn explained, blanching at memory.

Math frowned at the boy. "It isn't that bad, and it healed you of the coughing sickness."

Kellyn looked down at the bedspread, then up at Cory. "Sorry, Master. You did get me well again, but the cure was almost as bad as the sickness!"

"I suddenly feel better," Cory said nervously, starting to get up. "Much better!"

Taliesin held him back. "Oh no, you don't! Math, get your medicines. He'll take it. We'll hold him down for you!"

Cory's mouth fell open. "TAL!"

* * * *

True to his word, the prince held Cory's wrists immobile while the boy twisted his head back and forth, mouth cemented closed, avoiding the flask of foul green fluid. Fortunately for Taliesin, Cory's recent ordeal had weakened the link to the dragon as well as his body. His face was twisted into a grimace, wishing more than anything to get rid of the evil taste already in his mouth.

"It's for your own good," Taliesin told him.

"Let me," Kellyn offered, and his probing fingers tickled Cory's belly. As Cory started to giggle, Math immediately poured steaming green medicine into the boy's open mouth. The patient coughed, then his face turned sour.

"That's all of it," Math told them. "For now."

"Ugh! I'll get you for this!"

"Sure you will," Kellyn said, digging his fingers into Cory's stomach again. The boy laughed hysterically and Taliesin suddenly had to let him go. Cory grabbed Kellyn, throwing him to the bed.

"His strength has returned!" Kellyn cried in warning.

Math nodded at the lads. "Good! That means the medicine is working. I'll be back later—and with stronger restraints."

Cory stopped and watched Math leave, closing the great oaken door behind. "He's kidding."

"I don't think so," Taliesin warned him, but a smile told Cory otherwise.

"That wasn't funny! Do you have any idea—phewey!—what that stuff tasted like?"

"Yes," Kellyn giggled. "I had to take it for a week."

"You *traitor!* How could you put me through that?"

"It was fun to see someone else suffer for a change," Kellyn explained.

"Besides, you were asking for it," Taliesin added. "Why didn't you just act like a man and take the stuff?"

Cory's face turned dark. "You've never been doctored by Math."

"Yeah," Kellyn agreed.

Cory spun, looking down at him. "Oh, so *now* you're on my side!"

"Come on, Cory! It wasn't that bad!"

"Yes," Taliesin added. "Just think of what Arianrod is going through down in Abollydd."

The boy's face abruptly fell. "And Gwion."

Taliesin saw his friend's expression and regretted that slip, whispering, "I'm sorry."

"So'm I. I'll take the medicine, Tal. When I'm better we'll sneak off for Abol—"

"SHHH!" Kellyn hissed, putting a hand over Cory's mouth, and the boy nodded. Math heard all. Silently, Cory swore. Keeping secrets from their master was impossible!

* * * *

In another week Cory was up and around, pacing his suite and making plans with Kellyn and Taliesin by writing them down instead of talking, but the old wizard somehow knew anyway.

Shortly Cory was summoned to the throneroom once more, as he had been all those months ago, when he was bound as apprentice to Math. This time he brought along his friends for moral support.

"No," Math told them flatly, and all three boys complained at once. Both the king and Math glared at them, and the youngsters grew silent.

"Cory, you are not yet ready."

"And when will I ever be ready?" Cory demanded, but his eyes dropped when Math stared at him, long and hard.

"You will be. But there are a few things I kept from you. As you learned, there are two major Arts. I am a spellweaver. My craft is quick and powerful, but weaker than invoking, which change and cement the very fabric of the world. Incantations are the most powerful of charms.

"All things have a name. To know the name of a thing is to know its essence, and to have power over it. Vainamoinen is an enchanter, one of the greatest. He knows more than just words, he knows the language well enough to sing the incantations."

Math stared at the frail boy, long and hard. "If you are to face Asmodeus, you must learn to sing while you weave. That would make you an avatar, a master of the two Arts. You are already an archwizard with a dragon as a familiar. Learn from Vainamoinen and you would become invincible."

Cory stared at the polished marble floor, hardly daring to breathe. Math had high hopes for him, perhaps too high. He was hardly an invincible, all-powerful wizard. He was just a scared kid from another world. Then an image flashed before his eyes, of Gwion crying to him, reaching out to him with chained wrists.

"Cold iron would still stop me."

The sentence hung in the air for a long while. Cory looked up, and Math's eyes gleamed. "Good. Good! You are not so arrogant as I thought."

"It isn't arrogance," Taliesin injected. "Forgive me, Father. But I must speak. Cory wishes only to rescue the others. If we wait too long they may die. We were down there, and we know."

The king looked at his two young sons, and took a shaking breath. "I know. When you were in the slavepits I thought we had lost you forever. There was nothing left to do but pray."

Cory nodded, finally understanding why his reward was so great. The king never really expected to get Taliesin back! His cheeks turning red with anger, Cory stared at King Llewellyn and asked the question which burned in his mind all the time since he and Tal were cellmates in Abollydd.

"Why don't you go down in there yourself? You have an army, don't you?"

"Cory," Taliesin warned, gripping his foster-brother's shoulder firmly.

"And what would you have my soldiers do, hmmm? There are nine hundred Kelloids down there! An army of demons which my forces can barely hold back from the cities at night—"

"Your Majesty, the boy doesn't know what the Kelloids really are," Math said, and Llewellyn turned to the wizard, nodding. "Cory, I have told you that they are not demons by birth, but might as well be. But I haven't told you all."

Cory nodded, intrigued. He stood by the throne, close by his adoptive father; listening to the man he had come to call Master.

"Many centuries ago the Kelloids were powerful wizards. Enchanters and spellweavers all, they were led by the most powerful among them: a young avatar named Asmodeus. He was the last archwizard born before you."

Cory gasped. He knew archwizards were rare, but until now, didn't know how rare! It was centuries—*centuries* ago.

"They began practicing dangerous magic. Dark and powerful they grew. I have told you that there is no difference between magic, which it is like fire, to be used for either good or evil. Likewise there is no true white or black. All magic comes from our Maker, like everything else. But these wicked men twisted the magic for their own greed.

"In the end they transformed their bodies into something hideous, but impossibly strong. All of their innate power was locked up in their forms to maintain them, but they considered the sacrifice worthwhile. Their new bodies never weakened, got sick, nor aged. They had traded their mystic gifts for something unnatural. That is why they need the magegems to spellcast. They no longer can."

Cory swallowed, turning to the King to apologize, but Llewellyn spoke first. "They are an army of sorcerers, nine hundred strong. We cannot hope to defeat them."

Weakly, Cory spoke, his voice small and thin in the huge chamber. "Then how can I?"

Math did not answer. He only smiled.

Chapter 10

▼

SORCERER

Ilmarinen stayed at the palace with Cory while Math returned to Penllyn. The boy continued his schooling at Caer Dathyl, under private tutelage from Ilmarinen, who rarely took students. Ilmarinen, the greatest craftsman of magic weapons in the Twelve Kingdoms, taught the boy how to forge enchanted objects, how to heal the gravest of wounds, and also something of incantation. True to Math's prediction, Cory earned his sorcerer's cloak in three more months.

The boy stood in the throneroom, attended by all the great lords of the realm, as befitted an adopted prince of the Royal Family. Llewellyn ordered the cloak spun of the finest cloth, and Ilmarinen charmed it himself. Math, attended by all of Cory's fellow apprentices, invested the boy with his sorcerer's cloak and fastened it with a mystic silver amulet of Ilmarinen's making.

Trumpets blared, minstrels played, and the festivities began. Llewellyn sat at the head of the table, Cory just to his right, Taliesin next to him. The King raised his crystal goblet of wine.

"To my son Cory, the Sorcerer!"

"Prince Cory!" the cheers echoed, and the boy from Earth looked around him, seeing many great lords, most of whom he didn't even know. Oh, he was introduced to each of them in turn, put each name in the back of his mind as if learning a new spell, and went onto the next. But he didn't *know* them. Looking sideways at his closest friend, he doubted even Taliesin did.

"So, you are now the youngest," Manannan, the eldest, said to him. Cory nodded. "I hear you have done honor to our family."

The boy carefully put his goblet down on the fine white tablecloth. "Not really—"

"He's modest," Taliesin said, and Cory poked him under the table. "Ow!"

'Stop it!' Cory mouthed.

"Now, boys...." Llewellyn intoned, and Taliesin immediately looked up, stung.

"But Father...."

"So much for honor," a lord said from farther down the long dining table, and the guests all laughed.

Taliesin's eyes burned, giving Cory a look which said now-look-what-you've-done, but the boy seemed not to notice.

"Tell me Math, do you still think this boy has the makings of a great wizard?"

"I have from the beginning, my lord," Math answered the King, and Cory knew it was true; the old man had had his eyes on him ever since he read his palm, those many months ago. "If you remember, you were like these two, once."

"As were we all," another stranger agreed.

"Where does Vainamoinen live?" Cory suddenly asked, and Math was taken aback.

Slowly, the wizard regained his composure. "On an island, it is said, 'between the earth and the heavens.' But in truth, it is just a two month journey off the shore of Kaleva, straight west."

"'Just' a two month journey? Wizard, to what hell do you send the boy?" Sir Gereint asked.

Math's expression grew dark. "That is none of your concern."

But it is mine, thought Cory, who said nothing.

"I will go with you," Taliesin offered.

"No. You will stay," the king ordered.

"But Father—"

"I said no," Llewellyn bit off, "And that will be the end of it!"

"Yes, sir."

Taliesin eyed his foster brother, his heart full of worry. He secretly planned to sneak away with him, tomorrow.

* * * *

Warm wind whipped their cloaks and caught at their hair. It shushed past and around the tower, whispering through the battlements. In the light of the full moon, one boy silently approached the other.

"Tonight's a good night for it."

Cory knew what Taliesin meant, and shook his head. "No."

The prince scowled. "What do you mean, *'no?'*"

Cory turned around to face his foster-brother. "Math and Ilmarinen are right. I'm not ready yet."

Taliesin grabbed his arm. "Now you listen to me. Our sister is in there! With or without you, I'm going after her!"

"Then you'll go alone, and I'll have to rescue both of you."

The blond prince pushed the slight boy, who fell against the stone battlement. "How dare you! A curse upon your soul!"

Cory reached out to him and a gust of wind picked up from nowhere, forcing Taliesin back until he lost his balance and fell. That had been on reflex. Cory had almost prepared a more potent spell when he caught Taliesin's eyes and saw the fear in them.

"Tal, I'm sorry."

The young prince looked up at Cory and sighed, suppressing the awful urge to shudder. If this boy wasn't already a wizard, he soon would be. Trying to salvage what little of his grace was left, Taliesin got to his feet and forced a smile. "Don't be. My own stupid fault for provoking you!"

Cory returned the grin. "And mine for losing control. Math would have my head if he saw...." the boy caught himself, suddenly aware that his master might be listening.

Taliesin's smile grew wider. "Forget it, then. But at least give me a decent reason why...."

Cory shook his head. "I'm not ready yet. I can't face a horde of demons by myself!"

"You're the best sorcerer I know, and you won't be alone."

Cory slowly nodded, and cast his thoughts into his foster-brother's head. *'I know. You talk to Kellyn about it.'*

Taliesin, careful not to speak, only nodded.

* * * *

After leaving Taliesin, Cory went to the Inner Ward, where Benythonne lay sleeping on the soft grass; or was supposed to be sleeping, anyway. As he drew closer to the ward, Cory sensed that the dragon was awake through their special link. And the beast was not alone.

Cory spoke a charm to draw the shadows about him and approached the final portal, which opened into the ward. The youthful golden dragon lay at rest under a five-hundred-year-old oak, his head up and his eyes intent upon the robed figure before him. Cory's eyes glazed over as he strengthened the link to hear what his familiar heard.

"Watch over him. Powerful he may be, but he is yet young and impetuous."

Benythonne nodded the affirmative. As if he could do otherwise. The pair were bound together undo death.

Cory dimly saw the man from the front, in his mind's eye, but a shadowy hood covered his head. Still, the boy could swear he saw a slight grin on that face.

The figure started to turn. Cory ducked behind the archway, holding his breath. Who was he? And more importantly, what was his interest with Benythonne? Cory's fear at being discovered suddenly turned to anger. *He* wasn't the intruder here!

The boy moved into full view, and gasped. The stranger was gone. He ran out into the ward, looking around carefully. The man had vanished without a trace.

The young dragon looked at him with its wide amethyst eyes, and Cory went to him. The boy reached out to pat the beast's nose. "Who was that?"

"Math," the dragon replied in a young boy's voice. "He's worried about you."

Cory started to sigh with relief, then caught himself and shuddered. The master knew everything. Was he watching now?

"Come on, Benythonne. We're getting out of here."

*   *   *   *

Under the cloak of night, the boy and dragon sneaked out of the castle. Cory cast a spell of invisibility over them, and the pair flew off into the dark sky.

Dark trees and hills passed far below as Cory cast a final glance at Caer Dathyl. He would not return, he swore, until he had managed to rescue Gwion, Arianrod, and the others.

They flew over Penllyn's jagged peak, past the sanctuary in which Math's students slept, dreaming of earning the staff of power that marked one as a full wizard. They flew on, over the wild, untamed Bledig Woods where Cory learned his first spell. Finally the pair arced downward, coming in for a landing by the shore of the Dead Lake.

"Kellyn."

At Cory's call, the thin blond boy came into view. Standing next to him was Taliesin, who was dressed in full gleaming armor.

"You're great at invisibility, but you make enough noise to wake the dead."

Cory grinned and allowed his spell to pass, causing himself and the dragon to appear once more. "Speak for yourself. Tal's armor makes so much noise it's a wonder half the demons don't know we're coming!"

"It's a wonder Math doesn't know," Taliesin said. "How'd you sneak out without that old wizard finding out?"

"It was Kellyn's idea," Cory answered. "He said we should pretend to be giving up, when we really meant to go ahead with the rescue attempt."

"Aye, and it's an old trick, Cory. It goes back to some of Math's first students. We have occasion to keep some secrets from him."

"True enough," Cory said, and turned his gaze west. "The entrance to Abollydd is that way. We might as well get on with it," he sighed.

The boys started walking along the tall cliff which ran the length of the beach, their feet digging into the cool, soft sand. Kellyn cleared his throat. "Um ... guys ... any ideas on how we're going to get in?"

"Getting in isn't the problem, it's getting out that worries me," Cory told him.

"We'll get out," Taliesin said firmly. "Between my sword and your magic—"

"And my claws," Benythonne added.

Taliesin smiled. "And your claws, we'll give the demons a run for their money!"

Cory turned to him in surprise. "I must be rubbing off on you. Just how much did I tell you about Earth?"

"More than you know," the prince answered. A sudden noise attracted his attention, and Taliesin's hand immediately flew to the hilt of his sword. "Down!"

The four of them immediately dropped to the sand and crawled over to the relative protection of the cliff. Cory began weaving the spell which would turn them invisible once more, but stopped when two figures tumbled off the high rock face and landed right in front of them. One, a woman, quickly regained her balance and brought a long broadsword to bear upon her foe. The other was a Kelloid, armed with a whip in one hand and a steel net in the other.

The woman fought bravely and well, slashing the air before the demon, preventing it from advancing. Cory caught his breath. He would do far more than watch.

With a gesture, a single mystic bolt flew from his hand and struck the demon from behind. As the Kelloid turned in surprise, the woman moved closer and stabbed it. Black blood flowed from the open wound, and the demon screamed.

The Kelloid flailed about wildly, trying to slash the woman with his claws. Cory called up the wind, blew up the loose sand and gravel, and stung the creature's wounds with it.

"Stop playing, Cory!" Kellyn said. "Just kill him!"

"Why? This is fun!" Benythonne said, and rushed forward to clamp his jaws around the Kelloid. With a single, crushing bite, the little dragon snapped the demon's neck.

"Fun? *Fun!* Cory, you've got to have a talk with that dragon of yours!"

The boy waved the comment away. He started towards the woman, who seemed to be ignoring him. She was watching the top of the rise, where two more figures were fighting.

Oh, great! So much for our surprise attack!

"Keela!" a man's voice cried out, and the swordswoman turned to Cory.

"Don't just stand there, boy! Help him!"

Cory nodded and swiftly flew into the air with a single thought. In a moment he had cleared the face of the cliff and was flying over the two combatants. One, a young human male, was chained and dodging the cracking flail of a large Kelloid. The thick leather was weighed down by sharp bone, and swiftly found its mark. As the demon drew back to strike a second time, Cory caught the end of the flail and held it there.

The creature turned, and the boy had to choke down his old fear of these monstrosities. It had been a year, a whole year, and still he was afraid of them!

"Well, well! What have we here?" the demon said with a gleam in his eye. He playfully pulled on the other end of the whip, drawing Cory closer. "A lost young human. Come here, little one," the creature hissed.

With a look of disgust, Cory dug in his heels and stopped his forward movement. "*No*," he said with finality, and gave a tremendous yank on the flail.

Yelping in surprise, the Kelloid tumbled forward, landing on his stomach. Cory quickly sidestepped to avoid being crushed under all that weight, and caught a firm hold of the demon's muscular arm in the process.

"Careful!" the man warned. "He'll kill you!"

"I know what I'm doing," Cory replied, more calmly now. Indeed, once he had started to actually fight, the training Math had given him took control, and he had no time to be afraid. With the demon still struggling in the grass, Cory took a firm hold of the arm with two hands, and tossed the demon over his shoulder into the air. The Kelloid, unable to orient himself so quickly, went over the cliff and landed in the sand below.

"Kellyn! Watch out!" Cory cried, and ran to the edge, looking to see if his friends were in any danger. The demon was lying face down, unmoving.

"It's all right, Cory! You knocked him out!"

The boy paused there for a moment, then turned to help the man, who was on his knees from the treatment the Kelloid had given him. His long, black hair was disheveled and his tunic was slashed where the flail had torn through to the skin underneath. Cory pulled his dagger and knelt in the grass next to him.

"Wounds look superficial. I think you'll be okay," Cory said, carefully touching the cuts and whispering charms to heal them.

"You're one of Math's students," the young man said, regarding Cory's cloak. "What's with the dagger?"

The boy smiled. "A trick my brother taught me. Hold still," he said, and fitted the end of the blade into the keyhole. In a moment the lock opened with a satisfying click, and he went to work on the other one.

"Where is the Master?"

Cory looked up at him, and realized that he was wearing a sorcerer's cloak as well. "Caer Dathyl. Do I know you?"

The young man smiled. "I am Brent."

Cory inhaled sharply. "Brent the Black?"

"My reputation is exaggerated, I assure you," the young man said, and the two of them stood up after Cory undid the other shackle.

"What are you doing here?" the boy asked of the older sorcerer.

Brent frowned down at him. "I might ask the same of you. Or doesn't Math still punish boys who wander off at night, when they should be home in bed?"

Cory turned away. "That's none of your business."

Brent was surprisingly quick for one so ragged-looking. He snatched the boy's arm and turned him around. "It is. You came out here on a dare or what?"

Cory looked up at him. "No, nothing like that at all!"

"What then?" the sorcerer asked, his eyes piercing the young boy's, sneaking into his mind when Cory wasn't expecting it.

Brent gasped. "You must be crazy! Nobody can just walk into Abollydd—"

The boy pulled away, annoyance prevalent in his features. "I can, and stay out of my head! You have no right!"

Brent looked darkly at him. "I have more right than you know, pup. Math's students watch out for each other, and I'll be darned if I'm going to let you go into that cavern!"

Cory started to back away from the man, energy beginning to build at his fingertips. "Try and stop me."

Wearing an imposing expression, Brent took a step forward.

All at once the world began to spin, and Cory found himself fighting to retain his balance. The ground span beneath his feet and trees seemed to wind in circles about him and Brent. The stars shifted crazily in the sky, and the moon seemed to rise and set and collide with the earth. Before long the boy fell to his knees, his breathing labored.

Then it stopped as suddenly as it started, and Cory moaned, his ears still ringing. *What in Heaven's name did he hit me with?*

"Get up," Math's familiar voice demanded. Cory somehow managed to raise his head, but his vision was badly blurred. They were all back in the lush garden of Caer Dathyl's Inner Ward. Brent was kneeling not four feet from him, while Taliesin and Kellyn were lying on their backs in the grass, taking air in huge gasps.

Dimly, Cory realized that it wasn't Brent who cast that spell. *Math must've brought us back here. God, my insides feel like cold spaghetti!*

The old wizard didn't seem to notice, or care, that the victims of his spell were all disoriented to the point of being sick. He stood over Cory, eyes aflame. "What have you to say for yourself?"

For the moment, the boy could only look up at him with the expression of a small child caught with his hand in the cookie jar. "I—"

Math sadly shook his head. "I should have seen this coming. You are, and probably will always remain, an impetuous youth."

"Master...."

"I put my faith in you, Cory! How could you betray me like this?"

"But...."

"But *what?*" Math bit off, his long beard swaying with the movement of his tense jaw.

"This is what you've always told me to do," Cory finished.

The magician was caught off guard by that response. The boy was, of course, speaking the truth. From the beginning, Cory had been trained to do battle with Asmodeus himself, not just demons in general, as all the rest of Math's apprentices were. How then, could he feel angry with the boy?

Math exhaled audibly. "You have a lot to learn, young one," he said simply.

"You said that about me, once," Brent interrupted, his voice strong. Math spun around to face him, his cloak flying with the movement.

"You *dare*? Llewellyn ordered you banished from the kingdom!"

"I was called back," Brent told him evenly.

"By whom?"

"The king," Keela offered, walking up to stand next to Brent. She tendered Math a scrolled parchment. "Here is the royal command, with Llewellyn's own seal upon it."

Math took the paper with a look of disgust, and quickly scanned its contents. Then he handed it back, the expression on his face saying the order was irrelevant. "This does not erase your crime—"

"Crime?" Brent shouted. "We were in love!"

"—but as the king feels you are needed in this moment of crisis, I see no reason to question the wisdom of his choice. Stay if you will," Math continued, raising a finger to his former apprentice, "but stay away from my pupils."

Brent opened his mouth to say something, and then caught himself. He simply nodded his assent, and Math silently turned and walked away.

"Well, he hasn't changed," Keela said.

The tall young man regarded the boys, still balled up in the grass, all but senseless. "What else is new? You find us a place to spend the night. I'm going to help these poor pups."

Chapter 11

ISLAND OF MYSTERY

Brent found the boy hidden behind some evergreens in a secluded section of the Queen's garden. In the grass all about the kneeling youngster were open tomes of magic, with several small stones laid out in a pattern in front of him. The golden dragon lay by his familiar's side, resting, but ever protective of the child.

Without breaking pace from scribbling on scrolled parchment, Cory spoke. "Are you going to stand there all day or did you want something?"

Brent didn't try to hide his astonishment. The spell he wove about himself made his approach as silent as a fawn in the glade.

"You are as powerful as they say you are. How did you know—"

"My dragon sensed you, and I knew through him. We're tied together."

Brent nodded. "I know of familiars, but I've never had one myself. Few take the risk."

Cory didn't hide his distaste for what had recently happened. "Math branded me an impetuous youth, remember?"

Brent smiled and took a step forward, intending to advise the boy. "He did the same—"

Benythonne raised his head from the grass and stared at the sorcerer, grinning at him with a full set of razor-sharp teeth.

"—to me," Brent finished, and stopped dead in his tracks.

Cory raised an eyebrow and stopped writing. He finally turned his head to face his visitor. "I wouldn't come any closer. Benythonne doesn't know what to make of you yet."

Brent smiled nervously. A dragon, even a baby one, was the last creature a sane man would want jumping all over him. "Why is that?"

"You have an air of dark magic about you."

Brent formed a huge "O" with his lips. "That was Math's doing ... so to speak."

Both of Cory's eyebrows shot up, and the young man waved his hand to stop the boy's question. "A long story. Let's just say I'll never earn my wizard's staff."

The boy nodded, his long hair bouncing with the movement. "The others have told stories about that. Math threw you out, but nobody seems to know exactly why."

Brent grinned again. "And a lot of the apprentices have bets going as to what it was, Hmmmm?"

Cory smiled in answer. "Yeah."

"That, at least, I think I can settle. It was forbidden love that was my downfall."

"Huh?"

"Keela and I wanted to wed each other, but I was betrothed to another. And also, she was only a commoner. Both Math and the king would not allow such a marriage."

"So you got married anyway?"

Brent gave him a curt nod. "I disguised us with magic so the priest didn't recognize us. When Math found out, he exploded. So did the king, who exiled us both."

"Just because you got married?"

"We were almost burned at the stake. It was that close to treason, what we did."

Cory shook his head. "Now I'm really confused!"

Brent laughed. "So was I, for a long time. I didn't think Llewellyn would be so disappointed about my breaking the betrothal."

"But why? Who were you supposed to marry that the King got so mad about it?"

Brent squatted down to the child's eye-level, keeping the dragon in the corner of his vision. "His daughter."

Cory gaped. "Arianrod?"

"Yup."

Cory sensed something, and if Math taught him anything, it was to trust his instincts. "That's why you were at the gate to Abollydd last night! You were trying to rescue her too!"

Brent's smile widened and he raised his palms. "Guilty as charged! I figured I could finally vindicate myself by rescuing her. In fact, it was the king's idea, and I went along with it. But Keela decided it was senseless to—Waitaminute ... what do you mean 'too'?"

Cory grinned a nervous grin. "Tal and Kellyn talked me into it. He and I know those tunnels like nobody else—because nobody's ever escaped the Kelloids before—and Kellyn's my equal in spell knowledge. We figured we'd be able to sneak in, break Gwion, Arianrod and a few others out, and escape before they realized what was going on."

"Do you think you were ready?"

Cory rested his chin on his knee and blew between his teeth. "No."

"Neither does Math. Your plan can work, Cory, but you need more knowledge. You have to become a wizard first."

The boy shook his head. "An avatar."

Brent's head moved as if struck physically. "What?"

"Math wants me to become an avatar. That's why he's sending me to see Vainamoinen the Enchanter."

The young man looked away wistfully. "According to legend, an avatar is the living embodiment of messenger from the Maker, and a master of the two Arts of Magic. But there hasn't been an avatar since...."

Cory nodded. "Asmodeus."

Brent smiled widely at him. "No, the last avatar was Elphin, who's a year or two older than me. Asmodeus is an ancient demon, once an archwizard...."

The young man's voice dropped off as he stared into the child's blue eyes, understanding finally dawning. "*Maker*...."

"Yeah, they say I'm an archwizard. That's why Math's so scared of making a mistake with me ... and yes, I've heard whisperings of it. But what good is all this power they say I have, if I can't rescue those closest to me?"

Brent inclined his head. "Power is one thing—"

Cory nodded. "—knowledge is another. I've heard it before, from Math."

"And it's true, Cory. For if it's truly your destiny to fight Asmodeus, you will need every advantage. Be wary."

"I will."

Brent gestured to the books. "By the way, what's all this?"

"Pet theory of mine. Some things are different here, but a lot has to be the same."

"Huh?"

Cory leaned forward. With a simple mystic pass, all the tomes closed and set themselves neatly in a pile. "I'm not from your world, Brent. I was kidnapped here from Earth, where magic doesn't exist."

Brent's eyebrows rose. "No, I didn't know that. So what does a world devoid of magic have that ours doesn't?"

The boy smiled. "A better understanding of the laws of nature."

"What?" Brent asked, laughing.

"Let's just say I'm trying to transform myself into something that's very fast," Cory answered, gathering his things.

"An eagle?"

"Nope. Nothing alive."

Brent took a tome or two from the pile in Cory's arms, and the pair started walking. "The wind?"

The boy shook his head. "Faster. Much faster."

"Oh, come on! What is faster than the wind?"

* * * *

The busy dock was filled with people, sailors moving about and unloading heavy crates from ships in the afternoon sunlight. In spite of that, no one paid more than a passing glance when a shooting star landed on the edge of the wooden dock, and a boy and a dragon stepped from the blinding light a moment later. Because of the world-famous school on the island's north end, people were used to the usual pranks boys armed with magic could do. The sailors and burly dockhands shrugged their shoulders and returned to their tasks. One surprised worker, however, dropped a small barrel with a curse, splintering the wood planks at his feet.

Cory's spell, however, was not intended to scare anyone. Just get him there. "Well, it worked, Benythonne!"

The little dragon shook his head, trying to clear it. "I feel funny. Cory, what did you do to us?"

"I turned us into light! On my world, nothing is faster, and it looks like it's the same here too. We just made a two-month journey in less than five seconds."

The dragon was unimpressed. He weaved about like a drunkard, trying to maintain balance.

Cory giggled and wove a spell to alleviate Benythonne's dizziness. "Come on, we've got to find this Vainamoinen."

Helping his dragon along, they started down the long pier. Cory glanced around him, surprised at the familiarity of it all. The crisp air, tasting of salt and fish, filled his lungs and revitalized him. High above in the clear blue sky, circling gulls called to him. Cory smiled. It almost seemed like the docks at New York's South Street Seaport.

The planks creaked under his weight, and he stopped a man by tugging at his shirt. "Excuse me, sir?"

The burly sailor wiped his mustached face with a sweaty hand and sized the boy up immediately. "You're new?"

Cory nodded. "I was wondering if you could tell me—"

"Follow the street to Dunkirk, turn right, and follow that up the hill. It will bring you to the gates of the keep." So saying, the man turned around and returned to his work, seemingly mildly annoyed at being interrupted.

"Thank you," the boy said in a low tone, and started up the path the man suggested. He considered flying there, but some gut reaction told him that he shouldn't. Cory was prepared to cast a spell of disguise over Benythonne, but nobody seemed to be paying even the dragon much attention.

"Something really weird is going on," he said under his breath. "Who doesn't pay any attention to a dragon?"

The cold wind whistled through the alleys and down the narrow street, whipping his cloak behind him. The gutter was paved a lifeless grey, and the paint on some of the buildings was chipped. People wearing rags passed him, on their way to market or the town well, where women washed their clothes.

Three blocks past the well was a small side street marked Dunkirk. The ground began to incline, but Cory made his way easily enough. The small street wound about for another four blocks before abruptly widening into a large dirt road, the obvious edge of the town. Cory was about fifty feet from the road before he noticed that a group of youngsters was following him. Before he could turn all the way around, one of the boys was standing in front of him.

"Well, what do we have here? A new student, perhaps?"

"Maybe," Cory replied, stopping. Four more boys, all bigger than he, closed in from behind. One was reaching out to touch Benythonne.

"I wouldn't," Cory warned, just as the small dragon whipped his sinuous neck about and snapped his teeth just two inches from the boy's fingers.

"It's real!" the startled youngster cried. "The dragon's *real!*"

Cory turned to face him, arms akimbo. "Of course he's real! What did you expect?"

"We thought it was an illusion," a blond youth replied. "Where did you get a real dragon?"

"Mount Penllyn. He's my familiar. Waitaminute! Is that why everyone in town was ignoring us? They thought he was an illusion?"

"Aye," the tall youth replied. "Is it really thy familiar?"

Cory grinned. "Yeah."

"Wow," a boy about Cory's age whispered, gazing fondly at the dragon. "Can I ride him?"

Cory stared at him. "He doesn't usually let people ride him, and he's still a baby yet—"

"I am not a baby," Benythonne retorted.

Cory turned to his dragon as the other boys' mouths all fell. "You are too, and you're not going to carry anybody until your wings are stronger."

"HE TALKED!" the youngest of them said.

Cory nodded. "Dragons do that, but they don't talk often."

"I knew that," the oldest boy said with a sneer.

"Are you going to the school?" another boy asked.

"I guess so," Cory answered. "Where is it?"

All eyes turned to the oldest boy in the group, who cleared his throat. Normally, they led freshman astray their first day on the island, but this kid was different ... he had a dragon! "Just up the road. We'll take you there," he said to everyone's relief.

"Thanks. What did you say your name was?"

"Goewin. What's yours?"

"Cory," he answered, keeping an eye on his dragon. Benythonne was rearing on his hind legs and beating his wings. "Why walk? We can fly, and I'll carry one of you!"

Cory spun around, his cloak swirling in the air. "No! Benythonne, I—"

But it was too late. The little dragon had already risen into the air, and was swiftly gaining altitude. Benythonne's familiar was left standing on the ground, the words still in his throat.

"I'm gonna kill him! Excuse me, fellahs," Cory snapped, and quickly rose in a clean, straight line after the dragon. The boy called after the beast, demanding for him to slow down. Benythonne did, stopped completely, and began descending again.

But something was wrong, something Cory sensed through their special bond. The little dragon was beating his wings against the air, harder and harder, but making no headway. Misunderstanding lead to confusion and fear, which Cory shared.

Then, three thousand feet up, the boy started wavering in his flight as well. Instead of shooting upward with ease, he found his concentration slipping, and soon slowed to a dead stop. After hovering a few moments, something began pulling at him, dragging him back to the ground. Cory fought against it with all of his psychic strength, his eyes clamped firmly shut, desperately straining to stay airborne.

At length, his strength gave out, and the boy let out all his held breath in a single gasp, allowing the downward force to claim him. Cory landed on his hands and knees, taking breath in huge gasps. Next to him, Benythonne didn't seem to be any better off.

Goewin and the other boys went to his side, looking sadly down at him. "We were going to warn you about that," Goewin said, "but you took off too quickly."

Cory looked up, his hair disheveled, his face red and slick with sweat. "What?"

"This island attracts magic like a giant magnet. The stronger the spell, the stronger the attraction. That's why none of us fly anywhere. It takes too much out of us."

Cory looked stung. "You mean we're prisoners here?"

One of the other boys nodded. "None of us can leave this place until we learn how. That's the final test. The day we figure out how to leave is the day we become wizards."

"Wunnderful," Cory murmured, rubbing the dirt off his knees. He finally understood the reason why Math wanted to send him here so badly—Cory could not leave until he had finished his education and became a true wizard.

Goewin clapped him on the back. "It's okay. Come, walking isn't that bad."

* * * *

Cory felt very small standing before the great golden gate of the walled school grounds. A ten foot long doorknocker made of solid silver hung on the gate. The wall itself was constructed of white marble, with runes etched into its face. The words were so old Cory could only make out one or two of them, and that made him feel as if he were in second grade all over again.

Goewin spoke a charm, and the great silver knocker pulled back, resounding once, twice upon the gold plates like a bell. In a few moments the doors opened, and a tall man in a flowing brown cloak stepped forward. The man looked past the boys, completely ignoring Cory, and pointed at Benythonne.

"What in Maker's world is *that?*"

Cory cleared his throat, suddenly frightened. What he was afraid of he wasn't sure, but something about this man was more mysterious and frightening than Math.

"My familiar, sir."

The gatekeeper looked down at the boy, truly dumbstruck. "Familiar, you say? What apprentice has a familiar, much less a golden dragon?"

Cory felt some of his courage returning and held his chin up. "I am a full sorcerer!"

The man put his arms akimbo under the cloak. "Oh, are you now? And who is your master, boy?"

Cory's eyes burned, his fear turning to anger. He really didn't like this guy! "Math the Ancient," he said proudly.

The man began to laugh. "*Math?* That old fool never did learn wisdom ... and yet he dares to teach youths magic?"

Power built up in Cory's palm without his realizing it. In a moment he sensed the energy, ready to be hurled as a bolt or ball of power at any time, but he hadn't intended it.

The man stared at him, and the energy suddenly burned the boy's hand. Cory yelped, shaking his hand and kissing the fingers as if he had touched a red hot stove.

"Let that be your first lesson, child! Never raise your thoughts against your masters, much less with your feeble magicks!"

Cory only stared, suddenly afraid again. The boy hadn't known someone could twist his own power against him, and he definitely didn't like the idea.

"And answer me when spoken to!"

"Yes sir," Cory meekly replied, suddenly turning to his dragon. Benythonne was baring his teeth, ready to pounce and tear the gatekeeper to shreds.

Benythonne, No! Don't you dare!

The dragon looked at him. **But he hurt you!**

Cory put his still stinging hand to his side to reassure his familiar, but he knew that was next to useless; the dragon felt his pain. **I'm okay. Really.**

"That is the first wise thing you have done since coming," the man said, making note that he obviously had heard the telepathic conversation.

Cory felt like telling him that Benythonne would have killed him, but thought better of it. He might still have trouble getting the dragon inside the gate. "Yes sir. May we go in now?"

The gatekeeper stared at him for a moment, turned to the dragon with a cautious eye, and then nodded. "Aye, but *that* one stays in the ward."

"Yes, sir. Thank you," Cory finished, and bid Benythonne to follow him and the others inside. Behind them, the man closed and sealed the gate with lock and enchantment. It was not so much to keep the boys in as to protect them from the rabble who lived on the island, Cory realized.

The ward was enormous, larger even than Caer Dathyl's. A grassy field contained some trees, in which unusual birds flew and sang merrily. Cory told Benythonne to wait there while he followed the other boys into one of the larger buildings.

They paused where a couple of chatting sixteen-year-olds were leaning against stone pillars. Goewin asked one of them where they might find the Abecedarian, and they said he was probably in the kitchen supervising what this evening's "gruel" was going to be. One of them stared after Cory as the group of boys went down a large corridor.

True to their word, Tydorel the Abecedarian was in the great chamber, standing next to the ovens and over the vats, arguing with the head cook.

"You call this nutrition? It's all sugarcane and sweet plums!"

The cook winced, having seen the boys. "But the lads like it. They complain about the taste constantly!"

Tydorel made a face, rubbing his white beard. "Humph! It tastes well enough! Growing children need healthy food to concentrate on their studies—" the Abecedarian stopped in mid-sentence, sensing the students standing in the door. He turned towards them, wearing a look of annoyance.

"What is it?"

Goewin suddenly was possessed with the urge to play a minor prank, and gave Cory a shove, pushing the smaller boy out in front of all of them. "New student, Master."

Cory quickly regained his balance and stared at the old wizard, suddenly afraid. Tydorel was looking down at the boy from his height of over six feet, regarding him as something undesirable.

"Who gave you the right to wear a sorcerer's cloak?"

Cory swallowed. He definitely didn't like the way the adults on this island were treating him. Hesitantly, the boy found his voice. "I earned it."

Tydorel frowned so badly Cory thought the man's face would stretch out of shape. "You can't be more than *ten!*"

"I'm thirteen," Cory said softly; he was used to that, being small for his age. He began to wonder why he was so afraid.

"Harrumph! Thirteen, the age of pranks," Tydorel scoffed. "Take that off right now!"

Suddenly Cory grew angry. Who was this stranger to tell him to take off his cloak? "No!"

Tydorel strode forward. "Impertinent whelp! I'll tear it from your shoulders and beat you with it!"

Cory stepped back and cast a spell, quickly weaving a wall of force between the two of them. Tydorel was moving too quickly to stop himself, and slammed right into it, hitting his face against the wall.

Cory heard several gasps from behind him, and he knew he must have committed some unknown breach of rules. But frankly, he didn't care. This was the second adult to make fun of his hard work, and he was darned if he would allow it to continue. With a gesture, the wall turned an opaque orange.

Tydorel spoke two words and the wall shattered, its splinters flying to all parts of the kitchen. He took another step forward, then noticed that Cory was gone.

"Where is he?"

"That's for me to know and you to figure out, almighty wizard!" the boy's voice taunted from everywhere at once.

Tydorel stopped dead in his tracks, exhaling. The boys stared at him, wondering if their new schoolmate was going to spend the next three weeks in confinement, or something even worse.

But all at once, the elder's feature's softened, if slightly. The man drew breath and swore. "Maker take me for a fool! You are a spellweaver. I should have known! Come forth, I will not harm you."

"You won't try to take my cloak?" Cory's voice asked.

"I swear by the Divine Fires of Ebon, I will not try to take your cloak. But you had better have the right to wear it!"

Cory doused his invisibility, appearing right behind the Abecedarian. Tydorel whirled, staring at the skinny boy, wondering how such a young child could possibly have become a sorcerer so quickly.

"I do, sir. Here, I have something for you," Cory said, and produced a rolled parchment from under his cloak.

Tydorel took the scroll, broke the wax seal, and quickly read it. He frowned again. "*Vainamoinen?* Is this some sort of joke?"

Cory shook his head. "No. My master, Math the Ancient, sent me to be his student."

"Then you have come a long way for nothing, young one. Vainamoinen does not exist."

CHAPTER 12

CASTLE IN THE SKY

Goewin had taken a liking to Cory, and showed him around the school, introducing him to students and teachers alike. But Cory was made into a laughing stock, or at least that's the way he felt. The whole time he thought strangers were snickering behind his back, laughing at the boy who came to their island as the brunt of a cruel practical joke.

Cory didn't find it funny at all! How could Math have done this to him? Why not say straight out he was being sent to a magic academy, instead of lying and making him present that joke of a letter to the headmaster of the school?

The boys stopped to rest by a large marble pool surrounded by trees. Nearby, Benythonne lay in the lush grass, snoozing away while brave youngsters came close to have a good look at him. Cory tolerated it, so long as they didn't disturb the dragon's sleep.

"I still don't believe you did that," Goewin said, his bright blue eyes wide with awe. "Nobody ever stood up to Tydorel like that, and you humbled him!"

Cory turned his attention back to his new friend. "I did what?"

"You outmaneuvered the old geezer! Half the school's talking about it!"

Cory stared at him in disbelief, and after a minute a smile broke. "You mean that's why they're all snickering?"

"Yes! What did you think they were talking about?"

The boy sighed. "I thought they were laughing at me."

Goewin frowned. "Laughing at you? What for?"

Cory looked down at the sparkling water as it cascaded from the fountain, creating currents in the concave base. "Because of that letter. Math sent me here to see Vainamoinen, who doesn't even exist! How could my own master be so cruel?"

The older boy sighed, and put a hand on Cory's arm. "Hey, it's alright! We were all tricked, one way or another. My father sent me here, and never said one word about my being trapped on the island until I learned to be a wizard."

Cory looked up at him. "Maybe he didn't know."

Goewin's face turned to anger. "Oh, he knew! He was a student here! Before I came, he said I could come home to visit once in a while! The worst part is being trapped here, learning lessons on Midsummer's Eve, instead of feasting with my family."

Cory just stared. It was obvious his friend was fighting back tears. "I'm sorry."

The older boy turned away. "It's alright. Come, there's still a lot you haven't seen yet."

Cory hesitated. "Can't we rest a bit first? It's hot."

His friend smiled. "That's why I'm taking you to the lake."

Cory's features changed immediately. "Why didn't you say so in the first place? Let's go!"

* * * *

The heat of the day was chased away by cool water as Cory swam with his new friends in the large lake called Chalybeate. Night came soon enough, but the sweltering heat of summer remained. After lying awake in the small, hot room he shared with Goewin, Cory finally drifted to sleep.

The boy awoke hours later, to the sound of several birds singing sweetly through his window. Cory sat up and noticed that the silvery rays of Abydonne's full moon were shining on his legs. He rose, walked barefoot across the cold stone floor, and leaned on the windowsill, looking down at the courtyard. There, by the fountain, it seemed that every bird on the island was taking a bath and singing sweetly, almost seeming to call him by name.

Intrigued, influenced by a spell he didn't understand, Cory quickly dressed and left by the window, careful not to wake his friend. He flew down, landing softly by the fountain. At his approach, all the birds rose as one into the clear starry sky.

Cory swore, watching the birds fly off, wishing he had at least made himself invisible. Then he heard something scraping the stones and turned. It was Benythonne, approaching as silently as a dragon could.

"You heard it too?" Benythonne asked.

Cory nodded. "Why would those birds call us here?"

There was a hissing from the fountain, and both boy and dragon returned their attention to it. The water pressure had increased, and moonlight played upon it, forming an image. In a moment, the head and torso of a man appeared.

It was an extremely old man, with a long white beard and clear blue eyes. He was smiling gently at Cory, seeming to be pleased about something. The man nodded to himself. Then he started to mumble, "Aye, Math was right! The resemblance is unmistakable!"

Cory frowned at the reference to Math. "You know my Master? Who are you?"

The man's smile grew wider still. "You do not know me, lad? I am surprised you know not the man whom you have traveled so far to see."

The boy's eyes grew wide. "Vainamoinen! But Tydorel said you didn't exist!"

The enchanter frowned angrily. "And as I am sure you have already found out, Tydorel is an old fool. Come, lad. We have much to do."

Cory looked up at him. "Where? Into the fountain?"

The old wizard chuckled. "No, Cory! Go to Lake Chalybeate. I shall meet you there."

With that, the image faded, and Cory was left staring at flowing water. All around him, in the many windows surrounding the courtyard, people stared at the sorcery. Cory, of course, was blamed for it. Then Tydorel himself poked his head out the window, and screamed at the boy.

"What's going on? You! Don't you know what time it is?"

Cory just glared at him, then turned to his dragon. "Let's go, Benythonne."

Concentrating, the boy flew into the night sky, his familiar keeping pace. Cory looked over his shoulder just to make sure Benythonne was flying right, but then caught sight of the entire school staring at them. "Looks like we caught a lot of attention."

"Cory, we're gonna be in trouble for flying away like this!"

The boy smiled. "Don't be silly! Just be careful not to fly too high, or the island will pull us back."

"If you say so—Oh, wow! Cory, look!"

The boy faced forward again, and saw how all the birds were surrounding the lake and making quite a noise. They all seemed to be looking at the two of them, waiting for them. The lake itself was very still, moonlight playing off the water's surface like a mirror. Cory and Benythonne landed by the lake's edge, very close to the water.

Cory pursed his lips. "Well, now what?"

Benythonne lay down in the soft grass, almost surprised that the birds weren't scattering in fear of him. "I dunno. You're the sorcerer! Was that really Vainamoinen?"

The boy shrugged. "I guess so. He said he was. And he looked like a wizard."

The dragon stared at him. "Yeah, but it didn't seem right."

Cory sat down in the grass next to him. "What do you mean?"

"Well, wizards are ... you know, stern. Vainamoinen acted real nice to you."

The boy looked thoughtful. "Yeah, you're right. He treated me like a real person—"

"And how should you be treated?" came a voice which boomed across the lake.

Cory turned and saw another image of Vainamoinen staring at the two of them as it floated above the lake. Cory rose and swallowed. Maybe this guy treated him better than the others, but he still had the nasty, wizardly habit of sneaking up on a kid when least expected.

"Sorry ... it's just that every wizard I've met here has treated me like ... well, an apprentice."

The wizard frowned. "And is that not what you are?"

Cory smiled. "Yes, but—"

Vainamoinen smiled gently. "But I understand. You wanted to be treated with more kindness, with the respect that is your birthright."

Cory looked up at him, brightening. He definitely liked this guy. "Yeah. Only ... what birthright are you talking about?"

"Gaze into the water," Vainamoinen bid him.

Cory looked down at the wizard's feet, into the dark surface of the lake. Slowly, the water wavered, the moonlight sparkling off the crests of the waves. Suddenly, the reflection of a great castle appeared, and Cory frowned. He knew there wasn't any castle nearby....

Startled, he looked up, and saw it. Floating above the lake was a large rock, and on that rock was the castle, all of ivory, crystal, silver and gold. Both he and the dragon gasped. They had never seen anything so beautiful before. Something magical tugged at his heart. Somehow, that castle looked awful familiar.

"Come on, Benythonne," Cory said very softly, and flew off the ground. The pair rose swiftly, one thousand feet, fifteen hundred, two thousand. When they were close to three thousand feet up, Cory felt the island starting to pull him back. He saw that he was still a little way from the floating castle, and swore under his breath.

Cory decided not to let the island beat him. He stretched out his hands and cast the most powerful spell he knew, desperately trying to reweave the fabric of reality. In the back of his mind, he remembered another time, another place. He was nine or ten, swimming laps at summer camp with the other kids. His arms had ached for rest back then, but he refused to give in. He kept on, ignoring the pain, blindly heaving one arm over the other and pulling himself to the raft in the center of the lake.

It was the same now, except that it wasn't just his arms that were tired, it was his whole being, and he had the added weight of a dragon to pull. The boy touched the power deep inside him, and coaxed it. Cory knew the patterns, for Math had taught them to him. *Gravity*, he thought. *I must fight gravity....*

Just as he felt his strength slipping, something grabbed hold of them both and yanked them safely to the castle's base. Cory felt earth beneath his feet and opened his eyes, taking deep breaths and relaxing his concentration.

The boy stood five feet from the rock's edge, Benythonne next to him. Directly in front of them was a beautiful, lush orchard, and beyond that, the castle. Vainamoinen stood in front of a large oak tree, supporting his weight on a wizard's staff. His clear blue eyes pierced the distance between them, smiling at the boy. The old wizard raised his hand, beckoning them closer. Cory came, the dragon at his heels.

"Welcome home, Cory," Vainamoinen said, and put a gnarled but warm hand on the boy's shoulder.

*   *   *   *

The elderly wizard led Cory into the castle, and the boy noticed his new master had many servants. Lining the barbican alone were no less than twenty soldiers, all wearing Vainamoinen's standard on their tabards and shields. Dyrnwch, the chatelaine or head servant, was very beautiful, even for a woman in her fifties. She gave Vainamoinen a glass of sherry, and Cory a cup of hot chocolate, before showing the boy where his room was.

Like his suite in Caer Dathyl, Cory's bedchamber here was large and luxurious, and if not befitting a prince, it at least befitted a highborn noble. Cory tossed his cloak on a chair, kicked off his sandals and heavy outer clothes, and jumped on the bed. Suddenly lost in the softness of the feather mattress, which surrounded and caressed his body, the boy quickly fell asleep.

When Cory woke, sunlight was streaming through sheer silk curtains, which swayed in the light morning breeze. He noticed someone had covered him with a light sheet during the night and left him a pitcher of ice water on his nightstand. The ice had long since melted, but it was still cool, and Cory sat up and poured himself a glass.

Someone rapped lightly on the door, and Cory bade them enter. Dyrnwch came in, bearing Cory's flowing blue and white cloak. "I cleaned it for you, my lord," she said, and hung it on a brass hook by the door.

The boy smiled at her. "Thank you, milady. It means much to me."

The woman smiled at him. "I am not noble, young lord, but thank you for the compliment."

Cory frowned. "Where is Vainamoinen?"

"Having breakfast, lord. He wants you to join him after you bathe and dress," she said, and began to remove some fine silk clothes from the wardrobe, setting them down on a chair.

The boy nodded, stretched, and rose. He expected to feel cold stone under his bare feet, but the floor was covered with an expensive rug patterned with intricate symbols and runes. Cory walked into the bathroom, made a simple pass with his hand, and the marble tub began to fill with heated water.

All too easy, he thought, stripping down for his bath. *I can pretty much reweave the fabric of reality, and yet I'm not fully trained. Well, the old wizard is supposed to solve that, and then ...*

"Are you all right in there, milord?"

Standing in front of the tub wearing absolutely nothing, Cory nervously turned to the closed door and prayed she wouldn't just walk in. Quickly, he grabbed a towel and threw it over his naked body. "Yes, thank you!"

"I've laid out your clothes for you. If you need anything else, just call."

Cory waited until he heard Dyrnwch leave before he dared put the towel down and entered the water. It was surprisingly comforting, the heat soothing his aching muscles. Slowly, he slid down, allowing his head to go under.

Half an hour later, clean and dressed in a fine blue silk tunic and leggings, Cory skipped down the stairs to join Vainamoinen. The enchanter sat sipping something hot and silently watched as clouds drifted by in the blue sky.

Cory smiled at him and took his place at the table. "Good morning."

Vainamoinen turned, surprised. Instantly a smile came to his lips. "Ah, good morning lad! Sleep well?"

Cory nodded as a servant brought him a plate filled with eggs, bacon, and toast. "Yes. The bed is very soft."

"Good, good! Today I shall show you some of the castle's treasures."

The boy lightened. "Thank you, but I much rather would begin learning magic."

The old man frowned. "Enchantment, you mean?"

Cory nodded vigorously, his toes curled around the legs of the chair. Foremost in his mind was escaping this crummy island—pleasant though it may be—and returning to Gwynedd to battle Asmodeus and to free all those slaves.

"There is time enough for that, my boy. There are other forms of magic I would show you first."

The boy's face fell, but he tried to hide his disappointment. If he learned anything as Math's apprentice, it was patience. Wizards taught much, but only if you didn't push. Unfortunately, Cory's patience was near its end, and he was afraid Vainamoinen saw that.

But if the elderly mage did, he did not reveal it. If anything, he seemed content to do nothing more than sit smoking his pipe and watch Cory enjoy his breakfast.

Something large let out a yelp of joy, catching the attention of both the ancient magician and the youthful one. Cory smiled, a half-eaten piece of toast hovering in front of his mouth. Benythonne was soaring in the clouds above the castle's golden turrets, imitating the flight patterns of the colorful birds. Their special link let Cory share the sheer thrill of flight. Then the boy frowned.

"Master, how can he—"

The old man's chuckle cut off the rest of Cory's sentence. "I taught him the secret of the island early this morning, so he could go hunting. It won't let him leave, but he can fly higher and more freely now."

Cory beamed, putting down his toast. "And what is that secret?"

Vainamoinen gripped his pipe, removing it for a moment to stare at the boy with a gleam in his eye. "Ah, now that would be cheating. You are the student here, Cory. The secret of the island you must learn for yourself."

Cory sighed and went back to eating. "You can't blame a kid for trying."

Again the old man chuckled. "No, I suppose not. Now finish eating. Your eggs are getting cold."

The boy did so, suddenly aware that perhaps Vainamoinen shared a bit of his impatience, which he had never known in a wizard before. But it was clear the old man wanted to show him something, and that made Cory eat faster.

* * * *

Vainamoinen led his student down a hidden corridor in the castle, then down another, their entrances hidden with magic. The smooth stone walls were lit by torches which lined the hallway, and Vainamoinen's boots echoed down the empty corridor. It seemed to Cory that they had been walking almost forever.

Finally they came to a single door, sealed shut by golden chains and enchantment. Vainamoinen muttered a few words under his breath, and the chains fell free as the door swung open of its own accord. The boy followed his new teacher inside.

It was an unusually shaped, sunless room. Illumination came from tall candles and several of the magical items stored there. In the center of the room was a large crystal sphere which glowed a bright yellow. Cory went to it, holding his palm just over the shining surface.

"That is the Eye of Balor, Cory. You can use it to view anything you wish, but be warned not to let anyone else see it."

The boy turned around. "Why?"

The oldster was thumbing through some tomes which sat on a high shelf. "Because it will instantly kill anyone not born with the power to use it."

"Oh." Cory shuddered and pulled back his hand with a jerk. More cautiously, he looked around the rest of the chamber. The stone walls were all lined with books and scrolls, except one wall, on which were hung several musical instruments. Cory recognized some of the unusual ones from what Taliesin had taught him at Caer Dathyl, including a mandolin and a kantele.

"You play those?" Cory asked innocently.

Vainamoinen gave the boy a strange stare. "Of course! Just what do you think an enchanter does, Cory? I have to be something of a bard as well."

A smile slowly came to the boy as he realized how dumb a question it was. A bard was an enchanter, a musician who could sing his spells.

Enchanters did with words what spellweavers did with their hands, and the very best could sing the charms. "They seem very old, Master. And they radiate magic energy ... a lot of it."

The old man chuckled. "As well they should! Take a look at the kantele, lad."

Cory walked over and picked it up, gently turning it over. Except that the kantele was box shaped, it didn't seem all that different from a guitar back home, and that it had seven stings instead of six. The strings were of mystic silver, and the body of the instrument itself seemed bone-white. With a gasp, Cory nearly dropped it.

"It *is* bone!"

Vainamoinen nodded. "I made it myself, from the jaw of a giant pike."

Cory frowned at him. "A what?"

"A fish. A giant fish. It was going to gobble up a group of children who were swimming in Lake Eiriol, so I slew it."

"Oh," Cory brightened, and plucked a few of the strings. The instrument was in surprisingly good shape, although it seemed to be very, very old. Cory started playing 'Sing a Song of Sixpence,' and suddenly felt the familiar tingle in his hands, the telltale sign he was casting a spell. Only this time, the tingle spread through his whole body, making him feel giddy.

By the end of the song, he gazed at Vainamoinen, who looked very pleased. Then he glanced at a table, and there were six large copper coins lying by a book, pennies on Abydonne. Cory gasped.

"Did I do THAT?"

"You certainly did, lad. You want to borrow it for a time?" Vainamoinen nodded at the kantele.

Cory held it gently, then slowly nodded. In truth, he was afraid to fool around with such powerful magic, but he knew better than to insult a wizard by refusing. "Alright. You mind if I play it somewhere else?"

Vainamoinen nodded his approval. "Go to the garden. It's quiet enough there. Just be careful not to cause any earthquakes, hmmm?"

Cory giggled. "I'll try not to! Thank you, Master," Cory said, and kantele in hand, quickly left the room.

Chapter 13

THE ARCHWAY AND THE OATH

In the months that followed, Cory's skill as an enchanter grew. Math had taught him some enchantment along with spellweaving, but now he was learning from a master of that art. The boy learned to play the kantele, the mandolin, the harp, and others. Each instrument had its own effects, but Cory soon learned the most powerful instrument was his own voice. Once he knew the name of each thing, he could command it, even change its essence—an art which interfaced with spellweaving.

It was not uncommon for him to spend several hours in the room of magic treasures, poring over ancient tomes for knowledge. The boy was always careful to avoid the Eye of Balor, knowing its terrible power to kill as well as reveal hidden secrets.

Then one day, an idea, which had taken seed many weeks before, took firm hold, and Cory drew close to it. He stood before the mystic artifact for three quarters of an hour, just staring into its glowing surface, before he got his courage up to use it.

"You that can show me anything, pierce the Veil between the worlds, from this plane of reality to another," Cory said in the Old Tongue, then added the final line: "Show me the Earth, show me my mother."

The globe pulsated with eerie light, his own reflection shifting, swirling in its depths. Slowly, an image formed. Then Cory saw what the doctors and social workers and every other adult on his world had been preventing him from seeing. His mother was lying in a hospital bed, her pale face framed with uncombed, long, dark hair. A tube kept her breathing, and several machines monitored her vital signs. His eyes locked on those. While most of the monitors were active, one of the screens displayed a flat line. Cory turned away, finally understanding.

The boy cried openly, letting the tears flow down his cheeks and taking breath in great sobs. His mother never would wake up. She was brain dead. The machines kept her breathing and her heart beating, but she was *dead*. Only a warm corpse remained.

Dyrnwch found the boy there many hours later, threw a cloak over his trembling shoulders, and led him to his chambers. As Cory sat there on the bed, the chatelaine stoked a fire in the room's fireplace. It finally occurred to him to ask.

"How did you know to find me?"

Dyrnwch smiled at him. "You didn't show up for the meal I prepared, my lord, and you always do."

Cory broke into a smile, his face still wet. Dyrnwch was an excellent cook, and he was always early at the table, particularly if she had hinted at a tasty dessert. "I'm sorry I caused you to worry.."

"Don't be, lad. What did you see that got you so upset?"

"My mom," Cory managed, and fought back more tears. "She's ... dead."

The woman sat down next to him and put her arm around the boy's shoulder, shushing him.

Annwen, another servant, came in bearing a golden platter covered with a linen cloth. She set the platter down on a nearby table, and

Dyrnwch signaled for her to leave. The young woman did so, quietly closing the door.

"You must have suspected it for a long time, my lord. You yourself told me they refused to let you see your mother on your homeworld."

Cory shook his head. "They lied. They said she was asleep and would wake up—"

Dyrnwch rubbed his back, letting the sobs pass. Then she wiped his face with her handkerchief and gently asked, "Would you like some dinner now?"

Cory nodded. He didn't feel like eating, but having starved all day, his stomach complained otherwise. She nudged the boy under the covers and put the tray over his lap. The napkin was removed, and Cory saw she had prepared roast beef in special sauce, scalloped potatoes, vegetables, and custard for dessert.

Again, Cory said to her, "I'm sorry. I didn't mean to miss—"

"Now hush!" Dyrnwch said sternly. "I want you to eat your dinner and that will be the end of it!"

The boy smiled. "Thank you, Dyrnwch."

"You are quite welcome, my lord," she said, and noticed Vainamoinen standing in the door. She gave the wizard a look which said to wait, kissed Cory on the forehead, and left the room.

"How is the boy?" Vainamoinen asked quietly.

Dyrnnwch sighed. "He will be fine, my lord. Give him time."

"Does he know?"

Dyrnwch shook her head. "I don't understand why you don't just tell him, Vainamoinen."

The enchanter smiled. "I will, Dyrnwch. In my own good time. Although I would prefer it if the lad figured it out for himself."

The woman made a face and left. "As you will, my lord."

* * * *

Over the next few days, Cory became more withdrawn. He sat in the garden among the blossoms, alone except for the company of his dragon. The notes produced from his flute told of the sadness within. Vainamoinen watched unseen from his tower window, wondering what to do. It was not that he had not taken care of a child before, but he did not know how to heal such a wound. Slowly, the enchanter turned away from the window to read from an ancient tome of magic.

"Is he still watching?" Cory asked, momentarily ceasing to play.

The dragon nodded. "What's wrong, Cory? Are you okay?"

The boy nodded, but he couldn't hide the open lie from the little dragon anymore than he could hide his feelings. In frustration, Cory picked up a rock and threw it, watching as the stone flew out over the edge to fall on the island below. He frowned. In a moment, he got up and walked to the ledge.

The dragon's violet eyes twinkled with excitement. "You're gonna leave?"

Cory nodded. "All I need is the name of the island, Benythonne. I'm sure of it."

As the dragon watched, Cory stood there, contemplating the edge. Finally, the boy took a deep breath and said, "Let's go."

So saying, Cory jumped off the ledge into open space. Immediately both gravity and the island's powerful attraction grabbed hold of him and pulled him earthward. But the boy refused to give in. He concentrated with all his might, desperately fighting to stay aloft, but drawn inexorably downward.

Then a single word escaped his lips: "Avalon."

Immediately, the island released its viselike hold. Cory was able to fly more easily now, but ever there was the presence of the major spell which held onto him. Cory both celebrated and swore. He had prepared months for this, positive that once he had the name of the island, it would release him. But there was something more, something he was missing.

"What? WHAT!"

Behind him, Benythonne giggled. "I'm surprised it took you so long! Some sorcerer!"

Cory made a face and cast a harmless bolt of light at his dragon. "Oh, shut up!"

The boy arced in his flight, the magical beast following. Below them, the Island of Avalon was lush and green in the height of summer heat. Apprentices swam in the lake, some of the more observant of them pointing upward at Cory and Benythonne as they flew past. The school itself came up quickly, and Cory slowed to buzz the uppermost towers out of spite. He still didn't like the way Tydorel and the other adults had treated him.

Then he saw the gate.

"God! How could I have been so blind!" So saying, he came in for a graceful landing at the great stone archway to the keep. When he first came here, he could hardly make out a few of the strange words etched in the stonework. Now he could read all of them!

"It's a spell! The spell to leave the island!"

"More of an oath, boy, and not so loudly. We don't want the others to hear."

Both Cory and the dragon turned. The gatekeeper stood there in the sunlight, his face no longer hidden by a hood. It was a kind face, with a full beard circling deep green eyes. "My name is Carmichael."

Wary, Cory frowned, not going any closer. "Why do you hide the secret from all of us kids?"

"That should be evident from the words themselves. Have you read them?"

Cory nodded. "Yes, they have something to do with forsaking thrones, but I still don't understand."

Carmichael did not hide his disappointment. "You have not read the whole thing, boy! The whole point, the whole history of the island is there."

Still frowning, Cory turned back to the archway and read. Slowly, his eyes grew wide as understanding came.

"I knew who you were the moment I saw you. Welcome home, my lord."

Cory turned. "You ... what are you talking about?"

Carmichael sighed. "Speak to Vainamoinen, the Lord High Wizard. He will explain everything to you."

The boy took a step forward. "Waitaminute! That inscription explains the island and the school, but what's this about Vainamoinen, and why were you so hard on me when I got here?"

The gatekeeper stared at him for a moment, then laughed. "That's what's really bothering you? Be warned, Cory. You may be my rightful lord and master, but you are still just a child."

Cory made a face. "I'm no child, not any longer."

Again, Carmichael sighed. "No, I suppose you are not, but in many ways you still are. You wanted to know why I was so hard on you before? I was trying to teach you patience. But alas, you left us far too soon. Tydorel still hasn't forgotten that."

The boy broke into a smile. "Yeah, I'll bet!"

"I assume that was the night Vainamoinen called for you?"

Cory nodded. "Yeah, he brought me to his castle over the lake. It's nice, but it's not home. Oh, and by the way, I did learn patience. Just being trapped here until I learned enchantment did that."

Carmichael frowned. "I doubt that, but I'll keep you to your word, boy. Remember, Cory. If you ever have need of me, I am here."

"Thank you, Carmichael. Now, you're right. I must speak to Vainamoinen. There's a lot he still hasn't told me, and I'm sure he's hiding something from me."

At that, the man started to laugh. "Oh, aye! The enchanter hides a great deal, my young lord! Go to him."

* * * *

When Cory walked through the front entranceway, Vainamoinen was there, standing at the foot of the great staircase. The enchanter gave Dyrnwch a glance, and the woman left the hallway, her footsteps echoing on the cold stone tiles.

Cory swallowed. He didn't think it would be this hard to say goodbye, but now that he thought about it, it was. This man had never shown him anything but kindness, and how Cory had to say that his short stay was at an end. "The time has come, Master. I'm ready to leave."

Vainamoinen looked at Cory for a long, silent moment, then shook his head and lit his pipe. "I'll decide when you're ready."

The boy frowned. "But Master—"

"That is the end of it, Cory. You are not leaving until I say so."

Suddenly anger replaced sorrow in his breast, and Cory screamed at him, "You can't keep me here! I have to leave! I have to defeat Asmodeus!"

The ancient wizard shook his head. "No, you will not! I forbid you to leave this island!"

The boy's lower lip jutted out in defiance. Cory shouted in anger, stepping boldly forward. "You can't forbid me! You're not my father!"

A single, angry glare from Vainamoinen silenced him. "I'm your *grandfather!*"

"My grandfather?" Cory repeated in a hoarse whisper. A cold chill crept up the boy's spine and settled in the pit of his stomach. He knew. Somehow, he had always known. It had been there, staring him right in the face. The old man's kindness and his pride that swelled whenever Cory learned a new spell, the 'coincidence' that his last name was also the name of the island—it all fit!

The enchanter nodded. "I had hoped that you would have learned this on your own, but Dyrnwch was right. The secret was too well hidden. Our family history is as wrapped in myth and lore as the secret of the island itself."

The boy stared, wide-eyed. "You mean, we're ..."

Vainamoinen quickly corrected him. "*ONCE* were the absolute rulers of Atlantis, a great kingdom of Abydonne, until our fore sires in their foolishness, or stupidity, or both, destroyed everything! This little island is all that remains of that once great kingdom."

Cory nodded to himself, looking away at his dragon. "Well, not everything. They rebuilt. Gwynedd, Kaleva, Powys, Turlin...."

Vainamoinen dismissed it with a wave of his hand. "The Twelve Great Kingdoms are but shadows of what once was. And this island serves as a constant reminder of what we have lost. Never forget your heritage, Cory. Never, ever, forget what was."

Slowly, the boy nodded. Then he returned to the subject at hand. "So why won't you let me leave?"

Both Vainamoinen's white eyebrows shot up. "To fight that demon? Are you out of your mind? I'd sooner die myself than let you go!"

Cory frowned. "Is that why you're so afraid? Because you don't want—"

Vainamoinen nodded vigorously. "Exactly! I don't want what happened to your father to happen to you!"

In a low voice, Cory asked. "What *did* happen to my father? How did he get from Abydonne to Earth?"

"Garth was a little older than you are now. Your father discovered that Asmodeus was kidnapping human children from Earth for use as slaves, and when he traveled there to find some way to prevent that, he became trapped. Trapped on a world where magic doesn't work.

"There was nothing I could do but watch him through the Eye of Balor, and even that was clouded, for the eye can only see into that world on certain phases of the moon. When I saw his death in that dragon of cold iron, I lost all hope. Then came the day Math told me of you."

Vainamoinen hugged the boy, his only living relative. After a long moment, Cory looked up at him.

"I can't let Asmodeus' evil to continue, Grandfather."

The old man sighed. "I know. I used to battle him myself, before my body grew old and weak. Now I can no longer even leave the island. To do so would mean my death, for my heart can no longer stand the strain of the spell."

Cory's jaw grew firm and jutted out bravely. "Then it's up to me."

Vainamoinen stared at the boy, obviously fighting back tears. He held Cory's shoulders and shook him. "No! You are not yet ready. You are far too young!"

So saying, the old man buried Cory's face into his chest, holding on so tightly the boy found it difficult to breathe.

* * * *

Cory had read the note twenty times before putting a weight on top of the paper and blowing the candles out. He hated this. Vainamoinen was the only real family he had left, in this world or any other. But Cory also knew that he had no other choice. Only two people in all of Abydonne possessed the kind of power that was needed to defeat the demon horde, and one of them was trapped here forever. He left the room and flew down to the orchard, where his dragon waited.

Quickly, Cory drew the necessary inscriptions in the dirt around both him and the dragon with a stick. Benythonne watched with interest, sadness in his eyes.

"You sure we're really ready for this? You don't even have your staff yet!"

Cory stopped for a moment and sighed. "Grandfather has it, I'm sure. But sure as all get-out he's not going to give it to me, even though I did earn it!"

There was doubt in the little dragon's voice. "I dunno, Cory …"

"Will you put a lid on it? I've gotta concentrate."

Slowly, the boy began to sing. It was a sad song, calling out to the island, to the lost land itself. Once, millennia ago, there was a great continent. On it were two great kingdoms, Atlantis and Ys. Both were at the height of civilization, both ruled by royal families who possessed great magical powers.

One day the two kingdoms went to war. The conflict was so dreadful; the energies released that day were so mighty, that the land itself was torn asunder. All that was left was a pitiful little island named Avalon, after the ancient royal castle of the same name, which now floated forever over the lake that was once a mighty sea.

But the land remembered. It still clung to the past, crying out for lost dreams. It drew all magic tightly to it, trying in vain to rebuild what once was, and holding on especially to the remnants of the royal line—Cory's family.

Then, at the song's climax, Cory swore the most solemn oath of a wizard: "I swear by my staff that I shall protect the people and never rule over them!"

At once, the boy felt the island release both him and Benythonne. In a moment, both he and the dragon were transformed into light, and streaked across the night sky towards the mainland.

Chapter 14

WIZARD'S STAFF

"It was a night like this," Brent whispered into his wife's ear, and squeezed her tightly.

The young woman's hand tightened on his firm shoulder. "Please, don't remind me of what I made you give up, beloved."

"You didn't make me give up anything. I did it myself," Brent answered, and kissed her.

There was no sound, nothing but the soft gurgling of the fountain and singing crickets in the grass and rosebushes. The moon was waning, and so cast a soft glow upon the two lovers.

Then an explosion of bright light turned night into day for the briefest of instants, startling both. Brent nearly dropped Keela into the fountain.

"Maker! When I get my hands on the little apprentice who—"

"Sorry," an apologetic voice answered, "but I really didn't think anybody was going to be here this time of night."

Brent turned around at the boy's beckoning, and all anger immediately drained from him. "Cory! I haven't seen you in months!"

"Feels like it," the boy said, stepping forward.

The elder sorcerer gave him a hug, then frowned. "Where is your staff?"

"Long story," the boy said. When Brent gave him a dark look, he added, "Oh, don't worry. I've earned it. It's just that I don't have it, that's all."

"What's that supposed to mean? Where is it?"

"I just had a disagreement. Believe me, I intend to go back for it!"

The young man's frown deepened. "What are you talking about?" Then he realized what the boy was saying. "Vainamoinen?"

Cory sighed and nodded.

Brent nearly exploded. "Your new master? What happened? Why should he hold back your staff if you've earned it?"

"Because he doesn't want me doing dangerous stuff like going up against the demons of Abollydd, that's why!"

Now Keela frowned. "Isn't that what wizards do?"

"Not when they have an overprotective grandfather watching their every move, they don't!"

For a moment, neither of them caught the reference, but slowly, Brent's jaw fell. "*Maker*, then you're...."

"Vainamoinen's grandson and heir, yeah."

Keela sighed and looked at Brent. "It explains a lot. Both Llewelyn and Math have been acting really weirdly where this child is concerned."

Cory's hands went to his hips. "Child?"

Brent tousled the boy's long, dark hair. "Don't let it get to you. She still calls *me* a child!"

"If the shoe fits, darling...."

Brent sighed and turned the boy around by the shoulder. "Come, lad."

*   *   *   *

Prince Taliesin ran down the corridors, breathless. His bootstraps were loosely fastened, his hair uncombed. The boy was far too anxious to find his foster brother to care for anything else. He ran through Cory's suite, past servants who made the bed and cleaned up the morning's breakfast.

"He has gone to see Badger, my lord. If you hurry, you still might catch him."

Without pausing to thank the maid, Taliesin turned on one heel and ran back the way he came. Breath came hard, but he tried not to notice it any more than the beautifully woven tapestries covering the walls of the stairwells and halls he ran through.

Why would a wizard need to see a blacksmith? the boy wondered. Anything Cory needed now, he could simply conjure!

The mystery remained until he ran across the Inner Ward to the caer's blacksmith shop. Finally, overcome by exhaustion, Taliesin paused in the doorway to catch his lost breath. Badger, a thin, bearded man slightly taller than the young prince himself, was pounding away at a small piece of iron. Cory stood by the forge, his fine silk robes aglow in the scarlet light of the fire. Looking closer, Taliesin saw a soft, violet light also playing across the young avatar's features. The blue glow emanated from the trinket the blacksmith had crafted.

Suddenly, it hit the young prince like a bowshot. Cory had used his newfound mastery to enchant iron while it was still hot in Badger's grip! Once it grew cold, the dwoemer would be permanent, and no wizard could ever change it, for cold iron locked magic in place.

"FINISHED, BY MAKER!" Badger cried, holding the glowing metal aloft.

Cory watched in fascination as the blacksmith's tongs dipped their work into cold water, and steam leapt towards the roof of the wooden structure. The boy wizard nodded his approval as it was presented to him.

"Excellent, Badger. You have my thanks."

The lean man wiped his grimy brow with his forearm. "If it is useful to you, Highness, it is time well spent. Now leave me, I pray you. I yet have two swords to finish by weeksend."

Smiling, Cory turned to leave, and saw his foster brother blocking the doorway. His smile grew wider, "Tal!"

"Cory," the older boy said, still panting. "I came as soon as I heard! Father refused to wake me last night."

The young wizard smiled deviously. "Well, we couldn't disturb your beauty sleep now, could we?"

Tal gave his foster brother a playful slap, then nodded at the piece of metal Cory twirled in his fingers. "What is that thing?"

Cory grinned, and passed Taliesin a small, enchanted key. "Insurance. Come on, we still have a lot to do before we meet with Llewelyn in an hour."

Cory led him to the far side of the caer, where the Inner Ward lay stretched out in all its emerald glory. Freshly mowed grass held drops of dew, and sunlight played across the stream of the fountain. Near the flowing water, the whole of Math's school waited by a resting golden dragon.

At Cory's approach, they all dropped to one knee and bowed their heads in respect. At first thought, it seemed that was because he and Taliesin were princes, but Cory knew better than that. The other boys had always treated them as equals. That they should supplicate themselves now was a mystery.

Taliesin asked the question before Cory could. "Why are all of you kneeling?"

"We just found out, Highness. Our sovereign Lord Avalon deserves no less."

Cory stopped dead in his tracks, words frozen in his throat for a moment. "Brent told you!"

Kellyn nodded assent. "We are yours to command, your Grace."

The boy sighed, truly uncomfortable as a prince. Deep inside, however, he did like all the attention. The combination made for an upset stomach, which the boy did not try to hide. "For starters, you guys can get up. We still have to plan for tonight, and we don't have time to fool around."

So saying, Cory sat on the edge of the fountain, outlining his general strategy, and inviting suggestions. While his foster brother was thus occupied, Taliesin pulled Kellyn aside.

"Alright, what's going on?"

"Don't you know?" Kellyn asked, astonished that a prince so close to Cory would be one of the last to know. "He's Vainamoinen's heir, the Prince of Wizards!"

Taliesin reacted as if slapped. "HE'S WHAT?"

"Vainamoinen's grandson," Cory confirmed from ten feet away. "Now if you're through screaming at the top of your lungs, can you please pay attention? If something goes wrong, both of you will be stuck in the bowels of Abollydd forever."

Swallowing his astonishment, Taliesin could only stare in silence. Suddenly everything fell neatly into place. He had been told that Vainamoinen never took students, yet he had agreed to teach Cory on a word from Math. Also, the idea that an outworlder could possess such power as Cory's was an absurdity. The archwizards were rumored to be descended from some lost kingdom's most powerful avatars.

"—but what about the demons? Won't they harm the slaves if we try to rescue them?"

Cory shook his head. "Taliesin and I were talking about that. I don't think they would, but just in case, it will be up to you guys to protect the slaves while I go up against the demons themselves."

"Maker guide you, lord," Bron said, and Cory nodded.

"May He guide us all."

* * * *

The throneroom of Caer Dathyl was even more cold and imposing than Cory had ever remembered it, or perhaps that was simply the expression he was reading from King Llewelyn. His adoptive father was not pleased about something, and the boy hesitated to speculate about what.

Flanked by his foster brother and fellow apprentices, Cory approached the throne. He knelt on one knee before the King, his glorious cloak falling gracefully around him. For some reason he did not quite understand, the boy was frightened, feeling impending loss.

Mouth twitching, Llewelyn spoke. "Where is your staff, boy?"

Cory swallowed. He did not think leaving the island before he actually had the staff in hand was going to cause this many problems. "With my natural grandsire, your Majesty."

Llewelyn's eyebrows shot up. "You have family?"

The boy nodded. "Vainamoinen, the Lord High Wizard. I am his grandson, Majesty."

Llewelyn's eyes shot sideways, to lock directly on Math. "Why was I not told of this?"

Leaning on his own staff, Math looked incredibly old. He cleared his throat, blue eyes moving from the kneeling boy to the seated king. "I was not certain, sire."

Cory's head shot in Math's direction. *He knew! He knew all along!*

"Not *certain*?" Llewelyn barked. "Ebon's Fires, wizard! What sort of game did you think you were playing? You swore to me the boy was an orphan!"

"So he *is* an orphan, Majesty. Both the boy's parents are dead. That he has a living grandfather does not change that fact," Math explained, smiling slightly into his white beard. When the king began to sputter in anger, the wizard quickly went on. "But that does not affect the matter at hand. That the boy returned without his staff is no surprise, for Vainamoinen did not have it to award him at the completion of his training."

Cory's jaw fell so low it almost hit the floor. He could not help from blurting out, "*You* have my staff?"

With finality, the spellweaver bit off, "No. Not any longer."

"Who then?" Cory demanded.

Math's expression turned very grave, and now, more than ever, he looked like a tired old man. "Cory, do you remember a night many months ago, the night you brought Benythonne home?"

The uneasy feeling returned to his stomach, and the boy slowly nodded.

"Do you recall that a price was exacted of Gwendorianoah, when you took her firstborn hatchling as a familiar?"

Cory turned his head. He could not bear to look at Math, his adoptive father, or anyone else. Hoarsely, the boy whispered, "No!"

Slowly, Math approached the boy across the polished marble floor. "I am sorry, Cory. The dragon demanded an object of great power as just payment from you. Benythonne could not be returned, for the spell you used was permanent. Your future staff was the only thing which would appease her."

Cory could not say anything. Indeed, there was nothing to be said. Slowly, without asking leave to go, the boy rose and walked from the throneroom, head hanging low. Echoing in his head were the words his adoptive father said the day he was apprenticed: *Return him to me a wizard, or not at all.*

No one said a word to him as the ushers silently opened the doors to let the boy pass. Cory knew he was leaving for the last time, for his shame was the shame of the Royal Family.

The boy's feet scuffed cold stone as he left the hall and entered the Inner Ward. Benythonne stood by an oak, loyally waiting for him, his violet eyes bright with hope. The little dragon knew what had transpired through the bond they both shared, and sympathy went out to the boy.

Benythonne could not be returned, for the spell you used was permanent. Your future staff was the only thing that would appease her.

Cory looked up; his eyes wet, and saw his dragon in a blur. Choking back a sob, the boy threw his arms around Benythonne's neck and cried. "I'd never trade you for a stupid stick of wood anyway!"

The youngster remained there for a long time, clinging to his dragon and sobbing. Finally he felt a hand lay upon his trembling shoulder. Someone had come to comfort him, as Cory suspected would happen. Ashamed, the boy tried to shrug it off. "Leave me alone, Math!"

"It's not Math," a young voice answered, and Cory looked up. It belonged to Taliesin. Behind the prince stood all of Math's apprentices, looking forlorn. "I'm sorry, Cory. We all are."

"Thanks, but it won't help. Maker knows I've earned the staff, but I'll never get it. And now I'm outcast, just like Brent."

"Father didn't say that," Taliesin told him, his hand still on his foster brother's shoulder.

"No, but he thought it," Cory sobbed. "I don't know what I'm going to do now. There's nothing left for me but to return to Avalon and live with my grandfather."

The Prince's hand squeezed Cory's shoulder, making the boy start. "You're going to leave without helping us rescue Arianrod?"

Shocked back to awareness, Cory remembered his promise. After meeting with the king, they were all going to sneak out of the caer and try to rescue as many slaves as they could. The boy's jaw set. There was no reason to change their plan now.

"You're right. Before I leave, I'll make certain Asmodeus gets what's coming to him!"

Chapter 15

ABOLLYDD

Brent ran through the caer's stables like a shot, breathless, his face drenched in sweat. A glance inside told him his fears were true: ten horses were missing. The stableboy turned away from his chores, a look of guilt on his face as his green eyes met Brent's.

"Where are they, boy?" the young man demanded, closing the distance between them in huge strides. "Answer me!"

"Don't know, milord," the skinny boy answered with a quivering voice. Angry adults were bad enough. Maker only knew what an angry sorcerer could do to him!

"Brent, for the love of Maker's world, will you slow down?" Keela demanded, calling after him seconds before she herself cleared the stable's open door.

Swallowing, the youngster continued to answer. "Their Highnesses asked for mounts, but they didn't say where they were going. Did I do something wrong?"

Brent turned, staring absently at one of the empty stalls. "Abollydd. They've gone to Abollydd!"

The stable boy's blood ran cold at mention of the demons' stronghold, and he did not try to hide his horror, shuddering.

"We've got to go after them," Keela sighed, and quickly took a saddle down from its peg.

But the stableboy ran to her, terror in his eyes. He might already be hanged for helping the princes into danger, but he surely would be hanged if he let two more mounts go without so much as the horsemaster's approval. "Mistress, no!"

Keela had to hold back her battle-honed reflexes to prevent from flattening the child as he grasped her elbow. With a sneer, she demanded, "What?"

"I can't just let you take the horses, mistress," the boy explained. "My master will—"

The boy's voice stopped in midsentence, his eyes suddenly glazed over with enchantment. Keela looked beyond the frozen child to Brent, blue light winking out from his pointed fingers.

"You didn't have to do that," she said.

"Yes, I did," Brent insisted. "Cory and Taliesin are princes. A word from them is Royal Command, and these are their father's horses. But I'm only The Earl of Morfran's younger son. Magic was the easiest way out, for all concerned."

Slowly, Keela nodded approval. Spellbound, the child would escape punishment, and blame for bewitching the boy could easily be transferred elsewhere, as it was a group of spellweaving apprentices who took the mounts.

"Hurry, Brent. I don't think we have much time to waste."

* * * *

Cory stopped his horse as soon as they had cleared the forest, staring out at the Dead Lake. Salt air assaulted his nostrils, and sunlight shimmered off the crests of the water, hypnotizing in their effect. Yet it wasn't the water he stared at. High above, Benythonne circled in an ever increasing spiral, looking for any sign of trouble. In his mind's eye, the boy saw the whole of the landscape through the special bond he and the dragon shared.

Taliesin stopped his horse beside his foster brother. The gelding he rode shook its head, its mane catching wind blowing in off the lake. "The last time we were here—"

"I know," Cory whispered back. "This time we're ready for them."

"Is that Abollydd?" Bron asked behind them, wide-eyed.

"Of course, stupid," Jamie shot back, giving the younger boy a look of contempt. "Don't you recognize it from the pictures in Master Math's tomes?"

"Be quiet, you two," Jern injected, and the two younger boys did, staring up fearfully at the seventeen-year-old's muscular form. The young sorcerer turned to the princes. "How are we going to get in?"

"The entrance is over there, at the foot of the mountain," Taliesin answered him. "But that's not what's worrying me. Even though it's still daylight, they can set a trap for us down there. Have they spotted us yet?"

Cory shook his head. "No. Benythonne doesn't see anything, and I don't expect them to sense us, not with the wards I put up. We're all clear so far."

"Thank Maker for small miracles," Jern shot back. The boy's magic cloak flapped wildly in the wind. "Even between the two of us, Cory, I doubt we stand a snowball's chance against Ebon's Fires—"

"If you want to back out, do it now, you coward," Taliesin snapped, hand on his jeweled sword hilt.

Jern swallowed, staring into the prince's blue eyes. "That isn't what I meant, Highness. It's just that nobody's ever escaped from them before."

"We did," Taliesin said his voice like ice. "The Kelloids aren't unbeatable."

Cory shot his foster brother a glance. "No, Jern's right. Don't underestimate them, Taliesin. They could easily kill us all."

Taliesin gave Cory a cold stare, gripping the reins tightly. "I know what they are capable of, Cory. Don't forget I survived three months down there before you arrived. But if you're getting cold feet too—"

The young avatar shook his head. "Not on your life."

"Then let's do it," the prince said, and before the others could retort, he spurred the gelding into a trot. While riding, the boy undid the leather thong binding his sword in its sheath, getting it ready to draw. He did not look back, knowing the others must follow him. Taliesin intended to get them moving before they had time to dwell on the Kelloids' hideous tortures.

Cory swore. If Taliesin went out past the protection of the wards, he would be visible to demon detection! Gritting his teeth, the boy kicked the mare's flanks and bade the others to follow him.

Sand was pounded by hooves and flew in a hundred directions as the group rounded the lake, moving swiftly towards the mountainside. Concerned, Cory sent his thoughts directly to his foster brother's head.

Taliesin, you idiot! Slow down before you give us away!

"They don't know we're coming," the prince shot back over his shoulder. The wind caught his long blond hair, whipping it behind him. Taliesin blinked, his eyes half open in an attempt to see through the rushing wind. Finally, a dozen yards from the base of the mountain, he stopped the gelding.

"That has got to be the stupidest thing I've ever seen you do!" Cory snapped, coming up beside Taliesin's mount. Stopping behind them were the other apprentices, all with angry looks on their faces.

Taliesin ignored him, dismounting and tying the horse's reins to a nearby bush. Cory and the others did the same, still angry, but Taliesin was ignoring them. The prince drew his sword, holding it before him with both hands, then moved towards the cave entrance.

"Wait, you half-witted jerk!" Cory called after him. "Haven't you heard a word I've said to you?"

The prince kept moving, and Cory decided that he had had enough. With a word, the young wizard pointed at his foster brother's feet. The sand opened, swallowing the boy's legs up to his knees.

"Ebon's Enchanted Fires!" Taliesin swore. "Cory, release me!"

Cory walked leisurely up to him, a deep frown on his face. "You couldn't give me orders even before the king adopted me," the boy shot back. "Now, will you listen to me, or do I leave you sealed in the earth all night?"

Taliesin's face erupted in anger, resembling a black storm cloud ready to burst, but he held his tongue. As a toddler, he was told the faerytale of how Vainamoinen won his bride Aino, Cory's grandmother, by sinking a foolish young sorcerer into the ground up to his neck. The young man had saved his own life by offering the offended Vainamoinen the hand of his younger sister. The prince suddenly realized it was no faerytale.

"Well?" Cory demanded.

"You win," Taliesin capitulated. "But for Maker's sake, don't stand around gabbing all day. The Sun won't stay up forever!"

Suddenly reminded, Jern looked up at the sky, and saw that it was just after noon. However foolish his action, Taliesin was right. They didn't have time to waste. The boy checked to see that the others had tied off their horses securely while Cory raised the prince out of the sand again. As a final measure, Jern placed the most powerful ward spell he knew around the horses, that they too might be invisible to demon detection.

"Cory, the horses will be safe until sundown," the tall, thin boy told him.

Cory nodded his approval. "I see it. Thank you, Jern. Hopefully, we should be in and out of there quickly. Okay, let's go."

The thirteen-year-old wizard led his friends around the face of the cliff, towards an open stretch of beach. There, facing the Dead Lake, was a large opening in the rock, leading into darkness. Cory checked a final time to make sure his defensive spells were still in place, then nodded to the others.

"This is it, guys. I think it would be a good idea if all of you armed yourselves with the most powerful spells you know."

"Already done, my lord," Kellyn told him. In the boy's palm shone a hint of yellow light, which Cory knew to be the beginnings of a mystic bolt. "Lead on."

Cory nodded to his foster brother. "You know these tunnels better than I do," he said. "I think it would be better if you led the way. Just be careful to stay close to me."

"Yes, Mother. You keep us safe from their magic," Taliesin retorted, hefting his sword. "I'll take care of the demons!"

Cory shook his head and sighed. "You'll never grow up!"

"Excuse me, your Highnesses," Jern interjected, "But now is not the best of times to be arguing."

Cory and Taliesin both gave him a dirty look. While Cory outranked him, Jern was the eldest of all of them. "Watch your tongue, syrah," Taliesin snapped, and quickly entered the cave.

Towards the back of the group, Jamie cast some light, careful to keep the magic globe in his palm dimly lit. Thirty feet in, Cory recognized the spot where Taliesin had killed the guard just before their escape. He stopped, swallowing.

"Cory, what's wrong?" Kellyn asked.

"Nothing," the boy answered, shaking his head. "Come on, I think Taliesin has gone on ahead of us again."

"Yes, he did," Pellor confirmed. "I think he went that way."

"Darn!" Cory swore, and started down the tunnel again. His foster brother was now almost certainly past the protection of his spells. But he dared not send his thoughts out, for that would surely bring ruin down upon them all. The young wizard had to hope that the demons would not notice the prince, wandering about in the dark, completely open and defenseless but for a sword.

Cory led his friends down the tunnels, trying to remember the way. Even as they walked, a gnawing fear crept up his spine and settled in his stomach. He had been here a mere three days, and the tunnels which comprised the Kelloids' home were an interconnecting maze of passageways. They seemed to walk forever, past stalactites and an underground stream. Finally, he stopped, staring off into the darkness.

"You're not lost, are you, Cory?" Pellor asked, his emerald eyes aglow in the mystic light of Jamie's sphere.

Cory didn't want to admit it to the frightened boy, but grudgingly nodded assent anyway. It was not the way of wizards to lie. "Taliesin was our real guide. I just wish he hadn't—"

Cory stopped in midsentence. Something had just brushed past his wards, and was quickly approaching. On reflex, he raised his hand and conjured a fireball. But even as the flames came into being, Cory realized it was pointless. No demon could get past the wards without tearing the spell asunder first. Whoever was approaching was human.

"Tal?" Cory asked hopefully.

"Try again," a young man's voice answered, and soon the owner stepped into the magic light. His finely tailored clothes were drenched with sweat, and his eyes were bloodshot with weariness and worry. Behind Brent was Keela, sword drawn and ready, her nerves obviously on edge. "I ought to tan the hides of the lot of you for pulling this stunt!"

"Brent, thank the Maker," Jern whispered. "Maybe you can help us find Taliesin!"

The young man's blood ran cold. "The prince is missing?"

"Well, nine out of ten ain't bad," Keela retorted. "I say we cut our losses and leave this place."

"Shut up, Keela," Brent snapped. "This is serious! We came to Gwynedd to rescue one royal scion. If another was captured—"

"Brent," Cory bit off like a curse, staring at the adults in anger. "Time's Wind, I hope you had the good sense to shield yourself!"

The exhausted young man stopped dead in his tracks, staring blankly at the child. "Maker, I hadn't thought of that!" he said in defeat.

Cory's eyes rolled. "It's a wonder half of Gwynedd doesn't know we're here!"

"Oh, they *do*," Keela insisted. "It wasn't too bright of you, taking those horses. Which was, by the way, how we found you. You were careful enough to cover your tracks against magic, but you left a trail through the forest so obvious a city boy could follow you!"

Jamie swore. "Taliesin was supposed to watch out for that!"

"He was supposed to do a lot of things," Bron said. "He wasn't supposed to get himself lost, either."

"Enough," Brent said, cutting off all conversation. "All of you are leaving with Keela, now. You will take the horses and ride as fast as you can back to Caer Dathyl, while I look for Taliesin."

"Alone?" Cory asked. "You wouldn't stand a chance! You need us, Brent."

Cornered, the young man bit his lip. Cory was right, and he knew it. The lad was the only chance they had against the demons, for he was Asmodeus' equal in power. Slowly, Brent nodded. "Very well. But I want all of you to stay close to me, and do precisely what I say. Am I clear?"

The boys all nodded, grateful that an adult was finally taking charge of this messed-up rescue attempt. All of them knew it was blind luck they hadn't been captured by now.

"This way," Brent said, and Cory didn't raise any objection as they entered a tunnel leading away from the stream. It seemed as good a way to go as any. By the light of Jamie's still-burning globe, and by his own mystic senses, Cory searched for any sign of trouble. The boy found none. That worried him more than anything else. He knew they should have come across at least a few demons by now, but there were none, as if they had all left.

"This is a big place," Pellor said. "What if it takes us years to find the slaves?"

Jamie punched the boy from behind. "Be quiet, shrimp! You want to give us away?"

"To whom?" the twelve-year-old whispered back. "I don't see anybody!"

"That's what worries me," Cory said, and slowly, both Jern and Brent stared at him, realization setting in. They all stopped walking. "We haven't seen hide nor hair of anybody since we came in here, except you two. This has all the signs of...."

Brent finished the boy's sentence for him. "A trap! I've got the same feeling, pup. I think we should double back, and try another—"

The sound of metal grating on stone cut the sorcerer's words short. In the time it took them to whirl their heads around, they saw an iron grating coming into place, cutting off the tunnel behind them.

"Cold iron," Cory said tunelessly. "It *is* a trap, and we just walked right into it!"

"What gave you the first clue, young one?" A demonic voice echoed throughout the tunnel, making the hairs on Cory's neck stand on end. The boy had only heard it once, but he remembered the voice of Asmodeus. Next the sound of running feet came from down the hall, and they all knew they didn't have much time before they were all overwhelmed.

Quickly, Cory wove a mystic wall over the open part of the tunnel, reinforcing it with incantation. The result was that they were walled in, but at least he had bought them time to think their way out.

Brent nodded his assent. "How long do you think it will hold?"

The boy shrugged his shoulders. "Anywhere from a few minutes to a few hours, depending on what they throw at it. But either way, we can't stay here forever," Cory reasoned.

The young man nodded, walking over to examine the iron grillwork. Of them all, only Cory, Brent and Keela kept their wits about them. The young apprentices all stared about them, wide-eyed, like sheep led to the slaughter.

"Cory, can you lift this thing?"

The boy frowned. "Don't know. My strength always decreases to normal whenever I try to use it on cold iron, but I'll give it a try."

Cory braced himself, gripped the bars firmly, and tried to lift. The gate rose a precious few inches, but his face was red and his arms shook with the strain. First Brent, then Keela pitched in, and it rose another inch.

"Come on, you pups! Give us a hand!" Brent called, his voice tense.

Cory screamed in frustration, desperately trying to summon dragon strength. But the cold iron absorbed the mystic energy as soon as it was produced, like cold water absorbing so much heat. He also sensed several demons suddenly hammering away at the edge of his wards, relentless in their assault.

"We have company," Cory moaned, and tried to tap his own reserves in a last attempt to lift the grill. But just then he felt it getting heavier, and he had to let go. The grill crashed to the floor with a clang, which reverberated throughout the tunnels.

"Well, it's a cinch we're not getting out that way," Brent remarked. "If anyone has any bright ideas, now's the time to voice them."

"Well, we could always try surrendering," Keela quipped.

Cory made a face. "Don't even joke about that! You have no idea what it's like being their slave!"

Brent put a comforting hand on the boy's quivering shoulder. "And I have no intention of finding out, either. Are you all right?" he asked, suddenly realizing the boy's shaking had nothing to do with fear.

Cory shook his head. "I didn't want to tell you. I can feel the wards beginning to weaken. When they collapse, I'll get the brunt of it."

Brent nodded grimly. He knew all too well the effects of breaking a maintained spell on the caster. "Cory, release the shields. We can't risk you."

At first the boy hesitated, then he nodded, submitting to the elder mage's wisdom. But even as he began to unravel the threads binding the wards in place, he knew it was already too late. With ruthless speed, the shields shattered, the reverberations across the psychic rapport translating into white-hot pain in the boy's mind. Cory screamed, dropping to his knees.

Kellyn knelt next to Cory, knowing full well what that meant, and he tried to ignore his own fear by worrying about his friend. "You okay?"

Cory shook his head, trying to catch lost breath, blinded by pain. He knew the invisible wall was next, but at least that was a stable spell, not maintained by concentration. The boy lamely covered his ears when the Kelloids at last reached the wall and the youngest apprentices started to scream.

With a gesture, Brent altered Cory's spell, turning the wall opaque. Then he turned to Keela. "Now we can't see them, and they can't see us."

The woman stared, jaw line hard, fingers grasping the hilt of her sword so tightly her knuckles turned white. "This is insane! I say we just drop the darn wall and fight them!"

"Shut up," Jern snapped, kneeling in front of Cory, trying to help. "Nobody invited you along!"

Glowing hands moving in intricate patterns, the youngster wove a healing spell about his friend, desperately trying to relieve his pain. The anguish in Cory's eyes eased somewhat, and he seemed to focus on the older boy. "You'll be all right, Cory. Just try to rest."

"Can't," Cory said plainly. "No time."

Indeed, in that instant, the wall collapsed. Demons came at them by the score, all armed with whips and most with magegems. Sickly orange light mixed with the pure blue and yellow of Math's apprentices as the energies collided. In short order, the younger spellweavers were taken prisoner, until only Brent, Keela, and Jern were left standing. All three of them knew they had their backs to the wall and were overwhelmed beyond hope.

Still, they fought on for as long as they could. Jern wove his most powerful spells in an effort to protect himself and Cory. He knew their only hope lay in giving Cory the chance to recover, but still felt the effort was foredoomed. Even as the teenager felt his concentration slipping, he screamed the avatar's name. The younger boy only stared, trying to focus his mind enough to spellcast, but pain prevented him.

Through blurred vision, Cory saw Kellyn and the others struggling, captives of the demons. Keela's sword flashed scarlet, cutting a bloody swath through the demons. In a moment, her offense was caught short as orange light from a magegem shone in her eyes, and her body suddenly grew rigid, the sword dropping from her unfeeling fingers. Off to his right, Cory saw Brent drawing forth something hideous—probably a black magic totem—from his belt pouch, and called forth smoke and flames. Kelloids burned, screaming even as their flesh was scorched. Still they came, ignoring searing pain, grabbing hold of the sorcerer and slapping his body hard against the solid rock of the tunnel wall.

Jern was the next to fall. Three magegems sent bolt after bolt against the youth's thin, protective shielding, and it inevitably fell. Victim of the same malady that had struck down Cory, Jern dropped, whimpering, next to his friend. Rough demons' hands quickly snatched the two boys up.

The last thing Cory heard before he slipped into unconsciousness was demon laughter, and the familiar voice of his old jailer, Cambian. "Asmodeus will be pleased. We have the boy archwizard."

CHAPTER 16

▼

DEMON THRONE

Cory thought he was dreaming. Having a nightmare, really. Images of things he somehow knew were really happening were displayed in his dreams, and he couldn't wake up, no matter how hard he tried. He wasn't even in the dream, physically. Not in his own body, at any rate. The young boy dreamed he was a young dragon, golden wings furled tightly against his body, hardly daring to breathe. He was sneaking through the darkened caverns of Abollydd, and paused at this level. There was a great rent in the wall, and Cory could look down through this gaping stone hole to see the monstrous figures, some thirty feet below, discussing his fate. Belatedly, in his dream, Cory realized he was seeing these events through the eyes of his familiar, but he really didn't care. Cory watched and listened with a curious detachment.

Asmodeus sat in the great stone cavern, which served as his throneroom. Stalactites dripped water into pools, which reflected gold, silver, and platinum artifacts. Great pits in the stone floor burned with the constant flow of oil, the light playing off the crystals that encrusted every square inch of the high walls. The throne itself was all of gold, ebony, and onyx, and glowed eerily with energies, which could only be dark magic. The demon lords standing at the base of the throne awaited his pleasure, having submitted their report. The ancient creature, which had once been a human wizard, didn't seem all too pleased. The frown creasing his features would have torn the skin on a human face.

"So," Asmodeus began after a long pause. "Garth left an heir, and I pulled the boy from his Earthly exile with my own hands."

Ahriman grinned. "Then you do not appreciate the irony, my lord?"

Asmodeus stared at him, glowing yellow eyes drawn together as he snarled with anger. "Do you find this *amusing*, Ahriman?"

"Only in your blindness to potential, my lord," the Kelloid meekly replied. "The boy is possessed of extraordinary power. At the very least, he can supply a magnificent magegem, the likes of which we have never seen."

Cambian nodded vigorously, his foot talons leaving long streaks in the stone floor as he turned to face Asmodeus. "The sorcerer's brat could replace all the power he cost us when he undid your spell of eternal-night."

For a long moment, Asmodeus said nothing, considering. Neither of them moved, hoping his anger would not flare, and if it did, it would be taken out on a human. But slowly, the Demon Lord's eyes gleamed, and he smiled at them both. "No, I have other ideas for him. For the blood of House Avalon to serve me, as a slave or otherwise, is a possibility too tempting to ignore."

"Yes," Ahriman hissed, his pointed ears quivering with delight. "If we could put a spell of binding upon the child, a *geas*...."

"Better still," Asmodeus said, raising a clawed forefinger. "If we could turn him into a Kelloid demon, make him one of us...."

"How, my lord?" Cambian asked. "To cast the spell which transformed us all took most of your former power."

"Not as much is required for one, and I do not have to expend any of my own precious energies, not when the boy has so much to spare."

Both of the demons grinned hideously. "Wise, your Infernal Majesty. Should we prepare the spellbooks?"

Asmodeus nodded. "Yes, help me inscribe the pentagram and runes. Fetch one of the adult humans from the crystallizing chamber, Cambian."

*   *   *   *

Moaning, Cory's eyes fluttered, and awareness returned. He was sprawled on the floor of a cell, manacles binding his wrists, wearing nothing more than a slave's loincloth. His head ached, but no longer did it produce the blinding pain which impaired concentration.

Not that it matters anymore, anyway, the boy thought, and tried to raise his head. Pain and weakness answered, making the move impossible.

"My lord?" a young, familiar voice answered. Thin fingers applied a damp cloth to his aching forehead. "Cory, are you alright? I was so worried!"

The boy wizard's blurred vision began to clear, and he finally recognized the features of the boy who was tending him. "Gwion," he whispered. "You're alive!"

Cory stared into a grimy, sad face, at blond hair which had once been shiny and clean in the sunlight three months before. Slowly, the younger boy nodded. "I waited for you to rescue me, but you never came. And now...." Gwion's voice trailed off as he stared at Cory's chains, looking as if he was going to cry.

Cory's felt guilt stab his heart like a dagger of ice. Everything was happening just as he dreamed it, months ago in Caer Dathyl, as he knew it would. Trained by wizards, he had quickly learned that prophetic dreams have a quality all their own. Any time now, and Cambian would come down to torture them both. The boy swallowed in fear, resisting the urge to shudder in front of Gwion. Cory was older, and a fully trained wizard. He had known this was coming months ago, and so took steps against it.

"Put it out of your mind, Gwion. You *are* being rescued," the young magician said bravely, and tried to sit up. Dizziness assaulted him, but the boy shook it off, closing his eyes and trying to establish equilibrium. Slowly, his head cleared. Somebody was talking.

"Oh, *sure!* And just how we going to pull *that* one off?"

Cory turned. The voice was Taliesin's. "Tal! What happened to you?"

The prince sank to his knees, grasping the thick bars of his own cell, nearby. "I was captured, same as you. They made me watch your progress through a scrying glass, and I could see and hear everything you said, but couldn't warn you."

Cory forced a smile. "That's okay, Tal. You couldn't have done anything against them, anyway."

The prince sat up straight, trying to salvage what was left of his fifteen-year-old dignity. "And what's *that* supposed to mean? I gave them a scar or two to remember me by before they pulled the sword out of my hands!"

The boy wizard's eyes gleamed. "That isn't what I meant. They managed to capture all of us, together. Wandering alone through the tunnels, you didn't stand a chance."

Taliesin rested his fair head against the bars of his cell in frustration. "So, how are we going to get out of here?"

The younger boy swallowed, trying not to look into his foster brother's eyes. While Cory had known he would inevitably share a cell with Gwion, all of them being captured was a possibility he had tried not to consider when they were planning the rescue attempt. Now his oversight was painfully brought home. It would have been better had he done this alone, although he knew that wouldn't stand a chance either. For the first time, Cory thought about what might happen to them all if his plan didn't work, and desperately fought back tears. His chains clinked in unforgiving accusation when he wiped his wet face, and when he spoke, his voice cracked. "We'll get out. We *have* to!"

Cory then closed his eyes and tried to enter trance, slowing his breathing. Everything depended on the dragon. If he were captured too, all was lost. After a few minutes, Cory frowned, fear gripping his middle. The cold iron at his wrists even prevented communication with Benythonne! The bond was still there, unbroken, but he could not send his thoughts across it. He knew the little dragon was both alive and very close, but whether Benythonne were free or sitting in a cage was anyone's guess. Cory drew a shaking breath.

"We'll be out soon, I hope," Cory murmured, and looked up at Taliesin. The boy loved his brother, and would do anything he could to make sure nothing would harm him. "We'll get out of here, Tal."

The older boy frowned at him. "How? Even you cannot do magic wearing chains of cold iron."

Cory's forced a nervous smile and started to explain his plan. "Tal, you taught me my first spell. But before that, you also taught me something about cold iron which just might get us out of here."

The prince stared, wondering what wisdom he could have imparted on his younger brother that the best wizards in Abydonne had not been able to. Perplexed, Tal was about to ask what it was when all thought was interrupted by the soft flutter of feathered wings. He looked up and saw a swift brown hawk flying into the chamber, coming to land next to Cory and Gwion's cell.

"Good boy, Benythonne!" Cory said, the relief in his voice obvious. He immediately reached between the bars of his cell to retrieve the bird, coaxing the creature closer with words instead of thought.

The older prince's eyes grew wide. "*That's* your dragon? But how?"

"Shape-shifted into a bird," Jern explained from his cage, gripping the bars so tightly his knuckles turned white. "Cory changed him before we started for Abollydd, but he never told us why."

"Not exactly," the young wizard said, staring at the leather thong which bound their salvation to the bird's leg. "We share powers. That's the nature of having a familiar. I can fly, and I'm strong, while Benythonne has my shape-shifting ability."

Just as the small bird was waddling into Cory's grasp, something violently snatched it up, bringing a surprised gasp from everybody. The boy looked up, unbelieving, as the bird struggled in invisible hands. Mystic light flared, and the outline of a Kelloid shone, gradually solidifying. Cory's eyes grew wide as saucers. It was Cambian!

"Very clever, bratling! Too bad your plan didn't work," the demon said gruffly. Cambian pinned the small bird with one hand, holding a razor-sharp fingernail above its exposed breast, as if to stab it. "Your master ever mention what happens to you when your familiar gets killed? You lapse into a *coma*, boy. Get a fever. You can't eat, can't drink, and you lose a lot of body fluid quickly. A slow, *agonizing* death!"

Ashen-faced, Cory choked, looking straight into the demon's glowing yellow eyes. Cory knew Cambian wanted him to beg, and any delay would mean the little dragon's life. Slowly, the Kelloid lowered his claw to the bird's quivering form.

"Please, don't!" the boy said piteously. Warm tears flowed down his face, finally released. "I'll do anything! Please don't hurt him!"

"You'll do anything I say anyway," Cambian sneered. His claw touched the animal's breast and drew a thin line of blood, knowing the boy would feel pain too. The bird screamed, its struggles growing more frantic. All at once, a halo of golden light surrounded the small hawk, and it immediately began to grow. Cambian cursed, drawing back his whole arm to deliver a final, killing blow before Benythonne could complete the transformation.

But Benythonne bit the demon's wrist with an unnaturally sharp beak, slicing through thick scales and drawing black blood. Howling, Cambian threw the hawk to the ground, staring dumbfounded at his wound before putting the gore into his mouth. "Wyrm! I'll force a spike down your throat and roast you alive for that!"

Benythonne continued to grow. Within half a minute, the little dragon had regained his genuine form, and was staring at the Kelloid, opening a mouth filled with rows of razor-sharp teeth. Soft violet eyes now burned with anger, and wisps of dark smoke floated up from his nostrils. Cambian repressed a shudder, knowing if the dragon were old enough to breathe fire, the entire chamber would now be a blazing inferno.

The demon acted surprised, searching himself, as if a weapon were missing. Then he reached for his whip, taking a cautious step back. The dragon lunged, paws extended and mouth wide open. Benythonne's claws raked the demon, knocking him over. The two fell to the stone floor, savagely slashing at each other.

Kneeling in his cell, Cory clutched his chest, breathing hard. Helplessly, the boy shared his familiar's pain. Gritting his teeth, the boy tried to force words out, but he could only moan in agony. Bound by chains, he lacked the dragon's resistance to pain.

Gwion touched his friend's shoulder, not knowing what to do, his face a twisted mask of concern and guilt. Cory had come after him, and now was suffering for it.

"Key," Cory finally gasped.

Gwion stared at him, wide-eyed. He wished with all his heart he had the key to their manacles. If they weren't wearing chains, he could cast a healing spell, and Cory would not be vulnerable to Cambian's attacks.

"Get ... key," Cory whispered, eyes closed.

Gwion held him, crying. "I'm sorry, lord. I can't—"

"*Get it!*" Jern said from his cell, just above a whisper.

"I'm trying," Taliesin answered, his voice strained. Gwion looked up. The prince was reaching for a small glowing key, lying on the floor just outside of his cell. The little boy saw the thin leather thong tied to it, and realized that must have been what was tied to the hawk's leg. The thong must have snapped when Benythonne grew into a dragon again.

Still holding Cory, Gwion watched and swallowed. Taliesin was reaching for the key, his fingers scraping the stone floor just inches from it, but the chains at his wrists were hampering him. He could only fit one arm through the opening between the bars, and his hands were bound together. Frustrated, the prince swore and turned to Jern.

"I can't reach it. Can't you do any magic at all?"

Sadly, Jern shook his head. "Don't you have anything you can reach it with? A broom handle?"

"No! You think they supply us with everything we need to escape?" Taliesin retorted. Then he stopped, pulling his arm back into the cell.

"Wait-a-minute," he whispered, and shifted position. Taliesin sat up, putting his leg through the opening between the thick wooden poles. The boy smiled as his bare foot brushed the leather thong still tied to the key. "Yes, I can just reach it!"

Jern and Gwion held their breaths. Slowly, carefully, Taliesin tried to grab the thong with his toes, and at last snagged it. As the prince slowly reeled in their only hope of freedom, the boys nervously glanced at the fight nearby.

Preoccupied, Cambian had so far not noticed their escape attempt. The Kelloid was trying to get leverage, but the dragon kept him pinned to the floor. The demon swore in pain as Benythonne bit down on his arm, slashing his face at the same time with clawed forelimbs. Nearby, Jern saw, was a glowing orange stone. The boy realized Cambian must have dropped his magegem when Benythonne first attacked him.

"Pellor," Jern whispered. The other boy hadn't heard him. The twelve-year-old was watching the fight, his terror mirrored on the face of his twin brother, Seloy. The two boys sat huddled next to each other, faces pressed against the bars. "*Pellor!*" Jern repeated, and this time the boy turned in his direction. Jern pointed at the magegem, and Pellor's eyes grew wide.

As the boy reached for the stone, Cambian saw. He ruthlessly slashed at Pellor's hand, missing by scant inches. The boy drew his hand back, frightened but not cut. Pellor stared at the demon, knowing that if he tried that again, Cambian would probably torture him to death. His brother, held in captivity these many months, had told him horror stories.

"Time's Wind, no," Jern whispered, and turned back to Taliesin. The prince was carefully pulling the thong to him, dragging the key with it. With a smile of victory, the prince took the leather from between his toes and at last held the shining key in his hand. Instantly he jabbed it into his manacles, freeing his wrists.

"Highness!" Gwion called, and Taliesin looked up. He saw the boy reaching through the bars, Cory shivering on the ground behind him. The young prince swore. He had wanted to unlock his cell with the key next, but knew if he did Cambian would be upon him instantly. The little dragon was obviously tiring, and the demon might win the fight any second now.

Staring at Gwion's dark eyes, Taliesin nodded. "Catch," he called, and threw the key to him. The boy caught it, smiling. Cambian saw the movement and howled in anger.

"What are you doing?" Cambian demanded, finally having gotten enough leverage to sit up. "I'll torture all of you! Human filth! I'll make you all beg for death!"

Gwion jerked back into his cell with a sob. Frantically, he crawled over to Cory, unlocking his manacles with the enchanted key. The young wizard screamed as sensation returned to his numb hands. He sat there, breathing hard, tears drying on his reddened face. "Thank you, Gwion."

The little boy nodded and started unlocking his own restraints. "How did you get a key to the demon's chains?"

"Badger crafted it only this morning. I set the dweomer myself. It will open anything!"

Gwion rubbed his freed wrists, his eyes smiling for the first time in long months. "I can't believe we're free," he said.

Cory's eyes narrowed to slits as he saw Cambian ruthlessly hitting his dragon. The demon had the advantage now, crushing the brave little dragon under his greater weight, slashing again and again with razor-sharp fingernails.

"Not yet," Cory said tonelessly. He pointed at the wooden bars of their cell. Enchanted energy lanced forth from his fingertips, and the bars immediately turned to ashes, crumbling in a smoldering ruin. Cory stepped through the opening, his face a mask of anger.

"*Cambian*," he bit off like a curse. The demon turned and saw Cory walking towards him from the remains of his cell. The boy waved his hands in the air, weaving fire. Heat erupted from the ground, enshrouding both demon and dragon with flames. Benythonne didn't seem to notice, but Cambian screamed, trying to roll away from the fire. So doing, the demon brushed by the magegem, and it rolled into Pellor and Seloy's cell.

As Cory moved closer, hurling mystic bolts at Cambian, Seloy stared at the stone in wonder and fear and timidly picked it up. The boy shuddered, knowing he was holding the essence of dark magic. Yet he could not use it, even if he were not in chains.

"Hide it," his brother cautioned, and Seloy nodded. The boy dug into the hay which covered the floor of their cell, and buried the magegem under it. But light from the gem still glowed a dull orange, giving the illusion that the hay was on fire. Both boys swallowed.

"Not like that," Pellor said, and dug it up again. He stared at the magegem as it glowed malevolently in his palm.

"Maker, what are you two little idiots waiting for? Use the darn thing!"

The twins turned and stared at the occupant of the next cell, utter fear on their faces. "We cannot, Highness."

The girl frowned. Even three months of captivity could not completely mar her beauty. Long, golden hair fell in uncombed tangles about her slender white shoulders, framing eyes the color of the noontime sky. Princess Arianrod stared at them, unbelieving. "What do you mean, *can't*? You're supposed to be Math's apprentices!"

"Using dark magic could cost my soul," Pellor explained, moaning in fear.

Swearing, Arianrod decided not to press the issue. She turned instead to the conflict just outside of her cell. Cory had blinded the Kelloid with bright light, and the demon fell to the floor, screaming. Slowly, the demon began to transform into something else. Benythonne lunged, seeing an opening at last. On instinct, the little dragon clamped his jaws around Cambian's neck and tore out his throat.

Cory turned away, fighting the urge to be sick. Nearby, Gwion stared at the older boy, clutching the key tightly to his chest. Neither of them said anything, but a cheer rose up from the Kelloids' prisoners, from their cells.

"Hey, Cory. If you don't mind?" Taliesin said, calling him from between the bars.

Cory nodded at his foster brother, singing an incantation. Immediately, all the cells in the vast chamber began to glow as reality was altered. The wooden bars transformed into water, splashing all over, leaving the occupants drenched but free.

Quickly, all the children surrounded Gwion, who was opening manacles as quickly as he could. As soon as they were freed, the more puissant apprentices began setting up wards at the entrances. They wanted no nasty surprises until all of them were free of their cold iron shackles.

Cory knelt by Benythonne, singing charms to heal his familiar's gory wounds. One by one, the cuts closed and healed as if they had never been. Cory had learned his art well. As soon as that was done, Benythonne jumped up at Cory, licking his face. The boy giggled, falling back onto his rump.

Nearby, Taliesin embraced his older sister, lifting her off her feet. He stared at her, smiling. "You all right?"

"Of course, you little bugbear," she returned. "You had me worried for awhile. Was it you who planned this rescue, or did you get captured on purpose?"

"Very funny! No, it was all Cory's idea."

"I might've known," the girl said, smiling at the young boy on the floor. "I think I finally see why Father adopted him. He's exactly like you."

The prince frowned. "I think I've been insulted."

"Don't worry, you have been," Arianrod shot, and started toward Cory.

"You through playing with your dragon now?" Arianrod asked, hands on her hips.

The boy looked up, startled. He quickly rose to his feet, and his sister hugged him. "I'm glad you're all right, Arianrod."

Pulling away, the girl seemed close to tears. "Yeah, I was, but you two sure took your time getting here. Brothers!"

Taliesin frowned. "Took our time? Look, Arianrod—"

"Um ... Highnesses ... I hate to interrupt, but can't we continue this sometime when we're not being chased by demons?" Jern asked plainly.

Cory nodded. "Absolutely right, Jern. And this time, I hope my plan will—huh?"

The boy stopped, cut off by someone tugging at his elbow. "My lord?" Pellor asked. "I think you should have this."

Smile fading, Cory grimly accepted the stone from the little boy. It glowed eerily in his hand, almost seeming to shrink away from him. "Thanks. I know exactly what to do with this."

So saying, the young wizard turned to Taliesin. "You know these tunnels better than I do. Lead them out of here."

"What about you?" the prince asked, spine tingling at the word 'them.' "Cory, if you think I'm leaving you here—"

"There's no time to argue," Cory insisted. "Benythonne, Jern and the others will shield you from any magic the demons might use against you, but they should all be too busy with me to worry. I'll cover your escape."

"Your Grace, we can't just—"

Cory's expression turned to anger. "That isn't a request, Jern! As Vainamoinen's heir, the Prince of Wizards, I'm *ordering* you to protect these children!"

"My lord," Kellyn began, reaching out to touch Cory's shoulder.

"Don't worry, I'll be okay," Cory answered, and turned away before anyone could stop him. With a word and a single pass of his hand, the wards erected by Math's apprentices opened to admit him passage, then sealed again behind him.

Chapter 17

▼

EBON'S FIRES

Cory started down the darkened passage, letting dragon-linked night-vision guide his steps. Somewhere, dripping water echoed throughout the tunnels, and a cold draft blew his dark hair back. Behind him, the cries of his friends behind the mystic shields faded with distance. Cory was on his own, as he had planned, and they would all be safe. All he had to do was provide a loud enough distraction to draw every demon in Abollydd to him.

The boy swallowed. Closing his eyes, he tried to calm himself and think. There was no reason to fight them all, unprepared. The young wizard quickly wove invisibility about himself, coupled with a spell of silence. But he dared not erect wards again, not after what had happened before.

With a single goal in mind, the boy increased his pace, determined. The passageways were a maze, but memory of the place and his mystic senses eventually brought the boy where he wanted. A large chamber opened before him, lit by torches in the walls, and a pyre burning furiously in the center of the room. Crates and barrels lined the walls, filled with food and spices for feeding the many human slaves of the demons.

Cory noticed a single Kelloid moving heavy wooden boxes on the far end of the room, and stood, silently. He recognized the demon as the one who was in charge of Abollydd's kitchens. Without even moaning in effort, the Kelloid hoisted two crates, one under each arm, and left the chamber. Cory nodded to himself and walked over to the burning pit.

A thick cloud of smoke rose from the pit, everything inside a smoldering ruin. Everything the rescue party was wearing or carrying had been reduced to cinders.

Cory frowned, knowing that what he searched for would still be there. With a short incantation, something began to move at the bottom of the fire, and two pieces of clothing floated up from the coals, completely unscathed. Cory spoke a charm to cool the garment before it touched his naked shoulders, and stood there, letting his cloak drape itself about him. He paused a moment, feeling the cloth between his fingers, to assure himself that his Sorcerer's Cloak was really still intact. The dweomer woven into the cloth itself protected it from most forms of destruction, but the boy was still relieved to see that the warding spells had held.

Cory held out his hand as a second cloak folded itself neatly and deposited itself into his waiting grasp. The boy smiled warmly, thinking its owner would be pleased. Loincloths didn't provide much warmth. Before he started off again, he let the spell of invisibility drop as his cloak's enchantment took over. There was no need to duplicate a spell, especially when his energies could be spent better elsewhere.

The boy hadn't gone far before he came to an even larger chamber. An underground stream flowed through the room, and light from many torches played off the water and gem-encrusted ceiling. Were he less pressed for time, Cory might have stopped to enjoy the beauty of it all. While evil, the Kelloids still had some likeable traits, probably left over from the days when they were still human.

Stone slid on stone, echoing throughout the vast chamber. Cory whirled, seeing a heavy stone door seal off the path he had just come from. The boy swallowed. He had either set off some kind of a trap, or the demons had been following his progress all along!

Next Cory heard the sound of marching feet—many dozens of them. Kelloid demons came flooding into the chamber, armed with magegems, swords and whips. They looked around for a moment, their glowing eyes searching the darkness. The demon in their lead smiled hideously.

"Oh, what a clever little boy! Using a Sorcerer's Cloak to turn invisible," Ahriman mused, striding directly towards Cory.

They weren't kidding around with him, and Cory knew his enchanted cloak wasn't fooling anybody. Quickly, he threw up his hands and wove a web of light about the chamber in an attempt to slow them down.

The Kelloids came, not noticing the construct until it was too late. Gold energy discharged, sparking painfully into their thick limbs. Scores of demons cursed his name and pressed against the strands of mystic fiber, but the web held. Cory swallowed and stepped back against the sealed entrance, now that he had breathing room.

The youngster examined the stone door, and saw how tight the seam was, apparently reinforced with magic. There was no way he was going to get that door open in time, and he didn't want to waste his strength trying. This trap seemed horribly familiar, and he definitely didn't want to be captured a second time.

Heart racing with fear, Cory returned his attention to the inevitable. There was only one other entrance to the chamber, and the demons were blocking it.

The boy took a deep breath, trying to remember his training. Math had taught him that there was always an alternative to any situation. All he had to do was find it. The boy looked up, around him, searching for a way out. Sparks from the field caught on tiny shining gems encrusted in the ceiling. Those made him think of the magegem in his hand. Readymade power, available to discharge without sacrificing his own precious strength. But to use the stone itself was dangerous. Legend told that magegems always cost a mortal soul, and Cory definitely didn't want it to be his!

The crackling from the web grew louder, drawing his attention. The boy stared as his web discharged its power, and he knew it wouldn't last more than a few more minutes at most, unless he reinforced it. But then something caught his eye. It wasn't so much the burning of the mystic energy which was causing them pain as the light the sparks gave off. He knew that because every time a demon struck the web, it not only wreathed in pain, but the demons several feet behind it did, too.

Grimly, the boy nodded to himself. *He had them!*

Quickly, Cory snatched up a soft, chalklike rock from the floor and began inscribing a circle of runes about him with a trembling hand. Reactivation of the spell wouldn't take much, he knew, for his body was set for the last thing he had changed into. The web collapsed just as he finished drawing the last rune, and the young wizard quickly sang the incantation. Just as the first of the demons reached him, bright light flared as the boy's body transformed into energized photons.

The demons immediately surrounding him screamed in agony and frustration, for the boy had found a way to conjure sufficient demonsbane against them. Cory had remembered what every human child raised on Abydonne knew from the crib: the Sun could destroy the demons, but any very bright light would do the same thing. Demons fled the chamber *en masse*, tripping over each other in the attempt to get through a vast portal suddenly too narrow to admit them all.

As light, Cory could not cast any spells. But as he couldn't be harmed either, he simply floated there. Transfixed in horror at what was happening, Cory finally understood why light was so baneful to demonkind: the Kelloids' forms shifted, steam coming up from in-between their scales and thickly from their open mouths. Slowly, agonizingly, the demons transformed back into human beings! As the Darkness of Chaos was invoked in the original spell that turned them into demons, bright light canceled the incantation out. That in itself wouldn't kill them, but the pitiful creatures were all extremely old. Immediately, the march of years caught up with them, and the bodies of the former human sorcerers crumbled into dust.

The boy was frightened, and if he still had a human form, he'd shudder. He had never killed before, even by accident. All he had wanted to do was scare them off! Mindful that his very presence could slay, Cory lingered until the Kelloids who managed to make it out of the chamber in time could find some darkness to hide in.

Then Cory remembered his friends, and that he had to provide a distraction so they could escape unimpeded. The boy left the chamber, searching for the one sorcerer who could help him. Before, on foot, finding any specific room in the underground maze would have taken forever. But at lightspeed, it wouldn't take very long, he reasoned.

Soon his search led him to a crossroads of sorts. There, the second trap sprung. A huge crystal in the center of the room pulsated in Cory's presence, sealing the chamber and canceling his spell.

Cory knelt on the stone floor, feeling the cold seep into his unprotected knees. He took a deep breath, realizing that something had turned him back into a boy again.

"Some magic," he whispered, and stared at the crystal. Orange-red light flowed across the walls of the chamber, playing across his face, entrancing him. The boy felt all thoughts of fighting the demons desert him, leaving him with a sense of peace and contentment. At the last minute, Cory realized what was happening. With the last of his will, the young wizard closed his eyes and spoke a charm, shielding himself from the crystal's baleful rays.

The boy took deep breaths, sweat running down his brow. Demonic laughter filled the chamber, sending goosebumps up his spine. It was coming from the crystal!

"So, you are as powerful as the legends say you are," the crystal said in Asmodeus' voice. "But you are still young, boy. You cannot hope to fight all of us, and there is no need to. *Face me!*"

Shivering, Cory pulled his hood up before opening his eyes again. The cloak's spell of warding would protect him from any further attacks on his person, within limits. He quickly lowered his thin, shaking hands, hoping the demon wouldn't notice that. Things were bad enough without letting Asmodeus know how scared he really was!

Standing in front of the crystal was a man with blood-red skin, horns, and a long, barbed tail. Cory swallowed, his eyes growing wide with fear. This was no Kelloid!

"What's the matter, lad? I don't mean to hurt you. We can be friends," the fiend said in a sickening tone, in Asmodeus' voice.

Terror stricken, Cory stumbled back, tripping on his cloak and falling flat on his rump. The Devil laughed at him, taking a cautious step forward and offering the boy his hand in friendship.

"I could *never* be your friend!" the young boy retorted. "I read about you in Grandfather's library: The Angel of Death. Asteroth. Mephistopheles. Satan. In the stories, you're known by a hundred different names, and in all of them, you're *evil!*"

"Now, now, boy. There is no need for all this violence between us," Satan hissed. "Evil isn't all *that* bad. Why do you persist in defending the humans? You are above them, Cory. You were born with the power to rule over them! The humans are nothing more than maggots beneath our feet!"

Cory vehemently shook his head, forgetting to breathe. He stood there, muscles stiffened, as the Devil advanced upon him. All at once, black flames rose up from the ground, covering the walls, surrounding the both of them, and the room practically swelled with their heat. The boy swallowed, for they were the fabled Ebon's Fires. All at once he realized the handicap he had, as a wizard lacking a staff. Without the staff to focus his powers, he could not invoke the greater magicks, such as the Winds of Time or Ebon's Fires. This demon *could*, and Cory couldn't do anything about it!

"You do not know the glory that was Atlantis and Ys," the Devil told him. "These humans have tried to rebuild it, all to their sorrow.

Their twelve petty kingdoms would have been nothing more than duchies in our former realms, your Grace.

"Do you know why Llewelyn adopted you, the real reason?" Satan asked him with a sneer. As the boy was too afraid to answer, he simply went on. "The petty human kings have been trying for centuries to get true magic blood into their families! They wanted us, Cory. Llewelyn adopted you to *use* you!"

"No," Cory at last whispered. "That's not true!"

"Isn't it? Your foster brother told you how rare it was for a king to adopt a child! Think, lad! Why should a man with ten sons want to adopt another boy, unless you had something he wanted: real power!"

Cory thought about that, and swallowed again. Llewelyn had talked about power the day after he met him, and his very words came echoing back: *Return him to me a wizard or not at all!*

The Devil licked his lips. "You don't need them, lad. Consider: together, you and I can rebuild our kingdoms. But, you still do not trust me," he went on. "So I will give you a reason to. As a token of my good will, I will make you immortal!"

The boy stared, horror-struck. "You—you mean to make me into a demon," he whispered hoarsely. Satan nodded, holding out his hand.

"No," Cory answered, shaking his head. The Devil continued to coax him, but the boy had stopped listening. He tried to get his ragged breathing under control, trying to remember. Something was nagging at the back of his mind. Something was very wrong with all of this!

And then he realized it. Cory's head snapped up, blue eyes shining like sparks in the eerie ebony light. "You're not real! You don't exist! Math told me there was no Devil!"

"And you trust the ravings of an old man, when I stand here before you, in the flesh?" Satan answered.

"No," the young wizard said, determinedly getting to his feet. "You're a myth, and the Flames of Ebon are the final proof! You're using Asmodeus' voice, but even if he still had a wizard's staff, he can't use it anymore to conjure the enchanted flames! All of his magic is tied up in his demon form!"

The fiend's face set like cold stone. "If you think I'm a fraud, strike me down. Use your power, boy! I stand here before you, shieldless! A single mystic bolt is all it will take to slay me, and then everything I own is yours!"

Cory raised his hand, marshalling his power. A gold halo of light surrounded his outstretched palm, playing off his face. Satan stood there, hands out, ready to take the blow.

And Cory began to sing. All at once, the Devil realized what he was doing, and screamed obscenities, but it did absolutely no good. The young avatar invoked the Light of Truth, flooding the chamber with it. All at once, the "Flames of Ebon" disappeared, and Satan's form wavered like heat waves on a hot summer's day.

The boy gasped in shock. He had expected the Devil to disappear too, but in his place stood Brent, gagged and bound to a stake with chains of cold iron. Cory ran to him, and started to pull at the links, which were mercilessly tight.

Brent moaned through his gag, eyes rolling in frustration. Cory pulled the gag off, and the young man stared at him. "Forget the chains. You can't break them. But you can shatter the stake I'm tied to!"

Cory nodded and brushed his glowing fingertips across the wood, singing incantation. The stake started to hiss, then dissolved into gas. In a moment the thick stake was gone, and the chains simply fell off the sorcerer from the slack.

Brent nodded his head as the boy knelt to pick up the extra cloak and magegem he had dropped. "Thank you! I thought I was a goner for sure. What tipped you off that it was an illusion?"

"Math's lessons," Cory answered. "The Devil is a myth from Earth, as he is here. Once I realized that, the whole trick came apart. Even on Earth, Satan is known as the Prince of Lies. Asmodeus must have pulled my worst fears from my own mind, and conjured illusion against me."

Cory looked up, and saw the crystal still sitting there, pulsating like an atrocity. He swallowed, for it wasn't an illusion. Had he struck out with mystic bolts as Asmodeus had been goading him to, the crystal would have exploded, killing them both!

"God in Heaven, I almost—"

"But you didn't," Brent said, cutting him off. "You outsmarted him, pup," the sorcerer said, fastening his cloak clasp. Next he examined the magegem Cory had given him, and flipped it in the air, catching it as it came down again.

"Come, we still have to rescue Keela and the others," Brent told him, and led the boy down a corridor he hadn't noticed before.

* * * *

They had been walking for some time, shielded by wards conjured by Brent. Apparently, Cory's earlier spell had been lacking something, which the elder sorcerer willingly showed him. The boy shuddered in horror, for the missing ingredient was a few drops of blood, invoking dark magic.

"You're still priggish about it, aren't you?" the young man asked, turning a corner.

Cory just stared in the darkness. Slowly, he nodded, and then realized Brent couldn't see it. The boy cleared his throat and said softly, "Yes."

Brent grinned. "You're going to learn, pup. Lacking a staff, you're going to have to find alternatives. Dark magic is convenient, and lends a lot of power. Why do you think the Kelloids use it now that they can't cast spells by themselves anymore?"

The boy stopped, staring at him. Solemnly he said, "I will *not* use dark magic, Brent. To buy power with the life of another is ... obscene!"

Brent nodded at him, waved the boy onward, and continued. "Suit yourself. Just keep in mind that others do it, milad. Even the non-magi."

Cory saw what the sorcerer was implying, and didn't like it. He reached out, jabbing his forefinger into Brent's chest. "Don't you DARE! Asmodeus was lying about my father!"

Brent sighed, stopping again. Just ahead of them was light, apparently another cavern, but he wanted to get this straightened out first. "Sorry to disappoint you, but that was the one truthful thing he said. Llewelyn adopted you solely because you're an archwizard. He did it right after Math told him how powerful you really were."

Cory looked up, shocked as realization set in. The boy lowered his hand, stepping back as if punched. "Then that's why he banished you, after you refused to marry Arianrod?"

Brent reached out and put both hands warmly on the boy's trembling shoulders. "I'm sorry for telling you this, Cory. But don't feel bad about it. Of the two of us, you got the better deal."

The boy stared at him, and the sorcerer went on, "The king may have adopted you for the wrong reasons, but don't deny what he gave you: his love and a new family, when you were orphaned on a strange new world. He made you his *son*, Cory. Don't throw all of that away because of this!"

Slowly, the boy swallowed, ashamed at the feelings he was having. How could he be so selfish as to think that of his foster father? Llewelyn *had* adopted him, made him into a prince of the realm. Cory looked up, wishing he could see Brent's face more clearly, but also thankful that his own face was hidden in the dimness. "You're right, Brent."

"'Course I am," the young man said, and tousled Cory's long hair. "Now come on. We've got to rescue my wife."

They had not taken three more steps before they were back in the torchlight again, and Cory stopped dead. "MiGod, I know where we are! The Wheel is just down this corridor!"

Brent's back stiffened, the hairs on the back of his neck sticking up on end. "Oh, Cory ... if only you children knew what you were doing by turning that wheel."

"What?" the boy asked, filled with apprehension.

"Never mind, it's better if you didn't know," the sorcerer answered, and decided to keep the boy out of the crystallizing chamber if he could help it, before starting off down the corridor.

Cory stared after him, his curiosity taken. "Brent, what does the Wheel do?"

Brent let out his pent up breath. "Dark magic," he answered, and Cory wondered what could be so hideous that a sorcerer who used the Forbidden Arts could shudder at its memory.

They came to a pair of heavy double doors, set on cast-iron hinges. Cold iron decorated the doors themselves, finely wrought into demons' heads. That didn't stop them, though, for the doors were constructed of wood, and they had little trouble pushing them open. Inside, the demons turned around, mouths agape. Sixty children turning the Wheel didn't notice the two sorcerers until they started blasting away with concussive magic energy, and their demon guards went flying quite unwillingly.

Get away from the Wheel, Cory sent to the minds of the children, and wove protective spells to cover their escape as they ran to a corner of the chamber. Nearby, Brent sent bolts of pure mystic force, tying his own innate powers in with the magegem, which flared like a dying star in his hand. With a sure movement of his hands and a baleful glare at the Kelloids, Brent called up cold Arctic winds in the underground chamber. Kelloids were forced back against the walls under the bite of gale-force winds, and bonds of solid ice quickly formed under Brent's control.

Cory nodded to himself. The older sorcerer obviously didn't need any help, at least for the time being. He had just finished erecting the wards around the frightened children who sat huddled behind him, as far from the demons as possible. Cory gave the Wheel a look of contempt, and summoning power, blasted the solid wood into so many shards amid a crack of thunder. Remembering his brief imprisonment and bondage, the boy's anger grew white hot, and solid rock started to crumble at his rage. Smoke rose up, forming an opaque wall between him and Brent, and still he did not relent.

Cory, stop! Brent's voice echoed in his head. ***Don't waste your power! We still have to get out of here, and I doubt if Asmodeus has given up on you yet!***

Swift as thought, the boy sent one final burst of energy at the spot where the Wheel had stood, then brought his talent under control. Behind him, the youngest children sobbed uncontrollably, and Cory sensed they were just as afraid of him as they were of the demons. The boy turned, and then winced at the sight. They were all his age or younger, and all saw him as a black magician instead of their rescuer. Cory could have eased their worry with a simple charm, but chose not to, remembering that Math taught him there were some things magic should not be used for.

"I'm sorry if I scared you," he said simply. Then he turned, hurt by the look of terror in their moist eyes. Brent stood by the edge of a gaping hole in the floor, which Cory had just blasted open. The magegem fell from the sorcerer's hand, no longer glowing. Brent had spent all its power in this attack.

"I cast wards over the ice which are holding the Kelloids, and they should stay put for a while yet," he explained. "I want you to stay here and watch over the children. I'll be back shortly," Brent ordered. He had apparently not noticed, nor cared, that Cory had just alienated himself from his peers. Before the boy could answer, Brent jumped, levitating himself down into the darkness.

Chapter 18

PENTAGRAM

Cory stood still for a long time, listening to the cries of the children on one end of the room, the curses from the trapped Kelloid demons on the other, trying to ignore both and stare into the drafty black pit. How long ago had Brent left? It surely couldn't have been more than a few minutes, yet it seemed to stretch for hours. Finally, the high-pitched curses from the demons became too much, and Cory cast silence over that part of the room. That left only the whimpering of their young slaves, and he decided to at least do his duty.

The boy went to them, stopping cautiously ten feet from the closest. He locked eyes with a little blue-eyed boy, saw the chains still about his small wrists, and winced. *Why didn't I think of that before? I should never have left the key with Gwion,* he thought. Cory looked back at the Kelloids, thinking that one of them might have the keys to unlock the manacles.

Halfway across the room, he noticed something gleam in the torchlight. Cory's hood fell back as he bent to pick it up, and he smiled. *Thank God! One of the guards must have dropped his key ring when we attacked them!*

As the young wizard quickly went back to release the children, a gasp came from one of them. "It's Prince Cory!"

He looked up and saw the little red-headed boy who had said that. Cory immediately recognized the lad as Badger Blacksmith's apprentice, who had been kidnapped on the same raid as Arianrod. At the boy's exclamation, the others seemed to relax a bit. The fact that Cory was unlocking their chains also helped.

"Highness, what are you doing back in this dismal place?" little Aren asked, waiting his turn to be freed. The last time Cory had seen him, he was in the torture chamber.

"I'm rescuing you," Cory explained, grateful that the children's apprehension was disappearing. By blasting everything in sight he might have frightened them, but nobility and royalty were allowed their occasional rages.

After the last of the manacles fell clattering to the stone floor, and Cory had reassured the children he was not going to hurt them, he returned to his vigil by the pit. Still frightened of the Kelloids, the youngsters surrounded their prince and stood watch with him.

"What are we waiting for?" one of them finally built up the nerve to ask.

"Brent," Cory answered him. "But he's taking too long."

Aren saw the young wizard looking apprehensively at the trapped demons, and immediately understood why he lingered there. "Go and help him, Highness. We'll be all right."

Cory stood for a minute, looking at the multitude which had clustered around him. "No, I can't just leave you guys! You don't have any protection."

That made him think of Taliesin and the others. Briefly, he closed his eyes and entered trance, establishing contact with Benythonne. Taliesin and the apprentices had stumbled upon the torture chamber while looking for the surface, although Cory guessed Taliesin had led them that way on purpose. Having freed all the slaves in the chamber, they were now steadily making their way to the surface, with few problems. It was still daylight outside, and those few demons who were that close to Abollydd's gate were quickly handled by Benythonne and the apprentices. The boy smiled, glad that at least his close friends would be safe soon.

"Hey, Cory! Can you give me a hand here?" Brent called from the bottom of the pit, snapping the boy out of his trance.

After shaking his head to clear it, Cory looked down. "Brent! Thank God! I was starting to get worried!"

"Yeah, I was worried too," the sorcerer admitted. Cory then noticed Brent wasn't alone. Several adults were behind him, all looking as if they were having trouble just standing. "Help me get these poor wretches up there."

The boy nodded, casting a spell. The adults rose up through the crack in the stone floor, one by one. All were covered with grime, wearing loincloths and chains like their younger counterparts. One slave collapsed to his knees, and the sight of him made Cory sick. The poor man had a long unkempt beard and pale skin from lack of sunlight. But the worst thing was the look of emptiness in his eyes, which made Cory shudder. Immediately, the children started to help him, unlocking the manacles.

"What happened to them?" Cory asked when Brent finally rose up from the pit, carrying Keela in his arms.

"You don't want to know," he answered. But Keela spoke up, a mixture of anger and pain on her face.

"Oh, tell the boy, Brent. He'd not stay innocent very long in this place, anyway," she said.

Cory stared, Aren at his side. "What?" the boys insisted as one.

"We were in the crystallizing chamber," Keela explained, wincing at the memory. "The Wheel turns a crank, working a great engine which charges the crystals."

Keela and Brent exchanged a look, and she went on. "When the slaves are worn out, we are chained to the five points of a pentagram, with the crystals in the center. The demons then draw out our life forces, feeding the energy into the crystals."

Although he dreaded it, Cory looked at the memory in her mind, and shuddered. Seeing the boy's reaction, Brent nodded. "That's where the demons get their magegems. You wanted to know, pup."

Cory turned away in disgust, staring into the blackened remains of the Wheel. All the time he and the others were chained to the Wheel and whipped, forced into turning that monstrosity, they were helping to kill the adults below!

"Brent, what are you doing?" Keela cried.

"I've got to get us out of here, darling," the sorcerer answered.

Cory turned to see what was happening. Brent undid the bindings on a large sack he had tied to his belt. As he bent to spill the contents on the floor, Cory gasped. In front of the sorcerer was a large pile of magegems, apparently stolen from the demons' own stores.

"Like *that?*" she asked, agape. "Can't we just walk out?"

"Not in the shape you're in, no. And even if these children could carry all of you, it will take forever to reach the surface. Trust me, Keela. If there were some other way, I'd do it."

Cory believed that. Brent had an affinity for the black arts, and if he could get them out of here without sacrificing his new treasure of magegems, he would. The boy swallowed anger, that this adult he looked up to could be so heartlessly cruel; to use magic others had died for.

But the boy wizard didn't say anything. He merely watched in stunned fascination as Brent cast his spell, opening a gateway to the surface. At the dark sorcerer's urging, the magegems glowed bright as stars, and then abruptly winked out, to be replaced by a giant glowing pentagram in the center of the stone floor.

"Everybody through the gate before the Kelloids find some way to stop us," Brent ordered. He gave a young slaveboy a push into the center of the pentagram when they all hesitated. As the child's bare feet touched the inside of the circle, the gate flared. The boy disappeared, falling as if into the ground; yet the floor appeared to be as solid as it ever was.

Cory watched as Brent repeated the process with another child, and another, until they all got the idea and started going through on their own. Cory himself held back, inwardly afraid of the dark magic used. He turned away, looking thoughtfully at the entrances to the chamber.

Cory raised his hands, erecting rudimentary wards about the room. These wouldn't do much more than warn them of approaching demons, but they also wouldn't cripple him if the spell were suddenly broken. He finished in time to see the last of the slaves stepping through the large gateway, and Brent turning to him.

"Let's go, pup. Gateway won't last very long if Asmodeus gets wind of it," the young man explained, taking the boy by the elbow. Cory didn't fight him, even though he would have preferred to prepare himself before stepping into the vortex.

Orange energy crackled about Cory's legs as he stepped into the circle, and he fell as if into a pit, the gate swallowing him whole. Cory felt a sensation of bitterly cold mist swirling all about his body, creeping into his lungs. Even the enchanted cloak didn't help much against that cold. Dimly, he sensed Brent slide into the netherworld beside him.

Then, in midstream, Cory sensed something very wrong. They had stopped moving, and he had the feeling of being pulled sideways.

It's Asmodeus, the young man sent to Cory. ***He's onto us!***

Shock filled the boy's mind. With dragon's strength he quickly pushed Brent away from him, easily breaking the sorcerer's grip on his arm. Brent gave a cry of warning, but both knew it to be too late.

Sorry, Brent, Cory thought at him. ***But I can't let Asmodeus get you, too. It's me he wants. Just get the others to safety.***

Cory watched his friend vanish into the mist as they were pulled apart. Shivering, the boy gathered his cloak and cast a simple warding against the chill, even as his teeth chattered uncontrollably.

Abruptly the boy felt ground beneath his feet again, his knees buckling under the strain of coming to a tendon-wrenching stop. Cory took a tentative breath and shuddered, for hot air was a shock after all that cold. He spent a precious few moments gathering himself before daring to look around.

His eyes grew wide. He was kneeling in the center of a second pentagram, this one drawn not of orange light, but the scarlet of dried human blood. There was a lit black candle at each point of the star, with runes inscribed all around the circle. Even without trying, Cory knew the circle was warded, and it would be difficult if not impossible to step out of it. He was trapped!

The boy's head turned to the sound of laughter, by now familiar. Not ten feet from the circle was a podium with a great red and gold tome resting open upon it. Standing by the podium was a nine-foot tall demon, eyes glowing intensely with pleasure.

"I'm so glad you could join us, my boy," the Demon Lord hissed at him. "I have a few final preparations to make, and then I shall bestow that gift I promised you earlier."

Cory swallowed and tried to sound brave, but his voice cracked in the middle of his sentence. "You can keep your gift, Asmodeus," the boy said, getting to his feet.

A scaled eyebrow went up. "After all I've sacrificed to get you here? I think not. You will become a Kelloid demon, Cory. *Immortal!* And, of course, you and your familiar shall both serve me."

"No," came out as a hoarse whisper. Cory trembled, wishing it was just from his bare feet standing on the cold stone. Waves of icy horror shot up his spine, forcing him to shudder against his will. The demon grinned widely.

"Don't worry, boy. You shall not be alone for very long. Behold!" A large scrying glass appeared on the far wall. In the mirror, Brent led the newly freed slaves across white sands, toward the relative protection of the forest.

"Lo, the sun sets. Soon my forces will fly out into the night, and bring them back for punishment. Foolish human filth! Did you really think I would let them go?"

"You can't take all of them," Cory said with certainty. "And we killed a lot of you."

The boy immediately regretted saying that. Asmodeus gave him a look that dripped blood. Cory stepped back to the far edge of the circle, where the wards sparked painfully on his unprotected heels. He looked behind him and saw the corpse of the poor slave whose blood had been used to draw the pentagram.

"You shall help me get them back, when I'm through with you," Asmodeus hissed. "You will wring the life out of all of them in the torture chamber, boy. Or should I call you … *Draigswynwr!* Yes, I also know your true name. A raven in my service overheard Math when he named you! You are finally *mine*, child! You will be my slave *forever!*"

The boy shook his head from right to left, and another spasm of horror took him. Asmodeus had stopped talking to him, beginning to read the spell. Cory closed his eyes tight, frustrated at his helplessness. All at once he decided that he was *not* going to sit there like a lamb for slaughter. If the demon wanted him, he would have to fight to get him. Cory was determined to go out kicking and screaming.

The boy raised his hands, calling forth power. To his surprise, only a little glimmer answered. Fearfully, he looked at Asmodeus, who snickered to himself in between reading the words. Somehow, the Demon Lord had found a way to neutralize his magic! Desperate, Cory clamped his eyes shut, concentrating on his inner self. The boy was shocked to find most of his power was gone, stolen. However, he still had his reserves, that portion he had used to fight back the unnatural blackness conjured by the demons.

But Cory hesitated, remembering how sick he was after using it the last time, and decided to save that as a last resort. He had other resources, such as his dragon. Cory hated to draw on Benythonne's strength like this, but it was better than the alternative. Girding himself, Cory summoned power across the link. Light flared in answer, although delayed, as if something was draining the power even as it was produced.

Golden brilliance lanced out from his palms, striking the invisible walls of the circle. Gold sparks flew as the barrier was hit, and mystic light flashed on and off like a neon sign. Cory finally opened his eyes to see what was going on. The flames from the candles had climbed to six feet, and the blood lines of which the pentagram was drawn was beginning to run.

Asmodeus had momentarily left his tome, reaching for a large magegem necklace hanging on a nearby hook. Cory frowned, realizing that the demon had not been using any magegems before this, yet he had obviously placed wards powerful enough to hold Cory within the pentagram, and he was also casting the incantation without aid.

What's he using as a power source? The boy wondered. *Without a magegem, he can't be fighting me, draining me—God-in-Heaven, that's it! He's using my own power against me!*

Pausing to look at the threads, Cory realized he was right. All of his missing power was in the pentagram, drawn from his own being, by using his true name! Although panic welled within him, Cory fought the urge to scream. Having a fit was not going to solve anything, and just might make matters worse.

In his mind, the boy remembered another time, sitting cross-legged at Math's feet by a cheerfully crackling fire. His master had taught him that the threads could be rewoven into different patterns, reweaving reality along with it. The power contained in a magician enabled him to manipulate those threads; all he had to do was figure out which patterns he wanted them in for different effects.

That was simple enough, as the boy knew his own pattern better than any other. It was the first one Math had him learn, providing the basis for other spells, not the least of which was shape-shifting. Slowly, agonizingly, Cory nudged the threads back where they belonged. It was painful, because he was fighting himself. The psychic backlash was almost unbearable, but the boy endured. He was determined *not* to become a demon!

"So, you have begun to suspect, have you?" Asmodeus gloated. "It seems I have need of stronger measures to ensure your cooperation. We can't have you fleeing before the spell is completed now, can we?"

Cory ignored the snickering from Asmodeus, continuing to work. Suddenly there was a sharp stab of fresh pain, and Cory did scream, dropping to his knees. Orange light struck the field, blurring his vision, scrambling his thoughts, preventing him from spellcasting. Though his eyes were closed, he still heard the demon's voice echoing through his pounding skull.

"You are *mine*, son of Garth. You will be my servant until the end of time!"

Cory could not even gather his thoughts to answer, but silent anger grew in response, from the core of the boy's being. The pentagram's wards flared, shutting out Asmodeus' attack, although it still kept him trapped within its confines. Cory took breath in huge gulps as his vision cleared. He could think again!

"Ebon's Fires, it's not supposed to do THAT!" the Demon Lord screamed. Asmodeus realized Cory was beginning to learn how to control the spell, and knew it wouldn't be long before he escaped. Suddenly fearful, the demon began to read faster—but laid a careful hand on the dagger sheathed at his belt. The demon was determined that Cory should die by cold iron rather than go free.

With a gasp, Cory saw the threads again, and understood. The spell was drawn from him. He could work his will upon it, but only if he acted quickly! The next move was dangerous, but Cory had little choice. Gathering courage, the boy shifted two threads, and the wards flared red-hot, expanding outward with explosive force. Asmodeus was thrown back two dozen feet before he came to a screeching halt, flat on his back, the ancient tome lying in a scorched ruin beside him.

"A thousand curses on your soul, human! I'll destroy you for that!" Asmodeus hissed, saliva drooling from his scaled chin.

Cory had gotten to his feet, and was easily walking outside the circle of blood now. With the black spell broken, the boy's power had returned to its rightful place. Golden light arced between his hands, ready to form into mystic bolts of lethal force. "I think not," he said, and took a cautious step forward.

Orange bolts shot across the room in answer, conjured from Asmodeus' magegem necklace. With the speed of thought, Cory formed his unborn spell into a defensive shield. Sparks flew across the chamber in all directions, catching on old pieces of furniture and delicately woven rugs, setting it all on fire arbitrarily.

Releasing a yell of pure rage, Asmodeus discharged half the energy contained in his magegem. The boy was tossed across the room by the force, slammed hard against a stone pillar. Only his shield and the protective wards of his Sorcerer's Cloak saved his life, but the boy still fought for consciousness. Dizzy and weak, Cory tried to gather his thoughts as Asmodeus drew the dagger and advanced upon him.

Cory slowly raised his eyes, watching as his death quite literally approached. The Demon Lord's dagger had a sickly green halo, the telltale sign of a dweomer. Cory swallowed, trying to get to his knees. His arms were shaking with the strain, his back a mass of pain, breath coming hard. Blue haze gathered thickly before his eyes, unconsciousness threatening to claim him.

But the young wizard did not relent. He did not come this far to simply lie down and die! Dizzy beyond fear, he saw the demon approach as if in a dream, and was able to think. He could not hope to spellcast against cold iron. His only chance was to take Asmodeus physically. Whispering a plea of forgiveness to his familiar, Cory again drew power through their special link.

Immediately the pain diminished considerably, his strength returning. Just as the dagger flashed upwards for a death-stroke, Cory reached out and grabbed the demon's ankle. He yanked back hard, and Asmodeus fell backwards onto the stone floor.

"Brat! Sit still so I can stab your miserable, pure heart!"

Cory didn't give him the chance. The youngster quickly whispered an incantation, and the floor exploded under the demon, throwing him off-balance again. This time Asmodeus did let go of the knife, and it fell clattering to a far corner of the room.

Trembling, Cory fought his way back to his feet. His head swam with agony and dizziness, threatening him with all-consuming blackness. By the time the boy regained his stance and resources, Asmodeus was up again as well, beginning to spellcast.

Cory swallowed, knowing that in his present condition, he stood no chance at all of forming a strong enough shield. His only hope lay in attack, trying to keep the demon off-balance. Mystic bolts again lanced out, striking the floor explosively at Asmodeus' feet. The demon stumbled back; the Dark Lord managed to remain standing, but both his concentration and his spell were ruined.

"Very well," Asmodeus hissed. "I prefer finishing my enemies firsthand anyway."

Before Cory could react, the Demon Lord spread his wings and closed the distance between them. Asmodeus hit the boy in the chest with the force of a runaway van, brutally pinning him against a far wall.

Cory moaned, the wind knocked out of him. Only the fact that his familiar was a dragon enabled the boy to survive this far, but the demon's hands quickly closed about his throat as he fought for breath. Cory knew he had about two seconds before Asmodeus was positioned to snap his neck. Frightened, the boy responded with the training Math had given him. His arms snapped upwards, trying to break the demon's death-grip on his neck. Suddenly, the silver amulet Ilmarinen had crafted for Cory's cloak began to glow. Mystic energy sparked, forcing the demon to let go of the boy.

Cory gasped, drawing air into his tortured lungs, but Asmodeus was still upon him. The Demon Lord punched the boy's side, and Cory thought he heard a rib crack.

He's going to kill me, Cory thought desperately. *I've got to risk hitting him with everything I've got!*

At once, golden splendor emanated from the young wizard, intense as a star going nova. Asmodeus' form wavered under the assault of light, and for the briefest of instants, Cory saw a thin, wrinkled old man with veins showing in every square inch of his body. Then Asmodeus' own dark power kicked in, and his demon form returned.

Cory swallowed. This was a battle of equals, between archwizards. He knew that of the two of them, Asmodeus had the advantages of wisdom and physical strength. All Cory had were his youthful stamina and innate magic, both of which were waning. He had to do something, and quickly, or Asmodeus would surely kill him.

Then, out of nowhere, the boy felt a surge of energy fill his very being. Although his body still ached beyond belief, it resonated with pure magic power. Cory got to his feet, leaning on a wall for support. Asmodeus had not quite recovered from his last attack, and was still writhing on the floor; but Cory knew that wouldn't last for long.

Quickly, the young wizard wove the most powerful spell he knew, a Ward of Binding. The spell wasn't nearly as strong as the Winds of Time which Math had once used to imprison a black dragon, but it would slow down the demon's movements enough for him to try something else. Just as Asmodeus was getting to his knees, Cory's spell took hold, and the demon's motion ground almost to a halt.

Cory took a shaking breath. In spite of the mysterious new power lent him, his physical body was spent. He was only managing to stand by a combination of magic and adrenaline.

Then the necklace at the Demon Lord's throat glimmered, and he moved, like in a movie played in slow motion. Orange energy crackled, and wind picked up in the chamber, pushing the thin boy back. Still very weak, Cory stumbled and noticed the shining mirror on the wall behind him, which no longer showed Brent and the slaves, but a billowing, frigid cloud of nothingness. The boy frowned, for he at last recognized it. Asmodeus was trying to force him through the same gateway used to bring him into this world!

Cory conjured a bolt, preparing to throw it at the gateway itself. All at once, Asmodeus realized his mistake and the indoor hurricane ceased as quickly as it had begun.

"No! Don't! You'll destroy us both!" the Kelloid screamed, fighting in earnest to escape Cory's wards.

Bolt hissing in the palm of his hand, the young wizard glared at the ugly, misshapen mirror. Asmodeus had kidnapped dozens of unsuspecting children from Earth with that artifact, but it was also a doorway back to Earth, the only way back.

Cory's jaw set. With his mother dead, he had nothing on the world of his birth anymore. His life, his family, was here, on his father's world. With single-minded determination, Cory hurled the bolt.

Glass shattered with a boom that sounded like thunder from the end of eternity. Smoke and light filled the cavernous chamber at once, threatening to overcome him. Choking on fumes, Cory fell to his hands and knees, feeling the floor vibrate beneath him.

"Fool! You have no idea what you've done!" Asmodeus raged. Cory saw through tear-streaked eyes that his adversary was finally free of the Ward of Binding, and making his way to the door.

"I've stopped you," Cory answered as strongly as he could, but lack of fresh air made the words come out as an inaudible whisper. Thinking his battle over, Cory let his head sag, waiting for the earthquake he knew was coming to bury him under a million tons of solid rock.

Chapter 19

DESTROYER OF ABOLLYDD

Cory's nostrils flared and his eyes fluttered, awareness at last returning. It was dark and the air was stale, almost completely spent. Moaning, the boy brought aching limbs into motion, coming slowly to his knees. Red light bathed the small space, revealing a dome of jagged grey stone. As the boy's vision slowly cleared, he noticed the light was coming from five lines inscribed in human blood.

The boy's eyes widened, and he gasped, drawing hot air into his strained lungs. By pure stroke of luck, he had fallen inside the pentagram just before the earthquake hit. The wards had flared to life, restored by his presence inside the circle, saving his life.

But Asmodeus' prison might still become his tomb. He was trapped within solid rock, and the air was growing thinner by the minute! Cory somehow forced himself to remain calm, knowing that if he panicked he would use up oxygen faster.

Cory thought through his options, which were few. He could restore the air, but that was a long and complex incantation, and he dared not speak. That also used up oxygen.

Cautiously, the boy examined the threads making up the spell which protected him, afraid to make any sudden moves which might bring the roof down upon him. Most of his inborn power kept the pentagram active, so he couldn't spellcast. On the other hand, because the spell itself drew off his own power, he could control it easily. But what should he change the spell into, if he dared reform it at all?

The child closed his eyes, sweat running down his face and onto his parched lips. The cloak was hot, and he found himself wanting to take it off, but he didn't have the time. His thoughts began to swirl, knowing he would soon be unconscious again, and then dead soon thereafter. The boy fought off panic, knowing he had to think his way out of here.

But none of his training covered escaping a tomb of solid rock! There was a Spell of Enchanted Slumber. He would sleep, not needing air, food or water until somebody found him, usually a princess, and broke the spell with a kiss. But he knew that nobody would ever find him here. Similarly, he could change into light, and thereby stay awake, but he would still be trapped in that small space forever.

Gasping the last of unspent air, Cory opened his eyes again in frustration. There *had* to be a way out of here! Weakened, the boy leaned forward onto his hands, staring at the lit pentagram.

The pentagram! Of course! It's a natural gateway! Asmodeus used it to bring me here. All I have to do is recast the spell—just hope I have enough time.

The boy's lungs burned for fresh air. He was breathing mostly hot, used-up air now, which had very little oxygen left in it. Cory closed his eyes, knowing full-well that he could easily fall asleep like that, but he had no choice. Desperately, he sorted through the threads, no longer careful. Once he touched a strand and the ceiling rumbled. Cory was too dizzy from oxygen deprivation to give it much heed.

At last, he found it: the original spell used to draw him into the pentagram. Cory quickly rewove the pattern, knowing that as soon as the gate opened, the wards holding up the rock would collapse. But that mattered little, and he didn't have the time to think it through, just enough time to pray he was right.

Scarlet light flared as the gateway opened. The mountain came crashing down upon the pentagram, but Cory was no longer there; he had already fallen through the magic portal by the force of his own weight. Now floating limp in the void, cold harsh air rushed to him, but the boy welcomed it for once. It was air!

Cory was content for a long while, simply floating, filling his lungs. Eventually, though, his body began to shiver from the cold, and he knew that this place was as dangerous as the tomb. His awareness restored, Cory gathered his cloak for warmth and looked around. There wasn't a landmark to be seen, and every wizard knew the path had to be marked *before* the gate was formed.

However, Cory knew the way out was just a thought away. The boy concentrated and made contact with his familiar. The little dragon was lying in the shade of a tree, trembling from weakness. Cory felt a stab of guilt, for he knew he was at fault for Benythonne's malady. The young wizard was thankful that the return spell didn't require any effort on the dragon's part.

Using Benythonne's position as a reference, Cory uttered enchantment, forming a pentagram of golden light about his shivering body. With a puff of colored smoke, Cory suddenly found himself lying on the grass next to Benythonne, snuggling close for warmth. Completely exhausted, the boy couldn't say anything. It was a few minutes before somebody noticed him lying there and told Brent.

The sorcerer knelt by the shivering child, brushing dark hair across a pale face. Brent removed his own cloak and put that on top of Cory, then spoke a charm for added warmth. "Rest easy, little prince. Maker knows you've earned it this day!"

* * * *

Math knew of Cory's condition immediately, but the royal escort he dispatched took somewhat longer to reach the beleaguered party.

Servants bore their prince off in a litter after Math wove charms about his body to heal him. The boy woke just outside the gates of Caer Dathyl, drenched with sweat. Cory tried to sit up, but he still ached, his muscles refusing to cooperate. The weight of blankets and sheets won, holding him down.

A wrinkled old hand tore away the curtain in an instant, and Cory was greeted by a frown above smiling blue eyes.

"Master," Cory whispered. "I—"

"Hush, I know what you have done," Math said gently but firmly. "You need your rest now."

"But—"

"Hush, I said!" the wizard barked, and laid a hand over the boy's eyes and forehead. Math spoke a charm, and Cory drifted into forced sleep once more.

Brent was beside his former teacher in an instant. "Is he all right?"

Math slowly nodded. "He is. You did well. Llewelyn will hear of this. The prince would be dead now if not for you."

The sorcerer stared, not quite believing his ears. The wizard turned away, but although not another word was spoken, Brent knew the rift between them had finally been closed. There would still be underlying animosity between them, but the sorcerer saw that, at the very least, he would be welcome in court again.

A smile of contentment on his lips, Brent turned on one heel and walked off to join his wife. The two of them would finally walk through Caer Dathyl's gates in triumph.

* * * *

"Your Highness!" the butler hooted, chasing Cory across the suite with a cloak in one hand and sandals in the other.

"No, Cassidy. I've had enough," the boy snapped back, striding across the room in an effort to outdistance his servant. "Math kept me cooped up in here for an entire week! I'm going to see my father, no matter what anyone thinks!"

"I'm not trying to stop your Highness, but wouldn't it be better to walk into the king's presence wearing something on your feet, so you do not look like a common beggar child?"

Cory stopped dead, staring at his bare feet on the finely polished ceramic floor. The boy cursed, guilt holding him in place as the manservant knelt and put the sandals on him. "Sorry, Cassidy. It's not your fault."

"Quite understandable, your Highness. I was a lad myself once, and could never sit still while my nurse doctored me back to health."

The butler went on as he draped the Sorcerer's Cloak over his prince's shoulders. "In fact, it's a wonder you stayed in bed as long as you did."

Cory frowned. "Stop wondering. Math enchanted me. Spell finally wore off a few minutes ago."

The boy grew silent as Cassidy opened the door for him, and began to walk down the chilly stone corridors. At the end of the hall, Cory was surprised to see an honor guard of fifteen soldiers standing on the steps, preventing anyone from entering his apartment. The boy swallowed as the Captain of the Guard himself turned to face him.

"Your Highness is well?" Dyfan asked, his own scarlet cloak swirling with the movement.

Cory nodded, and then frowned. The guards could be there to keep him in as well as keep others out. "I'm going to see my father, Captain."

Dyfan gave a wary glance at the butler, who nodded his approval with a smile. The Captain's heels clicked smartly on the steps, and he saluted the boy. "At once, Highness. Company, fall in!"

At once, the soldiers came to attention, forming an escort on both sides of their prince. Cory's apprehension was quickly growing, for he felt his foster father's overprotective hand in this. Dyfan himself led the way, sword drawn and held in front of him. The way to the royal gardens was long and winding, and servants stopped to stare at Cory as the group passed by.

At last, they came to an open archway and stepped out into lush greenery surrounded by statues and fountains. Dyfan stopped before a group of finely dressed men and announced Cory. "Your Majesty, the Destroyer of Abollydd is here to see you."

Halfway across the garden, Cory stopped, his head snapping in the Captain's direction at mention of the new title. "Destroyer of Abollydd? Me?"

Deep-throated laughter met the question. Llewelyn was standing by the gurgling fountain, conversing with Math and a few other lords. Benythonne was lying in the shade of the castle, but came running up to the boy in an instant, sunlight shining off his bright golden scales. Cory laughed as his dragon licked his face.

"My son, you mean to tell me you don't even know?" the king asked, astonished.

The boy's answer was an innocent shake of the head, and he drew closer, passing servants who were laying out breakfast on a long linen-covered table. "The last thing I remember was shattering the mirror in Asmodeus' throneroom, and then there was this earthquake...." the lad's voice trailed off, and his eyes lost focus.

Llewelyn put his strong right hand on Cory's shoulder and smiled with paternal pride. "Abollydd is in ruins, and the demons who managed to survive the mountain's collapse have spread across the Known World. Cory, you have done what none other has been able to do: You have single-handedly rid Gwynedd of the demon horde!"

Cory stared, speechless. Math stood smiling at the boy, then glanced over to the side, where a lean young lord approached. "Aye, that you did ... but you did have some aid."

The boy turned to where his master was looking, and saw Brent wiping his hands of the pastry he was munching on. The sorcerer was wearing a tunic which marked him as one of Math's apprentices; the Master had apparently agreed to take Brent in and complete his training. Cory frowned, then thought about it. All at once, he realized what must have happened, eyes brightening. "That extra power which came from nowhere, when I needed it most...."

Brent nodded. "I figured you needed help, when I saw the dragon collapse from exhaustion. The apprentices and I pooled our magic and sent it to you across the link between you and your familiar."

Cory returned the smile. "Thank you, Brent. You saved my life."

The sorcerer gave him a coy look. "Think nothing of it, Highness. I owed it to you, for saving my life. Besides, had I not done so, your father would have had my head."

"If I would have left you your head first," Taliesin interjected, walking up to them. He regarded his foster brother, concerned that the younger boy might be too weak to even be standing. "You all right?"

"I'm fine," Cory replied, beaming. "What happened to all the slaves?"

"Returned to their families, except for the ones kidnapped from your world. Those orphans father placed in the care of Guild masters, to find a place in our world."

Cory nodded, feeling a stab of sudden guilt. Destroying that mirror was an act of selfishness. Although he had no intention of going back, the others must have dreamed of returning to Earth every minute of their captivity. The boy silently vowed to make it up to them.

As if reading his thoughts, Math put an understanding hand on his arm. "Your act also rid us of the Kelloids, Cory. If you feel guilt for mistakes made, also feel pride for the good you have done. The demons have plagued the countryside for centuries! Now they are gone, all because of you."

The boy nodded. "I see, Master. Then responsibility means making some small sacrifices for the greater good?"

Math and the King exchanged looks. "He will be a philosopher, this one. Have you been teaching him the works of Alvis?"

The spellweaver bowed his head. "A wizard must know many things, Majesty, as must a prince. I have tutored your youngest son well."

"Indeed you have," Llewelyn said, eyeing the boy.

Cory's face fell, looking up at the King with a sinking feeling in his stomach. "No, he hasn't. I've failed."

Llewelyn frowned. "Failed?"

The boy nodded slowly. "You bid me to complete my wizard's training. Father, can you ever forgive me for not having my Wizard's Staff?"

The King frowned at the boy, still half-smiling. "Forgive you? Cory, you are my son! What gave you the idea I might be disappointed with you?"

The boy stood, voice so low it was nearly inaudible. "Asmodeus."

The King laughed. "And since when have you ever trusted the words of a demon?" Llewelyn said, throwing his arms about the boy and holding him close. "Listen to me, Cory. You have made me very proud of you, and in my eyes you do have your Wizard's Staff, for you have earned it many times over."

The boy buried his face in his foster father's chest, hugging him back. Cory hid his tears that way, knowing in his heart he had at last found what he had been searching for: a home and a family.

THE END

GLOSSARY

ABOLLYDD: (pronounced Abol-lithe) Stronghold of the Kelloid **DEMONS**, located in a mountain in central **GWYNEDD**. Human children were enslaved there, and only the demons knew what happened to them when they grew up.

ABYDONNE: A magical world in a parallel dimension, co-existing with Earth. Magic works here because the laws of physics are different than in our universe. Legends from this world have reached Earth and influenced our own history and literature. See **MABINOGION**.

APPRENTICE: A child sent to live with a master and learn a craft (in this case, magic!) A boy began his apprenticeship between the ages of nine and twelve, and usually completed his training in seven years.

ARCHWIZARD: A **WIZARD** descended from an ancient royal line of magicians. An archwizard has more raw magical power than his fellows, and a racial memory of spells, so his apprenticeship goes by in one-seventh of the normal time.

ASMODEUS: Supreme Lord of the Kelloid **DEMONS**. Also known as Asteroth, Mephistopheles, and many other names.

AVATAR: A master of the two Mystic Arts of **SPELLWEAVING** and **INCANTATION**. While all magicians receive training in both, most usually specialize in one or the other. Few have the ability to master both Arts.

CAER: A Welsh castle, usually built into a mountainside or a large hill for greater protection.

CAER DATHYL: Capitol of **GWYNEDD**, built by **MATH** hundreds of years ago. This castle was actually Math's stronghold in Welsh folklore, and was also the home of Gwydion and Lleu Llaw Gyffes.

CAER LEON: One of King Arthur's strongholds, the other being Camelot.

CANTRIP: A very minor spell, taught to a beginning apprentice to build his confidence. Any human can perform a cantrip. These include cooling water, lighting a candle, or calling a pet over without speaking.

COLD IRON: The one bane of all magic. It prevents magical energy from flowing, and locks spells in place. A magician chained by cold iron is powerless, and edged steel weapons can kill most supernatural creatures. Magic swords are made by setting the **DWEOMER** while the iron is still hot from the forge; once the metal has cooled, the enchantment is locked in place.

DARK MAGIC: (also called Black Magic or the Forbidden Arts.) Use of the powers of darkness, or the taking of life for magic power. Its use is shunned by most wizards.

DEMON: A supernatural creature, completely evil, usually immortal. They have bat-wings for flight, are very strong, and are very hard to kill. The few methods of slaying a demon include direct sunlight and **COLD IRON**.

DRAGON: One of the most powerful races on **ABYDONNE**, born from the war which resulted in the Great Fall of Mankind. Dragons come in a variety of breeds, including golden, copper, silver, black, sapphire, thunder, and emerald (the most common.) All dragons have powerful strength, can fly, are resistant to fire and most normal forms of injury, and can live 3,000 years or longer. Dragons can gain knowledge from eating people, and can thus spellcast or shapeshift after consuming a magician. The natural enemy of dragons are unicorns.

DWEOMER: The permanent spell set into an object by a **WIZARD**.

ELDERS: Wizards of lore and legend, protectors of **ABYDONNE**'s Twelve Kingdoms, still alive due to magic.

ENCHANTER: A magician who specializes in **INCANTATION**. Most wizards are enchanters.

FAMILIAR: A psychic bond between a human magician and a creature. Familiars share each other's feelings, powers, and traits.

GATE: A spell used for getting from one place to another quickly.

GWYNEDD: (pronounced Gwen-eth) One of the Twelve Kingdoms of **ABYDONNE**, known for its rolling hills, lovely mountains, and peaceful people. Protected for the past several centuries by Math the Ancient.

INCANTATION: One of the two major Arts of Magic, in which a long spell is recited and/or runes are drawn out, precisely using the **NAME** of an object to affect it.

KALEVA: One of the Twelve Kingdoms of **ABYDONNE**, located just north of **GWYNEDD**. A scenic country of mountains and snow, known for its population of wizards and sorcerers, the greatest of whom was **VAINAMOINEN**. (The *Kalevala* is a collection of myths from Finland.)

LORD AVALON: A title held by the male members of House Avalon.

MABINOGION: Literally, "Tales of a Young Hero." A collection of stories dating back to medieval Wales, the cornerstone of Welsh mythology, and basis for the world of Abydonne. It's counterpart in Finland was the *Kalevala*.

MAGEGEMS: A crystal which contains raw magical energy, which can then be used for casting spells. See **DARK MAGIC**.

MAKER, The: God.

MATH (the Ancient): An **ELDER**, one of the greatest wizards of **ABYDONNE**, a **SPELLWEAVER** by specialty. He teaches a group of young **APPRENTICES** at Mount **PENLLYN**.

NAME: A person's true name was kept a very close secret. A magician who knew a person's soulname had complete power over him. Cory's true name is *Draigswynwyr* (Dragon-Wizard.)

OLD TONGUE: The original language of Mankind, used to **NAME** everything in the world, and thus control it with magic. (I used Welsh for the magic words in this book.)

PENLLYN, Mount: Literally, "Lake-Head." A mountain in **GWYNEDD**, where **MATH** runs a magic school.

PRINCE OF WIZARDS: A title held by the heir of the Lord High Wizard.

RING, The: A mountain range in southern **GWYNEDD**, which forms a circle. Home to dozens of **DRAGONS**.

SORCERER: The title of a junior magician. Most **APPRENTICES** earn this title by age sixteen or seventeen.

SORCERER'S CLOAK: The cloak awarded to an **APPRENTICE** of magic when he earns the title of **SORCERER**. It is woven by the boy's master, as a gift, and usually has several **DWEOMERS** woven into the cloth.

SPELLWEAVER: A magician who specializes in spellweaving. One of the two Mystic Arts, the other being **INCANTATION**. A spellweaver uses telekinesis to move **THREADS** of force into new patterns, which in turn redefine reality.

TAPPING: Drawing energy directly from **THREADS** for different effects, especially to enhance psychokineses and telepathy. A minor Art.

THREADS: The mystic lines of force that define reality. The most powerful of these are called Ley Lines.

TOME: An ancient book of magic, sometimes in the form of a scroll.

TWELVE KINGDOMS: GWYNEDD, KALEVA, Powys, Turlin, Cardigan, Brython, Gaul, Armorica, Rheged, Ulster, Talis, and Highland.

VAINAMOINEN: The Lord High Wizard, and one of the **ELDERS**.

WIZARD: Title of a senior magician, a master in one of the two Arts of Spellweaving or **INCANTATION**.

WIZARD'S STAFF: Awarded to a **SORCERER** when he earns the title of **WIZARD**. It is usually made of ash, rowan, or oak, from a sapling tree that was fed a potion containing some blood from the apprentice magician and his master, binding the living wood to both. The staff enables the wizard to access the higher magics. *Elaeth* is the name of Cory's Wizard's Staff.

ABOUT THE AUTHOR

All writers craft stories from their own life experience, and this epic tale is no exception. In the tales are hints of summer vacations to the Catskill Mountains; long days spent swimming in crystal clear lakes and playing amongst the tall pine, oak and maple trees. The oaks were of course an enchanted forest, the bird high in the green boughs Merlin's own owl, Archimedes. For Larry grew up in New York City with a healthy, overactive imagination. At the age of five, the boy's great-aunt Dorothy presented him with a copy of **The Wonderful Wizard of Oz** by L. Frank Baum. This was followed by **A Wizard of Earthsea** by Ursula LeGuin, and trips to the movies with his dad to see **Fantasia**, **The Sword in the Stone**, and **Escape To Witch Mountain**. By the time little Larry was ten, he was playing Dungeons and Dragons, and the World of Abydonne was taking form in his mind. Told by his mother to stop daydreaming in class and write his stories down, Larry opened a fresh spiral-bound notebook, and began his career at the tender age of ten.

Lawrence J. Cohen graduated from Brookdale Community College, where he first learned the craft of professional fiction writing from Professor Carl Calender in 1985; further formal education under Professor Oscar Muscariello at Jersey City University into Europe's mythology and folklore, including the Kalevala of Finland, and the Mabinogion of Wales, led to the crafting of **The Dragon's**

Familiar, his final project for his bachelor's degree in Creative Writing in 1988.

Lawrence J. Cohen has also penned the following manuscripts (originally typed on a Commodore 64, of all things) which with Hashem's help, will soon see print: ***Dragon's Orb***, the sequel to ***The Dragon's Familiar***; ***The Sword of Arakron*** trilogy; ***Wizard's Crusade***, a time travel story; ***Castle Ravenwood*** set in yet another magical world; and ***Odyssey***, a Star Trek novel, among others.

ACKNOWLEDGEMENTS

No writer practices his craft in a vacuum, and this novel is no exception: To my parents and grandparents, my former teachers and professors: Mrs. Cynthia Jacobs, 6th and 7th grade, Mr. Shark, 8th grade; Mrs. Judy Garguilo and Mrs. Ann Hunt, Manalapan High School English Dept.; Professors Carl Calendar and Gene Snyder, Brookdale Community College English Dept., Lincroft; Professors Oscar Muscariello and Emily Berges, Jersey City State University English Dept.; my old friends and fellow role-playing gamers: Jose Sanchez (Star Trek and Dragonlance), Tony Mendez and Tom Hudson, for role-playing and for editing my manuscripts; and finally, in memory of two childhood friends, gone but not forgotten: Mark Steven Collins (1963–1977) and Gerald DelGeorno (1965–1981.)

978-0-595-51413-7
0-595-51413-8